WITCH OF THE WILD BEASTS

CATHERINE STINE

Konjur Road Press
Forays into Fictional Magic

Synopsis: Is Evalina's supernatural bond with animals her curse or salvation? In 1854, when a cruel doctor kills her brother, Evalina's "wild beasts" come to her aid. She's imprisoned for witchcraft in Philadelphia's Penitentiary amidst extreme medical mischief. Evalina and fellow inmate, Birdy devise a risky scheme to get justice. If they fail, not only will the doctor's evil deeds continue unchecked, but Evalina and her crew will surely be hung.

***

For news of books, events and sales subscribe to Catherine's newsletters or visit her website
catherine stine.com

***

Other books:
Witch of the Cards
Pictures of Dorianna
Fireseed One
Ruby's Fire
Heart in a Box
Refugees

🌼 Created with Vellum

EVALINA

In my lonely cell up on Cherry Hill, I drew the furry creatures toward me. "A bit of bread? A scratch on your heads? A song?"

They peeked in through the gnawed chinks in the whitewashed walls. Tiny things with trembling threads of whiskers, they sniffed, inching out, snouts first. Darting, they lined up in front of me, their inquiring heads cocking one way and then the other.

I coaxed the feathered beasts, too. Doves and gulls crowded on the sill outside my narrow barred window. They scratched and pecked to shuffle as close to the opening as they could.

I fed them all with breadcrumbs saved from my prison breakfast.

They were my heart. My soul. Though they uttered no English, they spoke my language. They never called me Evalina Stowe, my given name, or Eva, my nickname, but most importantly they never called me *murderess.*

1 - FOUR MONTHS PRIOR

The buzzing sounded like sandpaper on dry wood. It was impossible to concentrate on my pattern cutting. I placed the long scissors on the tailor's table and gazed up at the high window across from me where the sound was loudest. There, on the inside glass in the uppermost right corner, was a wasp's nest as big as a fruit bowl. How odd! Only an hour earlier, I had climbed up the stepladder to polish the same pane. It was free of any hive.

As I wondered how it was possible to build the intricate structure so fast and what had whipped the wasps into such mad activity, a tremor rose in my own chest of fear and outraged sorrow. *Why?*

Even more winged beasts emerged from their checkerboard holes and circled the ceiling. *What is this?* I asked them silently. They only swooped lower and began to loop around me.

The chimes jingled on the door of Conklin's Tailor as Dr. Horace Dowdrick entered. He gave the front counter a sharp rap with his brass walking stick. The wasps scattered.

"My order," he groused. "Hurry! I'm a busy man."

I rushed from the pattern table to the back storeroom to alert my little brother Todd, who helped hang waistcoats and fetch skeins of thread. "Psst! It's the angry sawbones," I whispered. "Can you get his newest order?"

"Yes, Eva." A handsome boy with a gentle manner and dimples, Todd took after my flaxen-haired mother, who used to joke that with my raven hair, wild-eyes and dramatic moods that pirates off Delaware Landing had dropped me on her doorstep.

My employer, Mr. Conklin was out, so I dashed to the front desk and began to tabulate the order. He took long lunches and often returned sloppy drunk. Thus, one of my tasks was to take care of the payments.

I didn't mind that, though I resented waiting on Dowdrick for he was rude. He called me a lazy guttersnipe and had conniptions over how long I took, but it bothered me most when he yelled at my brother. Truth be told, his outfits were complex matters to cut and piece together. He ordered plaid double-breasted fronts, paisley wool and silk-quilted vests, more suited to the fop than the surgeon.

"I will finish your invoice Doctor," I promised as his over-sweet hair oil hit my nose. I breathed it out in a guff and said, "Please, have a seat." Gesturing to an empty chair facing the desk I made haste to add up the total. Better he stay here than to yell at my brother, as was his way.

At age seventeen, and supporting both Todd and myself, I was lucky to have any job. But especially this one on Spring Garden Street, in Philadelphia's most respectable area for homes and businesses. My employer entrusted me with simple repairs, the cutting of his patterns, and the greeting of customers, while he dealt with tailoring and complex fabrication.

"Foo! Get going you atrocious insect!" Dowdrick swatted

away a wasp that had returned and was buzzing about his face. "Make haste, girly, this shop is infested!"

"Doctor, patience if you please. Your order is being gathered as fast as possible," I replied, my stomach twisting.

Dowdrick sat for another moment, drumming his fingers on the wooden armrests and swatting away a second wasp. Then he rose and wandered toward the back. I glanced up, but could no longer see him, as Mr. Conklin had arranged racks of new suits in the far section.

There was another sudden swell of buzzing. The swarm careened around the shop like a kite in a storm.

A moment later, the doctor's scolds and my brother's stifled cries rang from the storeroom. I swore the wasps could hear my terrified heartbeat, for as I rushed back they flanked me on either side, creating hissing winged walls.

I threw the door open to find Dowdrick trying to choke the life out of my brother. "You clumsy sloth!" Dowdrick screeched. "How dare you throw my fine suits on the floor!"

Todd gurgled, his face reddening and eyes widening.

"What in the devil are you doing?" My heart pinched in terror as I grabbed the potbellied lug's shirt and tried to pull him off my brother. The man's perfumed stink made it hard to breathe. The wasps followed my lead, charging and stinging him about the face.

"Go!" he screamed as he swatted them. Momentarily, the wasps retreated. He pushed me hard while his other hand gripped Todd by the hair. "Lay off, wench or I'll tear your brother's pretty hair clear off his skull!"

The wasps renewed their attack, plunging their stingers in Dowdrick's pudgy cheeks. He batted at them, flattening a few. But not before I saw welts rise.

Thank you, wasps. They fairly sizzled with righteous anger—but on my behalf? Impossible!

In that second of distraction, Dowdrick struck again, grabbing Todd's shoulders and yanking them brutally. "How dare you treat my clothes like dirt!"

"Eva, help!" Todd's wails filled the room. His eyes were watering, his cheeks purple.

"Shoo!" bellowed the doctor, swiping away a new swarm. Todd yelped again as Dowdrick pulled his head back by a hank of hair. "Silence this no account boy!"

"Let go of him then!" I screeched.

Dowdrick's eyes were absolutely mad—bloodshot and out for the kill. Instead, of retreating, he spread his sausage fingers around my brother's neck and squeezed mercilessly.

"Stop! Now!" I kicked the doctor's wide calves and struck his fleshy back with an iron pattern weight, used to hold fabric and patterns firmly in place. It merely glanced off him and plunged to the floor.

The wasps dove in once more and set upon his eyes. His protests thundered in my ears. Were they intentionally blinding the doctor? Why would they harm him and not sting me? No matter the consequences, I had to insure this demon would do no more violence to my brother. I snatched the long scissors from the tailor's table and plunged them into his side. Dowdrick fell with a resounding thud.

I ran to Todd, who had also dropped and lay horribly still. In a sweating panic, I pressed my fingers on his wrist for a pulse. "Wake up!" I shook him. "Todd!" His head rolled ominously. His eyes were glazed. I listened to his chest for any movement, any trace of a patter.

My brother's heart had stopped.

I bent over him and sobbed.

It was not the first time this monster had mistreated my brother. I had heard him scream at Todd before but nothing like this! A pulsing fury overtook me. The wasps, still in angry hordes, careened about the shop, knocking down pins and patterns from the long table, causing a vase of roses to crash on the floor.

Inexplicably, they dove onto Todd and stung him about the ears. A few sank their stingers in my arm. "Off!" I screamed. "I beg of you!" I waved them away as my tears streamed down.

The liberty of crying for my brother was not to be. Mr. Conklin was fumbling at the rusty doorknob, now back from his luncheon and no doubt deep in his cups.

Stay out! I thought. *Give me a last minute with my poor Todd!*

Throngs of wasps left my side and hovered by the front door. How could they know I wished my employer to be detained? A fierce whirring in my chest said they did.

Two bodies lay face up: Dowdrick, who was Mr. Conklin's wealthiest client, with a bloody scissors jutting from his side, and my dear brother Todd, an innocent pawn of this sinister day. The shop was in shambles—shattered glass, waterlogged pattern pieces, hundreds of wasps still circling, so many they couldn't have possibly come from one nest. There was to be no more sleeping in the shed behind Conklin's. Surely I would be jailed, surely hung. I'd seen people thrown in prison for less.

Escape droned the wasps. Or was it my own tortured mind?

I gave my brother a last desperate hug and kiss on his cooling forehead before I fled from the storeroom and out the rear door. It opened onto an alleyway lined with carthorses, vegetable peelings and dung. Still weeping and in utter shock, I fled down the dark cobbled streets of Northern Liberties.

2.

I ran.

And ran and ran, tears streaking back either side of my cheeks.

I wasn't sure where I was headed. Only that I needed to get away, to hide. I ran down Spring Garden to Ninth Street, and then over to Brown Street.

There, my heart wrenched anew along with a fresh gushing of tears. Instinctively, I stumbled toward a certain building just off the corner. Stopping a few houses from it I gripped a light post and stared at the house as I gasped for breath.

Its front gate was still painted black and its flower box under the right window still brimmed with tea roses. But it was no longer comfortably disheveled with chipped bricks and shutters at gently sloping angles. The shutters now stood straight like toy soldiers in formation. The curtains had changed from warm yellow gingham to starched lace, cold and white as snow. The Stowe nameplate above the door had been removed. In its place a carpenter had installed a transom with fancy stained glass. It was opened an inch or so to allow in the summer breeze.

I wanted to scream into it, "I lived here! I was born here!"

I longed to rap hard on the brass knocker, have my mother thrust open the door and fold me into her generous arms as she used to do. I needed home, family, and the comfort of her hug. For time to go backwards.

For my brother to still be alive.

But Todd lay dead on the tailor's floor. And my mother and father had perished five long years ago from the cholera. I yearned to go back and recover Todd's body to honor him with a burial, even in an anonymous dirt pit. But it was far too risky. I was penniless. The police and night watchmen were surely on the lookout. They'd throw me in prison or worse.

I looked again at the house that was no longer ours— sold to pay for my parents' burials and debts. A paralyzing pain tore through me.

This place belonged to a family with enough money to repoint the bricks, replace the missing and rotted roof shingles and the tilting chimney. How was it that I'd lost every vestige of family in seconds? I choked back a wrenching sorrow.

I snaked along the side walkway, scurried to the back, ducked through some loose slats in the fence they hadn't seen to repair. Crouching underneath a bowed honeysuckle bush I sank my head in my hands. My mind needed to stop racing long enough to figure out what to do next. I rubbed my forehead and brushed tears away. Peering out through my fingers, I saw a skittering movement. A curious squirrel darted forth and then two yellow warblers hopped my way, studying me. Somehow they helped me to slow the horrific visions of Todd that charged inside me—Todd's bluing face, spittle bubbling down one side of his still but opened mouth.

"Do you feel my breaking heart?" I whispered to the creatures. Their eyes stayed steady. As if they trusted me, as if they understood English.

I pictured my mother, pale on her sickbed weeks before she died and murmured to her now as more tears fountained down my dress. "I was only trying to save Todd from a madman, Mama. I needed justice. Does that make me a monster?"

Abruptly, footsteps sounded on the walkway between the houses. I stayed stone still as the squirrel scrambled under the low hanging branches and the birds hopped inside the tangle of upper ones.

It wasn't the neighborhood watchmen hunting me—only a boy talking to his father about a toy sailboat. I breathed out slowly. It was risky hiding here.

When their voices faded I dipped through the loose slats and dashed back into the ally, and along it toward the Delaware River. Overhead, birds flew, brightening the sky with their flashes of yellow. More warblers. Could the ones from the honeysuckle bush be in that number? The mere idea gave me a faint comfort.

I ran until my lungs burned and until I reached the cover of trees along the loamy riverbank behind a small, manicured park with benches. Much like the squirrel, I burrowed deeply into the woods. Finding an oak with a trunk spreading in all directions, I leaned back on its rough bark.

The warblers stayed in the trees, chattering as the sun set. I stayed up with them, unable to sleep. It wasn't cold even after the moon rose yet I shivered with more dreadful visions—the tailor's grim discovery, his fevered call to the morgue, the bodies being hauled out on dirty stretchers, crowds gawking on the street and venturing guesses as to where the girl had run off. I shuddered violently and wrapped my arms around my chest. My belly growled but I had no appetite. I didn't care if I ever ate again.

I suppose I fell asleep at dawn for the next thing I recalled was the pink sun crowning the trees. Then nothing until I awoke again, to a man jabbing me with a stick.

"What's a pretty lady like you doing out here?" he asked, a leer in his eyes. "Want a bit of fun for a quarter?" His question hung in the air, along with the reek of sour liquor.

My heart in my throat, I leapt to my feet. Staggering back, I realized my legs were asleep, and now prickling. "Get away! Don't bother me!"

The man, in a soiled blue vest and striped shirt dropped the stick and held his hands up in feigned innocence. "I was just trying to see if you was alive, Miss. No harm done."

"Well, I am. You can see that plain as day. So get away! Shoo!" I made a show of batting at the air to which the man began to guffaw. This scared me more than his prodding at my skirts. Perhaps he was demented.

"Feisty one, eh? Shall we thrust and parry?" He held out the stick and lunged forward in a drunken fencing stance.

"Dratted man, get gone!" I screeched and commenced running on half-numb, wobbly legs. I sped deeper into the web of trees, immediately doubting my judgment, for I was penning myself in this way. Behind me there was a loud crunch of broken branches and a pained, "Oomph!" I dared a peek. The man had fallen and was stumbling to his feet.

I kept on running away from the river through the

trees, until by some miracle I found my way to Front Street, which I knew paralleled the Delaware. My lungs and throat were scorched. Turning quickly, I could no longer see him. There was no choice but to rest or I would faint. Tall brick warehouses that spanned blocks lined this stretch. A whitewashed sign announced *Cartwright's Shipping Parts*. A few steps after this loomed an arched entrance to their back lot so I slunk in to search for a hiding spot. The scruffy lot brimmed with weeds, broken glass and saplings spiking their way up through missing bricks. I was about to leave when I saw piles of wooden pallets along a sidewall. Quickly I ducked behind a stack and sank to the brick ground. I rubbed my sore legs, adjusted my torn dress over them and brushed off leaves and dirt.

Finally safe from the threatening man, I closed my eyes, tucked my legs further under my skirts and tried to rest. With every breath I missed my brother. The pain was as bad as if my insides had been gutted. "Oh, Todd, I was supposed to protect you. I'll never forgive myself. How can I exist without you, without my family? Yet I must. You would want me to," I muttered. My stomach growled plaintively and my dry throat begged for water. How would I sustain myself? I'd run off without even a nickel in my pockets. I dared not approach anyone for the watchmen were surely hunting for me.

The fruit and bread vendors set up along Market Street. Not all knew me. Perhaps I could beg a heel of bread. Oh, the shame of it! But what else could I do?

Close by were wisps of talk and laughter, to which my heart thumped hard. Was the man lurking about? Had a warehouse worker reported my presence?

More chatter—but it was the high voices of children or

at least those closer to my eighteen years. Still, I did not trust anyone, so I stayed crouched behind the pallets.

Louder voices and footsteps stopped inches from me. I kept as still as a statue and tried not to breathe.

"Who are you? Come out of there!" someone ordered. An older boy's face appeared—brown scruffy hair, bowed brows over accusing eyes and a hint of whiskers on angular cheeks. "Show yourself, girl!"

More faces stared in—some younger ruffians. All boys.

Blood pounded in my ears as I crawled out. "What?" I growled, making a show of strength in case I had to defend myself again.

The brown-haired boy, maybe fifteen and taller than me eyed my work dress. He guffawed. "Why, it's a regular proper shop lady on the run! Putting on airs as if she's a huckle-berry above a persimmon!" His crew laughed heartily. "What'd you do, rob the register or what?"

"Steal the wardrobe?" asked another.

"Did you go whole hog with your boss and his jealous wench found out?"

Their disgraceful accusations emboldened me. "Shut your dirty mouths!" I exclaimed. "You know nothing of me and none of that is true."

"Then what?" The tall boy's eyes grew more serious.

I couldn't tell them that I stabbed my employer's client, could I? No, not even this street gang. For who knew whether they'd spill the gossip to a watchman for a handful of coins or a hot meal. "I... I ran into terrible luck," is all I admitted.

"I'll say." Wry amusement returned to the boy's eyes. His friends laughed, too.

"Just tell me," I asked, "how do you eat? How do you get clean water out here?"

The boy snorted. "Why should we? You ain't told us nothin'."

"I'm in trouble. I... I can't say more."

The boy shrugged. "Ain't our problem, Missy."

"Yeah, bully for you!" chimed a heavyset boy with matted hair and a tattered red jacket. "You ain't so special. We all got problems. Leave our place. Go find your own."

Tears pricked at me but I blinked them away. This was no time to show weakness and emotions. "Go ahead and be ornery," I countered. "I'll find my own food."

Without another glance their way I burrowed out of the pallets and tromped down the walkway, glass crunching underfoot.

One of the kids called out after me, "Steal from the blasted vendors!"

"Already thought of that. Maybe I will!" I snapped.

As much as I wasn't sure I could eat, my belly screamed for food. So, the idea of some kinder soul handing me a biscuit gave me the strength to trudge blocks and blocks to the Market Street vendors. I was weak, growing dizzy under the heat of day and terrified of being recognized. To avoid this, I kept to the shadows.

Carriages clattered by and though there were some inquiring stares, no one pointed accusingly or yelled for me to stop. No one chased me or handcuffed me. I began to hope that the scuttlebutt was more about me having to flee from a shop robbery gone bad someone *else* had botched. After all, why on earth would anyone figure I'd want to murder my own dear brother? I dared not dwell on this because I'd collapse in a lake of miserable tears. I pushed on.

Halfway there, I noticed a shiny object glinting up from the sidewalk. A lost pair of spectacles! What a stroke of luck.

I grabbed them and brushed off the grime. One of the glasses was cracked but I put them on anyway. It would help disguise me from those who might know me from the tailors. They made the view blotchy but any little thing might help.

Finally, at the southern end of Market Street, I stared up at the rows of vendors with a dawning worry. Mr. Saxon who sold sausages would recognize me and ask questions. The old grouch Maude with her raven's eyes that made sure no roving hands prodded her cakes and muffins was one to avoid at all costs. I ducked around her, terrified to engage. It was a brisk market day, with housewives hauling babies and baskets, and men taking time to buy lunch before returning to their employment. Taking a restorative breath I gathered my nerve to approach an aproned bread seller five booths past Maude. "If you please, a taste of a bread for a hungry girl?" I asked with pleading eyes.

"Where's your money, Miss? I've got to sell my wares, not give them away." He looked me over disapprovingly.

My face heated up. I hurried on, passing the booth with the two girls who sold vegetables with their mother, for they also knew me and the shame of begging was too great. One of the girls screwed up her face at my spectacles and mussed dress.

I had some luck at the fruit stand, run by a young man with ruddy cheeks and an easy smile. He handed me a single banana. "I can't sell this one because it's turned all brown." He also offered me a sip from his water flask.

But then, he too gave me a warning. "Don't think that you can beg from me daily. I am almost as poor as you, and I have a family to feed." When I nodded without a word he added, "I wish you better times."

"Thanks, sir," I murmured and scurried away to devour

the banana in three ravenous bites. It wasn't much but it would do.

Late that afternoon I returned to the riverbanks, though not where I had encountered the lecher with the stick. I journeyed closer to Delaware Landing, where the vessels came in from over the seas. After careful observation that no other street wanderer or randy devil was anywhere nearby I rested under a close circle of maples.

I hated begging, but it was unsafe for me to look for work right away, and I could not figure out how else I would eat. I wasn't very good at it either, as my face would boil with humiliation and my voice would wobble. More than once, a vendor shooed me off with his broom or raised fists.

A week, then two crept by. I begged in the morning and went back to the park to nap, sleeping until dark. Gradually, I ventured out from my river sanctuary after businesses closed and working folks returned to their homes.

I grew bolder as to where I walked and where I lay down to rest. It seemed that no one was looking for me after all. Perhaps they *did* assume I was the lucky one who dodged death from a murderous thief at Conklin that afternoon. For even with the cracked spectacles an observant detective or watchman could pick me out.

I slept in horse stalls and on cobbled side alleys with the feral cats. Once again I crept back to the house on Brown Street and ducked under the honeysuckle, though the family's hound rooted me out with his baying when the moon was up. I tore out of there, and kept on the move.

I was quick-footed, hardscrabble, and still, after almost a month in desolate mourning for my brother. I regretted not sneaking back to Conklin's to recover Todd's body and honor him with a burial. But that dream was folly.

On Market Street by the stalls, I sometimes spotted the tall, sour boy I'd met by the shipping warehouse but we never again spoke. Other street urchins bobbed and weaved like water buoys around the vendors' carts, too, and I watched how they nabbed their victuals. There was one small boy I took special notice of—he had wispy blond hair and a deft hand. He looked no older than Todd, maybe six.

The first time I spoke to him, he tapped me on the shoulder when I was bent over in the ally, lonely, exhausted and crying for Todd. "Miss?" he said softly, staring at my ragged dress.

"Yes?" I brushed away tears and tangled hair as I stared up at him. "Who are you?" That face... where had I seen him? He could have been my brother's twin, with his puff of corn silk hair over green eyes.

"I knew your, brother, Todd."

I startled and choked down a fresh round of sorrow.

"I heard the news, Missy. Sorry for your loss. Todd was my friend."

Looking closer at the boy's face, it dawned on me. "Ah! I did see you talking with Todd now and then."

"We played at marbles sometimes. Before my mother passed."

"Oh, so sorry!"

"Me, too. I miss her like you must pine for your brother." He hitched his sagging trousers. "You hungry, Missy? I've seen you begging, but you won't get much that way. Even the rich ones are tightfisted." He broke into an alley cat grin. "I'm good at nipping food. I can show you how. It's best done as a team anyhow."

In two days, I'd only eaten one mealy peach and a stale

cracker. "That would be wonderful." I struggled to my feet and brushed off my dusty skirt. "Your name?"

"Lewin, 'cept they call me Lightning, on account of they never see me coming I move so fast." Another sly grin.

"Ha! I'm Evalina."

He led me to the baker's stall on Market Street and signaled for me to ask the vendor a question. "How much for a hot cross bun?" I asked, pretending to dig in my pockets for change. As I did, Lightning swiped two buns and was halfway down the street before I caught up to him.

"You *are* fast!" I said and took a famished bite from the confection he handed me still warm, delicious and dotted with raisins.

"Stick with me. You'll never miss for a meal."

It was true, for by day's end, I'd also eaten a current tart and a meat pie, and washed it down with fresh cider. My guilt eased slightly. It was simply a way to stay alive until it was safer to look for work.

We began meeting in mid-morning by a certain tilting street lamp on Market and worked our charms for the day's fixings. One would distract, the other would snatch the biscuits or if we were lucky, meat pies.

One afternoon as we sat in the Delaware River Park watching the ships float here and there Lightning revealed something disquieting. "I heard word the mad doctor strangled your brother."

My breath caught. "Oh? Who told you?"

"Don't matter no more," he said mysteriously. "That sawbones has wicked rages. He beats the tar out of children for no good reason. Many people. He even kicked my mother once."

"How horrid! What a monster!"

Lightning paled and nodded sagely. He looked so much

older than his six years then. My heart broke for him, for Todd, and all of the victims of the vicious doctor.

Lightning chewed the last of his tart and licked his fingers. "I also know where the sawbones practiced medicine. On Haines Street. I've swiped coins from his waistcoat, too."

"You're a brave boy," was all I could say.

Our conversation haunted me all night. Other urchins helped me get food, but Lightning was the only one who touched my heartstrings. He knew who I was, not just as a thief. No matter we'd come from two worlds—me from the poor yet educated class, him from the gutter.

We both belonged to the street now. That's how fast fortunes changed.

And then, the very next morning he never showed up by the tilted street light. I finally asked his street friends where he was.

"He's gone, Miss. Snatched away to prison," the boy said solemnly.

The news hit me like a gut punch. All I could do was to stumble into the woods behind the river and double over in wrenching pain. He was almost family. Just another reminder that loved ones could vanish in an instant. Lightning, oh, sweet boy...

I guess even lightning can be trapped in a bottle.

A month later, I finally found employment. It was my luck to be wandering by the docks at Delaware Landing when a fleet of boats came in, teeming with immigrants from across the great Atlantic.

One Robert Gaul was signing them straight away to

work at his Somerset Farms in Kensington. I quickly slipped in line. He needed young folks, full of pep to scare away birds from his corn crops.

"Can you stand the sun for hours on end? Can you swing a stick hard enough to thrash out varmints?" He peered down at me. Up close, he was intimidating, tall, round-faced, with hairy nostrils and a dark mole quivering on one cheek, all situated under a grimy top hat.

"Yes, sir." The idea of harming an animal hurt as much as if I'd hammered a nail into my own arm. But I was weary and sad about robbing food from the vendors, who were almost as poor as I. Plus, I needed a safe corner to sleep in. More than once, I'd kicked away drunkards and lechers in the wee hours who I'd caught pawing at me. "I'm strong and like being outdoors," I answered. At least that was the truth.

Bird Girl I was called.

Bird Girl I was.

But not the kind Mr. Gaul imagined. Every dawn, I would be sent to the fields with other Bird Girls. We would traipse up and down the rustling cornrows while banging our cane sticks. Up the winged beasts would rise in droves, clearly terrified. Beating their wings against the blue sky, they would turn momentarily, peering at me with mournful eyes.

Or so I felt. My co-workers laughed at me and told me I was daft. "Too much sun!" they would say. "Don't look up, they will lay their loads on your head."

"It is a shame to beat them," I confessed to Betsy Ainsley, a new hire like me. She was a Scottish girl fresh off an overseas boat. "They're so defenseless."

"What else can we do?" With one hand, she shook her stick at the stalks. With the other, she shaded her pale, freckled skin from burning.

"Don't know," I replied, "but I'm loathe to break their wing bones."

"Avoid trouble, Eva. I'd hate it if you were let go. He's terribly strict." She nodded toward Gaul's farmhouse, a rambling thing with wraparound porches and bushy red azaleas in front. Then she hurried off, looking back once with a faint grin.

Would the birds come to me if I silently called them? Would they hear my thoughts through the sky? I gazed down the cornrow at two birds, settled on the half-ripe cobs and remembered when I was a tiny girl of three years or so. I would leave breadcrumbs and corn kernels on the open sill I'd snuck in my pockets at dinner.

Gazing out over the row houses and chimney tops I would call for the animals. "Don't be scared, lovelies. I am your friend. Rest here." After a time, they would swoop down, peck up the crumbs and fly off. I'll never forget the joy of it, of wanting to leap up and down but staying put so as not to frighten the creatures.

After a time, they stayed even though they'd devoured their treat. They tipped their heads at me as if they could understand my words, "Pretty wings. Bright beaks. Sweet ones."

One dusky evening, I pulled my chair to the window and sang softly to five birds huddled on the sill when my mama's voice rang out from behind, "You have a magic way with the wild ones, Eva, like my granny, who animals flocked to."

Startled, my beloved birds thundered off, the black sky a torrent of gray feathers. I spun around. She was my mama so it wasn't right to be cross, and it was fascinating news that

I was like her granny. But in my child's way of thinking, I was so horrified that the birds were frightened off, I vowed to never again scare them. So I stopped calling them to my sill.

My mind spun forward, to where I now stood in the cornfield with the hot sun beaming down, and the birds still perched on the stalks. Another one had settled in. I would not flush them out or smack their wings with any stick. Instead, I decided to talk to them as I had when I was a child.

I faced them full on and lay my stick on the ground. "I understand why you like corn. I like it, too. It's sweet and delicious. Don't be scared. I am your friend. Never be afraid of me." In answer, some fluttered closer. A lilt of joy rose in me as it had those years ago. "Trust me and I will help to protect you." The third one lifted off the stalk and drifted down so close I could have touched it. "Lovely," I whispered. "Wild beast of the field."

So my way with animals wasn't a onetime fluke after all. I had rediscovered my passion. "Come to me and I'll house you, train you, and feed you as many yellow kernels as your bellies will hold. I'll protect you from these murderous Somerset farmers, who would beat you or cook you and pick apart your grilled bones."

More birds hopped out of the stalks, peering at me with a beaked suspicion. Then finding me safe, they sailed over and perched along my arms.

After this, I stopped scaring the birds from the corn altogether. But to keep collecting wages I still marched up and down the rows. If I saw a fellow bird girl I would stop and pass the time of day, speaking of music or weather; not often of food, since our rations were paltry. In addition to Betsy there was Mary McMalley and Sarah Bailey, both Irish immigrants from boats at Delaware Landing. I was finally feeling safer after the dreadful death of my little brother and my months of near starvation. I was crawling out of my shell and daring to smile.

Then one hot afternoon we heard the rumbling of Mr. Gaul's wide carriage tearing toward us in the rutted dirt road between the fields. Mary was five rows over, Sarah a good twelve, and Betsy another fifteen or so. I bent toward my row and pretended to flush out birds, only tapping lightly on the stalks as I warned the birds silently. *Hide, hunker down, this man will mosey on to his home and out of the field soon enough.*

Gaul's carriage did pass, yet I couldn't help but peek over my shoulder at him. He was staring down at me, with black eyes and a displeased frown. He tugged on the reins and the horses slowed, snorting with relief at a chance to break from working in the sweltering heat.

My heart throbbed with a vague panic as Mr. Gaul dismounted and strode over. What did he want with me, a lowly bird girl? His boots riled up clouds of dry dust, which wended their way over and made me sneeze. I'd never spoken to Mr. Gaul other than to accept the job and be directed to the German field hand, who showed me to my living quarters, a tiny room behind the stone silo with a horsehair mattress and a curved ledge to place things on.

"Girl, what do you think you are doing?" Gaul demanded, his bushy brows crossed, his face a stormy sky.

"Sir?"

"You heard me! You were only pretending to work as I rode by. *Pretending,*" he repeated with disgust. "This is unacceptable, you understand me?" he went on without waiting for my reply. "Your name?"

"Evalina Stowe, sir." All at once I was shrinking in my boots and growing outraged. My irritable disposition was my least reliable suit. I was moody and sometimes tempted to let fly a rude retort. So, I bit my tongue. I needed this employment. Especially when I thought of all of the famished days that had preceded my hiring, when I was forced to pilfer from food carts and taverns. When outraged proprietors chased me with their own sharp sticks.

"Hear this, Miss Stowe, you'd best get every filthy bird out from my corn or I'll send you packing on the next boat to Ireland." He grabbed my flushing stick from me. "Bird Girls must flush birds like so." With this, he gave the backs of my legs a hard whack. And another, wicked one. I winced but did not cry out.

A rally of birds streaked up from the cornstalks and swirled around us, squawking loudly. I could sense their outrage.

Mr. Gaul batted them away from his top hat, but not before I saw with vengeful glee one had soiled his black brim with an oozing blob of white shit. Gaul didn't notice. "Itching to go back to your motherland, are you?" he jeered.

I wasn't Irish, and I hadn't sailed here on any boat. My mother had been born right here in Philadelphia on Brown Street. But I dared not say a word to challenge him. I could feel the rustle of the birds, their extreme agitation, readying for battle.

Mr. Gaul climbed back in the carriage and thwacked his whip. The chart horses galloped off in a spreading constellation of yellow dust as if they also understood he was in danger.

Ever since I'd begun to talk to the birds and save them from thrashing I built comfortable houses in my room on the ledge with the finer twigs of maple and pine. I used thin bark ties to connect the thatching. It was easy to steal them corn. The silo was right in front of me, and accessible through broken stone chinks. It was unlikely Gaul would miss the corn. After all, the barn rats ate much of the haul as it was.

I gave my small charges fluff from the mattress and old ribbons from Conklin's I'd saved in my stockings to pad their nests. I taught them simple words: come, go, sing, beware and hide. I taught my smartest bird, a ruby-throated grosbeak I named Speckle, to carry a message to my co-workers Mary and Betsy. It read *I have extra corn pudding, come feast with me after work!*

Speckle carried the message to the right people, for though Betsy could not come, within the hour Mary knocked on the stone silo.

"How did you get the bird to do tricks?" she asked as she eagerly took a portion of my homemade corn pudding, from kernels I'd skimmed.

"I have a knack, I guess." I stroked the top of Speckle's head ever so softly.

"Quite!" Mary exclaimed, taking another spoonful of corn pudding. "Did you have to practice for years?"

"Not that long." I shrugged. My luck with bird training continued to fill me with a rare delight, and perhaps my granny had passed the strange talent on to me. This was all I understood.

Until a week or so later.

I was curled in bed resting after a hard afternoon in the heat of the field when I heard a set of determined boots approach. Peeking out of my small window, I nearly fainted from fright when I saw Mr. Gaul's large figure silhouetted against the gilded sunset.

He crooked his beady-eyed noggin in my half-opened door and pushed his way in. "Evalina Stowe!" he called.

I had no time to hide my birds. They'd been contentedly

perched in their twig houses, but at the sound of his shrill voice they began hopping and madly tapping at the twigs with their beaks.

All at once Mr. Gaul was by the ledge, toppling my bird-houses and smashing my stores of corn feed. "You loathsome thief! What the Sam Hill have you been doing in my barn, Bird Girl? How dare you steal my corn and feed it to these lice-bitten devils! You should've been scaring them out of my fields, not providing them room and board. Are you mad?"

Fury boiled in me and I steeled for battle. I leapt off my bed and desperately tried to salvage the twig houses, scooping them up in my arms.

As fast as I did, Mr. Gaul rapped them with his cane and they crashed back down to the floor. "You dare defy me, scalawag!" he yelled, beating me anywhere he could find bare skin. My birds began to circle him. I sensed their ire rise along with mine. Moving in, they pecked at his ears, his fleshy nose and his brows, as they closed in on his eyes.

"Gah! Get your familiars off, witch!" he screeched, and beat me ever more viciously. I would've tried to run but he gripped me tightly by my arm. The racket brought farmhands and fellow bird flushers running. My birds circled Mr. Gaul closer and closer until their sharp claws were embedded into his arms, drawing blood. "Witch, get them off!" he shouted, and as a wave of red hot anger flew from me, my best bird, Speckle, hovered right above Mr. Gaul, glowering at him like an uncanny human. Mr. Gaul pushed me away. He let fly a string of horrid curses just as Speckle made a dive for his opened mouth and hurled herself down Gaul's throat. Gaul's face reddened. He spun in frantic circles and thrust his fingers down his throat as he tried in vain to pull Speckle out by the tail.

I was in utter shock, standing rock still with my hands over my mouth. The others too, were frozen with stares of shocked fascination. During this, Mr. Gaul made ghastly choking sounds.

Still, no one was helping, least of all me. Among the farmhands and barn workers there was no love lost for Mr. Gaul. Gaul's wild eyes looked over accusingly. He wagged his finger at me.

The German farmhand, as if released from a spell of his own, took a few steps back and uttered, "Die hexe! Magische Kraft!"

Mr. Gaul's face turned chalky, soon followed by a queer shade of gray. He collapsed on the floor writhing, hands clamped around his bulging neck—around my brave Speckle who had sacrificed her life for mine.

Then, Mr. Gaul went horribly still, and the farmhand's words were quickly translated. Almost the entire crowd rallied to the chant, "Witch! Black magic! She's killed him!"

My reputation as witch was set no matter how I saw myself. Mary McMalley shouted, "She's got her familiars, the devil lady does! I saw them in her handmade cages. She stole the expensive corn to feed them and they sat on her arms." "Hang the witch!" cried the horse trainer. "That spotted bird was sucking from her teat in the field!" a field hand claimed. "She never flushed out the birds in the fields as she was told to." Mary McMalley's face curdled into a scowl. "The witch chose filthy birds over people." Mary's accusations hurt the most because I'd thought she was my friend. She'd seemed delighted by my birds when she visited. I'd even served her some of my special corn pudding. The only Bird Girl who hung back and didn't join the jeers was Betsy Ainsley. My wounded heart warmed for an instant when Betsy gave me a kindly smile.

But looks of sympathy don't prevent arrest.

The German farmhand hogtied me in front of the barn and knotted the bindings firmly around a hitching post. All of the Somerset Farm's employ stared, their eyes reflecting the horror. No doubt they would do any amount of Hail Mary's or latrine cleaning to escape my fate. That night three burly prison guards in hobnail boots wielding bats shackled me and hauled me off to the penitentiary.

In the dizzying speed of three months—May, June, July—I went from Pattern Cutter to Bird Girl, to Witch, to Murderess.

3

The first night I cried until the thin sheet was soaked with my tears. I wept for my lost brother, gone to Heaven too early. I wept for Speckle's strange martyrdom, and yes, the loss of my freedom. Then I slept like the dead until dawn, when the wondrous sun beaming down through the skylight woke me. My own skylight? How very unusual.

It was unearthly quiet. I was utterly alone. Not that I'd ever imagined what prison would be like. But I'd heard tales of the Walnut Street Prison—the noises, the disputes, all types of rowdy humanity crowded together in grubby cells. Bodies touching, unwanted advances, bloody boxing matches, wailing orphans, people being sick on the floor, or openly fornicating.

Here, I had my own bed and fancy toilet too, which I'd never had before. Twice weekly, the wardens would pull a cord, and the rushing water would wash away my waste like a miraculous invention from a future world. That first morning the deafening rush of water terrified me but then I was astonished at the mechanics of it all.

I had a table and two chairs but no pencil or paper, and

the walls were whitewashed clean of scribbles from earlier prisoners. The space was rectangular, maybe 9 x 14 feet, and the heavy door had a slat for food trays. It was early August and though the thick structure of the prison held in the cool, the heat of the day sapped it away until the air became terribly close. They dressed me in a charcoal gray dress with a gray apron over cotton pantalettes, a petticoat and corset. Sewn on the bodice of the dress was the number 113.

I had no precise way of marking time, but it seemed like hours before I heard footsteps. "Stand back," someone said. A woman's voice; this surprised me for I'd assumed all guards were men. I did as I was told. With the clink of a lock, a second rectangular opening appeared in the door like a postal slat. "Can thee read?" she asked me.

"Yes, Miss."

She pushed a wooden drawer through the opening with a piece of newsprint on it. I read with a gnawing horror:

Pennsylvania Inquirer
Price Two Cents * July 26, 1854 * Price Two Cents

Editorial
Witch Evalina Stowe Commands Animals
to Murder!

Miss Evalina Stowe, an eighteen-year-old last living at Somerset Farms in Kensington PA. was charged with two grisly murders, and possibly a third. A night watchmen discovered a horrific scene three months ago at Conklin's Taylor on Spring Garden Street where Miss Stowe and her seven-year-old brother, Todd, were previously employed. Dr. Dowdrick, a customer and professor at the Eclectic Medical College on Haines Street was found lying in a pool of blood with a long-scissors plunged in his side. Todd Stowe, deceased, was strangled. The confounding aspect was that thousands of wasps were attached to Dr. Horace Dowdrick for no discernible reason. The proprietor said that Stowe was the last person there before the dastardly deeds.

This case remained unsolved until a second murder occurred on July 8 involving Miss Stowe, employed as a Bird Girl at Somerset Farms. The farm's owner, Mr. Gaul, was murdered in cold blood by one of Miss Stowe's own trained birds. According to eyewitnesses Miss Stowe mesmerized the bird into flying down Mr. Gaul's throat and choking him. Many, such as Mary McMalley, a fellow worker at Somerset Farms, believe Miss Stowe is a present-day witch and her devil's familiars are birds, which she controls through dark commands and spells to murder.

This shines light on the earlier incident at Conklin's Taylor; namely that she commanded the wasps to sting Dr. Dowdrick by the hundreds, thusly stunning him enough to stab him. In an enlightened city such as Philadelphia, with its tenets of civility, the fact that a beastly witch lives amongst us, practicing the dark arts is deplorable.

How many more witches live in the shadows of the city? Miss Stowe is imprisoned in the Pennsylvania System's new Eastern State Penitentiary, built on a former cherry orchard. This prison emphasizes humane treatment, modern toilets, and the ability to serve in isolated penitence for one's sins. Most believe that criminal behavior is a moral disease, thus its cure lies in quiet contemplation. Could a witch become a moral citizen? One can only wonder. In the meantime, mothers keep your children far away from small animals exhibiting strange conduct and the women who own them.

Second murder? I'd thought there were three? Perhaps in all of the mad confusion...

"Well?" asked the matron on the other side of the door when I finally put the paper down on the tray. "What might thee say about this? Are thou remorseful, Evalina?" I dared peer through the narrow opening to see a pair of penetrating but concerned hazel eyes under a crisp black bonnet. A Quaker lady, then. This explained the "thee" terms. "Well?" she asked again. "Did thee commit the heinous crimes thou are accused of?

I dared not pin her down to how many murders there were lest it shine an even worse light on me with this pious woman. What could I say? I recalled my mama's own line. "Perhaps I do have a way with animals, Miss."

"But are thou remorseful?" she persisted.

I thought about this. If there had been a way to save my brother... if I had been physically stronger... if I had only checked earlier to see that Dowdrick was up to no good in that storeroom... "Yes, Miss. I regret not saving my brother, Todd."

"So, thee did not commit Todd's murder?"

"No, Miss. Never!" The idea sickened me. "I loved my brother."

"What about the stabbing of the doctor? And the wasps, did thou order them to sting?"

I drew a pained breath. How could I be sorry I'd stopped Dowdrick? This refined Quaker woman compelled me to be honest to a fault by her gentle piety. "I did not order the wasps to do the stinging, Miss. How could I have that power?"

"They call thee a witch. Are thou one?" The woman's voice trembled. It was clear that she was nervous my answer might be yes, and I might harm her, too.

"No, Miss." My own voice shook with fear and outrage.

"Well, then," uttered the woman, as if she was unsure where else to take this conversation.

"May I ask, what is your work here?" If I could get the Quaker lady's mind off witches and murders maybe I could learn valuable tidbits about life in the prison.

How to survive here.

"I deliver a messenger of inner light," she remarked with pride and conviction. "I will help counsel thee and lead thee to the Lord; to the deepest remorse and atonement for crimes. To a more moral and loving life."

"But Miss, I *am* loving. I loved my brother, Todd." I tamped down a sob. "I didn't murder anyone. Certainly not my dearest and only brother! Dr. Dowdrick attacked him. Dr. Dowdrick killed Todd, Miss! And my pet bird flew down Mr. Gaul's throat of her own accord. I beg of you, please believe me. I'm no witch! I don't converse with the devil! Please! Listen."

A weighty pause. "Shall we recite the Lord's Prayer followed by a moment of silence?"

The sob of frustration welled back up. But I swallowed it. Weeping would not free me from this place. "Yes, Miss."

"Amity is my name."

"Thank you. Amity. Your surname?"

"Just Amity at the present time." She said this not unkindly, or in a scolding tone, but in the gentle and patient way she had conducted the other parts of the conversation.

Was the name Amity similar to the words amiable or amnesty? Friendly? Forgiving? I could only hope. At any rate, hearing her name made me less terrified. It meant she was willing to converse. We recited the prayer together.

My mother had taught me the Lord's Prayer years ago, along with proper English and the reading of books. This was something I'd always cherished about her. Though we were poor, my mother managed to acquire a stocked bookshelf and teach me to read: *The New England Primer of ABCs*, *Folk and Fairy Tales of the Brothers Grimm*, but most importantly *The House of the Seven Gables* by Hawthorne.

In it, Colonel Pyncheon had accused a man named Maule of being a male witch and paid dearly for it. Maule's waves of terror at his hanging made his house rot and fall. The story was still sharp as tacks in my mind. He had cursed the Colonel as he died.

For that matter, Grimm's witches held power in their dark spells. They exacted their revenge, even though many of them were ruined in the end. Still, I felt a lilt of hope, a pang of useful anger. What was a witch exactly? Could a regular girl such as I who did not consort with devils have powers? It seemed impossible. Yet, if I was to be deemed a witch, perhaps I could wield power, at least long enough to get me out of here. I imagined what it would be like to lull the guards to sleep, or put a spell on the vermin to chew an exit tunnel. Even better, I could coax a flock of birds to lift me in their beaks and fly me out through the skylight to freedom.

Shame, Evalina! This line of reasoning is far from Quakerly! Though I'm not a Quaker, I dare not offend her. I had encountered the Plain People on Market Street and sometimes at Conklin's Taylor when their black coats needed pressing. They were soft-spoken and carried themselves with dignity.

My mother told me they worshipped in a place on Arch Street that had no preacher. Only silent worship on hard benches without cushions. *It is wrong of me to daydream such magic with Miss Amity standing on the other side of the bars.* I pulled myself back to the task of prayer, to uncertain redemption.

At the prayer's mention of walking through the Valley of Death, cold terror coursed through me. This prison might have a fancy skylight and running water, but make no mistake, being locked in here all by myself would require strength and fearlessness in the face of the ghastly unknown.

If I wasn't a witch with powers, I had no supernatural defense. If I was, did that mean I was cursed in the eyes of God? Did it mean that even my coaxing a bird out of its nest was an act of the devil? My mother had taught us Bible prayers. But she'd also taught us to think for ourselves, not to blindly follow the flock. Pondering these matters made me miss my mother on top of the heartrending pain I felt for my bother's loss. The silence was weighted with desperate questions I dared not ask yet. Except one:

"Will you visit me again, Amity?"

"I will." Her voice was kindly, and sounded young.

"Thank you."

"One more question, Evalina, please..."

"Yes?"

"Are thou sorry for stabbing the good Doctor Dowdrick?"

He was no *Good Doctor* as Amity called him, and yet... "I was only trying to keep him from harming my brother. I am no cold-blooded killer. You must believe me. Do you?"

"I will speak with thee again soon," was all she would say about the matter. "In the meantime, recite the Lord's

Prayer, think on Jesus and his apostles, and pray for thine Inner Light to grow and shine with the sweet light of penitence."

Had I killed someone? I had likely caused the demise of two men. In both cases one could say it was warranted, though my roiling emotions stirred up a dangerous brew. Outrage fueled righteous action but caused explosive damage. I was my own charge of dynamite. I twisted in silent agony. If things had turned out slightly different, Dowdrick would've been the one in prison for killing my brother without just cause. I craved true justice. What more had Mr. Conklin told the night watchmen and the newspapers? Pondering Amity's proclamations, I gripped the cell bars inside the wooden door and listened to the muffled padding of her departure.

4

Just before sundown, a tray of bread and water was pushed through the narrow drawer slot. But the person on the other side was not Amity, rather a man who would not answer any questions. He said only one thing: "Prisoner 113, food. " His voice was gruff and low. "When done, push the tray back out." All business.

I snuck peeks out of the slot when the tray was inserted. The man wore a brown jacket and pants. Odd thickly knit socks were pulled over his boots. He was broad and tall, with a bristling black beard.

Late that night I awoke to muffled laughter and the clink of a key in a lock. I jumped from my bed, my heart hammering, hoping against hope the bearded guard was freeing me.

"Sir?" I called. "Mister? Can you let me out? The walls are closing in on me. Please, let me out." I leaned my head against the bars inside the heavy door and above the food slot and perked my ears as best I could.

It was clearly the sound of a lock being turned, and the squeak of a door being opened. Not mine, though. The cell next to me. More laughter. The bearded guard's low voice. Earlier, his tone had been gruff. But now it was warmer with a distinct rich tone to it, like dark ale. I strained to make out words. The brick walls were thick, yet there must've been chinks because I could hear bits of conversation. 'Bad boy!' Muted laughter. 'What will… give old Dolly?' The strains of a folk song sung way off key. 'Laddie' something and 'Lassie' something. More guffaws. Then silence until much later when the door squeaked again and the key again turned in the lock. Soft footsteps padded down the hall.

"Dolly?" I pounded on the wall. "Is there a Dolly in there?" I felt like a lunatic doing this, but what else could I do but try? I repeated this refrain a few times. And then came an answer:

"Keep your trap shut! The guards… come running." Her tone was mocking and commanding, and yet oddly womanly. Like sandpaper on lace.

"Dolly? I don't mean to get you in trouble, but—"

"Get *you* in trouble, Miss Dull Wit! Shut it!"

Right then, I heard footsteps approach—different sounding ones, at a faster clip. Muffled yet resolute—the gait of a man. So I kept quiet and huddled on my bed. This guard paced back and forth for an hour maybe more. Dolly, whoever she was, knew what she was talking about.

I must've fallen asleep waiting because in the dead of night, I woke to rapping on the bricks. "Miss Dull Wit. Hey, you! Ear to the hole by the back of your bed."

So, that's why I could hear her. Darn, no candles to light my way. I stumbled to the back of my bed and raised the thin mattress. Ah! In the pitch dark, I felt a pinkie-sized indent and put my ear to it. "Yes! I'm here."

"What are you in for?"

"They say I'm a witch. They say I murdered people," I answered as loudly as I dared.

"And did you?"

"I suppose so. Not really."

She released a riotous snort. Or was it a thunderous fart? Hard to distinguish with only one teeny chink in the wall. "Dull Wit, you must know. Don't con the Madame of Number 12 Juniper Street."

A *madame?* Was this a French lady or...? "My pet bird flew down my boss's throat and killed him."

Another derisive snort, followed by an explosion of mirth. "That's a rich one!"

I had to admit, the image of the foul Mr. Gaul choking on a bird was satisfying. It did serve to shut him up for good! Yet, I felt a pang of grief picturing poor Speckle's struggle in the confines of the man's hot, sausage-like windpipe. "Not so funny for my bird."

"Did you cast a spell?"

"I... I don't know."

Something hit the wall. Her shoe? "Oh, bullocks, Dull Wit! You must know. If you don't, you'd best find out!"

That made sense in its own odd way. I should know what this talent was I had for animals. I suppose my granny had gone through this same worrying decision, so I shouldn't be too afraid of the devil to try. "Yes, Miss, I should discover the scope of it." *But how?*

A firm thud. She must've thrown her other shoe at the wall. "Stop calling me Miss. No innocent M*iss* am I. I am Madame Dolly Rouge. Or just plain Dolly."

"Then, Dolly, how is it a guard came into your cell? And if he opened the door then why then do you still remain there?" If Dolly was no wilting lily I should be outspoken, too. I could feel my ire rise like the rapid vibration of cicadas. "And do not call me Dull Wit! My name is Evalina Stowe! Or Eva to you." As my anger festered, I felt a flitting movement on my cheeks. I was stunned to feel a rush of winged insects scurrying about. Then they left me to buzz further over. If only I could see them. I missed the luxury of candlelight.

"Hey! What are you sending over here, Witch?" Dolly began to beat at the wall with what must be her shoes. "Stop them, Eva! No more Dull Wit, I promise! Stop them!"

I closed my eyes tightly and willed the insects to stop their infestation.

"I beg of you, cease! I'm scared of bugs. They're on my face. Help!"

My eyes were still closed. My emotions seesawed from anger to a smidgen of sorrow for Dolly. "Never call me Dull Wit then. Swear on it."

"I swear on my father's grave."

Inside, I chuckled. This power was real. I had managed to cow this bawdy woman. With my eyes still shut, I stretched out my arms and fingers, and felt the hitch and tickle of insects crawling onto my palms. I soothed them into a state resembling sleep. Mesmerized them, I suppose was the proper term.

"What are you doing?" Dolly called in a wary tone.

"Casting a spell on the insects. Putting them to sleep. It worked!"

"What the Dickens!" she said, "You and I should form a team. I sweet talk the guard, and then you cast a spell on the rats to terrify him into giving me the keys."

"You already have the guard eating out of your hands, Dolly."

She cackled. "Old Whiskers gives me candy, coins and kisses but no keys. Never the dratted keychain. How do we manage that, girly?"

"Evalina or Eva to you."

"Oh, bullocks."

5

The next morning, sunlight filtered down through the narrow skylight that Amity had called The Eye of God. She explained they were built in the ceilings of cells so prisoners could look up to pray, and God could watch over them, even speak to them—a sort of forced introduction. Though mostly what it meant to me was that day had come and I could finally see. She also warned me not to try and climb up to escape—that there were wardens ready to shoot at any time. Powers or no powers, this terrified me.

Glancing down at the places the insects burrowed through the night before, to my delight I counted three thin beams from Dolly's cell shining through tiny holes in the putty. Chinks in the armor of the penitentiary! Perhaps, I could even send tightly rolled messages like seafaring papers in bottles.

I made sure no guard was outside pacing. Then I knelt down and said, "You just might have yourself a deal, Dolly Rouge."

Nothing. No movement. No rustle.

"Dolly? Madame Rouge? Are you in there?"

More silence. The hairs on the nape of my neck stiffened. It was my turn to kick on the wall with my boot. Still nothing except that it brought the fast-walking guard over.

"Prisoner, you cannot bang on the wall."

"Sorry, sir."

"The other prisoners are paying quiet penitence. Your noise interrupts their prayers. You should be praying too," Fast Step scolded. "No more shenanigans or you will be punished."

"Yes, but sir? Is the prisoner next door to me all right? Is she sick or... ?"

"Not your business, Prisoner 113."

"Evalina Stowe, sir. I was just... well, I hoped she hadn't been taken ill, that's all."

"Number 113," he yelled, "your only business is to pray and think on your sins."

I plunked down on my bed and listened to the guard pacing for quite some time. All during this I also listened with hawk ears for the sound of Dolly's voice, in vain for her snorts of laughter, or even her calling out 'Dull Wit.' It was not to be.

What had become of Madame Rouge? Had the guards overheard our conversation last night? If so, why would they punish Dolly and not me? Was she in trouble for entertaining the guard with the bushy beard? Was Blackbeard in trouble as well? Would the warden hang them both? All of these unanswered questions rolled inside my head, which began to throb along with my heart pounding at a sickening clip.

Hearing high-pitched squeaks I quickly turned my head to the sound. A mouse sat in the corner to the left of the door! Another one wriggled under the door and then a third popped up from a tiny hole in the same corner. In my lonely cell up on Cherry Hill, I drew the furry creatures toward me. "A bit of bread? A scratch on your head? A song?"

They stared up at me flicking their whiskers. All three were gray. The biggest one had a white spot on his snout. Their varying sizes reminded me of the Goldilocks story.

"My head is pounding," I lamented, as if they could understand plain English. To demonstrate this I made a show of rubbing my brow.

They raised themselves up on their hind legs and pointed their snouts more intently at me. So I went on. "When tonight's bread comes, I'll feed you a portion. And then, start your training." I wasn't sure how I would train them, or what exactly I would get them to do, but here they were. It was a rare opportunity. Dolly had told me I should discover the exact scope of my talent for animal magic. Find out if I was a real witch, as the Somerset Farms people had accused me of being.

The tiny beasts broke their poses and raced toward me. I choked down a draught of panic at their rapid approach, at their shiny eyes and nakedly pink tails. I sensed that inside their jaws were teeth that could pierce rawhide.

Yet they did not bite, or claw at me. They simply climbed over my body and sniffed as if getting to know my enormous furless being. Once satisfied, they dashed off me, and settled by my side. I dared to extend my index finger and lightly stroke one mouse's head. It was warm and terribly delicate. The critter flinched but didn't bolt. Then, as if by some hidden instruction from the boss mouse, they trailed one after the other down to the floor and into a previously unseen hole in the corner floorboard. More escape routes.

I looked up. Indeed, there were miracles as great as the sun streaming down through the Eye of God.

After what seemed like a week Dolly still had not spoken no matter how many times I yelled her name. I sensed an empty cell, and I was petrified—that she had died. Perhaps they had hanged her.

Maybe I was next.

I struggled not to let my thoughts dwell there. Instead, I focused on exercising and on training the mice.

Once a day, the guard would stop by my cell door and demand I don a woolen hood. This detestable bit of fabric was hot and itchy, its only ventilation being two eyeholes.

After my hood was tied and knotted with lashes at the neckline, the guard would grasp a pulley and raise a back door in my cell that led to a small outside space, enclosed on all sides with metal bars. Though the bag was on my head, I could feel the guard's eyes on me—hot, prying, mean—waiting for me to do something strange. Their staring at me felt like a violation of my privacy and, speaking of penitence, even to my damaged soul. I hadn't figured out the prison layout. But in the next months I should surely try. If only I could meet other inmates and talk with them.

I paced round and round and round like a model prisoner and tamped down my urge to gather my mice around me. They would have liked the earthy scent of the outdoors, but the guards would have called them my familiars and smashed them underfoot. After I'd finished my dozen laps, I would sit on the cobbled ground, and imagine hauling up the heavy stones and digging a hole all the way out to Fairmount Avenue with a shovel, stolen from the groundskeeper. Escaping back to the dangerous but free chaos of the streets.

This went on for a week. I knew this because I began

counting out the days by scratching marks on the underside of my table with my shoe heel. Every night when the guard with the black beard pushed my bread though the slot I would eat my share and save corners of it for training. Sometimes there would be rice and a small piece of meat. Twice green beans, cooked within an inch of their life.

I tore off bits of my sheet and my undergarments to provide the mice with snippets of things to carry. The goal was to get them through the hole to Dolly's cell with a message.

Every day that dragged on without her return my panic ramped up. For if not Dolly, who would I send a message to? No one seemed to inhabit the cell to my other side, and the few times I dared call out when the guards had walked off, no one had answered me. The mice were rebellious at first, speeding willy-nilly with the shards of cloth, or disappearing with them into their underground den. No doubt these pieces were padding their family nest. My efforts to lure them to me, and to keep my commands calm and friendly—augmented with tasty morsels finally paid off. By week's end the first mouse I'd seen, the biggest one, wriggled into the hole that led to Dolly's cell with my sheet corner in his teeth and his pink tail twitching.

I had written on it with pricks of blood: *D! Give a sign you live! E.* I fretted that the mouse would chew up my message, or return it unread.

I sent the furry critter mental pictures—of dropping it on Dolly's floor and shimmying back.

Miracle of miracles, he returned without it! Maybe my prayers recited with Amity were working after all. If so, then was being a witch as evil as people assumed? I hoped not. I didn't feel evil. When a witch prayed could it transform her into a good witch? I couldn't think of any in the Grimm's tales. Was there such a being? Again, my head filled with unanswerable queries, so I returned to practical matters.

I fed the mouse an extra hunk of bread from the stores in my folded sheet. He regarded me for an instant before scurrying to the far corner of the cell. Greedily, he devoured the entire piece by himself. Jauntily, he cocked his head and licked his tiny paws.

"You deserve it," I whispered.

6

Despite my animal companions I was painfully lonely. If not for them, I would surely go mad in a matter of months. I missed my brother terribly and the isolated penitence was unusual torment. It made one's mind race with a constant stream of twisted fantasies. I imagined the guard placing a noose around Dolly's neck. I'd never seen her but I pictured her tall, amply built with commanding black eyes and cascading hair, like an Indian Queen. I imagined the guard hanging me, too. I pictured him binding us together, cutting us into bloody meat cubes and feeding us to the unsuspecting inmates. This foul image had me avoiding the next gray slice of meat slipped through the meal slot.

I saw myself, Prisoner 113, in the same cell for my entire life, my emaciated body drying into a crooked pile of bones. And the worst: I pictured Dowdrick creeping into my cell, hurling the woolen hood over my head and cinching it tightly with rope. Tying my hands behind my back and calling me foul names. *What will you do to me now, you filthy strumpet, you evil Witch of the Wasps?* I could almost hear him asking. *You think you're so powerful that you can get away with stabbing me and leaving me for dead, do you? Think again*! He would work himself into a rage, his cheeks bloating like waterlogged beets. And finally, he would lance my belly with the same long scissors I had plunged into him and sit there laughing as I bled dry.

These waking nightmares left me sweat-drenched, weak and lost. If only I had someone to talk to I might be able to crawl from the depths and breathe.

Once in a blue moon I heard another prisoner screeching, "Help!" or "I'm going raving mad!" It was frightening, but also a comforting reminder I wasn't alone. They were women's cries; it meant we were on the women's ward.

I would call out, "I'm here! I'm going mad, too!" The guards' loud scolding quashed my outbursts instantly, and no one ever called back to me. This scared me worse, because I imagined the inmates being punched or kicked into quick submission.

The line between normal logic and delirium was blurring.

I tried to talk with Blackbeard, but as lighthearted as he'd been with Dolly, with me he was hard as granite. "Prisoner 113, do your time," he would say. Or "Prisoner 113, I'll sew your mouth shut." After this, he would penalize me by pacing back and forth and banging on my door each time he passed by.

When the bearded guard took his leave, I called out to the second guard, who I called Fast Step. Mostly, he ignored me, or if anything, he picked up his pace. Only once did he pause by my door. "Is it true you're a witch?" he whispered.

I wasn't sure how to answer. I didn't want to say no, because I might need the advantage over him in the future. If I said yes, he might run off, spooked.

I finally said, "Let me out and I'll talk. Let me out and I'll show you."

All he did was race away, his footsteps at a fever pitch.

Many a night, I tried to test these so-called powers by closing my eyes, raising my arms toward the door and with every fiber of being, willing the key to turn and let the door spring open. It was not to be. If I had a magical ability to communicate and coax, it was only over the wild beasts.

After three long weeks according to my scratched calculations under the table, Amity paid a visit. I flew to the door and gripped the interior bars as if this would save me from drowning.

"How are thou, Miss Evalina? Has thee been praying to the Eye of God? And reciting thy prayers with all thy heart and soul?" she asked through the narrow slot in the outside door.

"Yes, Amity, yes!" Was it true? Not really. Yet it wasn't *untrue*. I was praying that my mice would become better trained. I was praying for Dolly's return. I was praying to be free of my dreadful visions.

"Let us pray together then. The Lord's Prayer."

We recited it slowly and with feeling. Indeed, it was healing to hear another's voice align with mine in spirit. I peeked through the food tray slot. Amity was pretty in a crisp beige bonnet with ruffles and she looked to be only a couple of years older than I. Her gaze was reassuringly straightforward and compassionate. I was relieved and grateful for every moment with her.

"Does thee know who Charles Dickens is?" she asked when the prayer was done.

"Why, yes. He's the author of *Oliver Twist*, is he not?"

"He is indeed. I am impressed that thee knows of his work. And that thee reads."

"Oh, yes! I was quite the bookworm, Miss. I remember Master Dickens's lines from *Oliver*. "We need be careful how we deal with those about us, when every death carries to some small circle of survivors, thoughts of so much omitted, and so little done- of so many things forgotten, and so many more which might have been repaired!"

"An obscure line, but well said."

"Am I able to read books in here to pass the time?" I asked. "Oh, that would be so lovely! May I?"

When Amity hesitated I feared I sounded too needy. I suppose she was only pondering how to say her next thoughts. For she finally answered, "Charles Dickens visited this penitentiary some years ago, and he wrote a treatise about it."

"Fascinating!" I would say almost anything to keep Amity talking.

"Quite." She sniffed. "He determined that isolated penitence is unhealthy for one's soul. Evalina, what does thee think of this?"

Was this a trick question? Might one particular answer give me a failing grade? I knew Amity believed in the healing power of penitence. It was my turn to hesitate.

"Speak truthfully, Miss Stowe," she demanded. "To lie is a sin."

My throat seized up. I coughed to loosen it. I was undecided on the issue of penitence. Though I figured it could just as easily change someone as not, so I leapt in. "The power of penitence is real, Miss Amity. But must we prisoners pray alone? Humans are social animals. Even wolves live in packs."

She sighed deeply. "Indeed. But these prisoners suffer from a moral disease, and this is why they commit crimes. If they are grouped together might they not be agitated, be tempted by the others to commit additional crimes?"

"Some." I admitted. "Not I though. I am a good person, Miss Amity! Please believe me. I never stole money, I never used the Lord's name in vain." Heaven knows what I did to inspire my precious Speckle to choke Mr. Gaul…"

"Does thou think thee could mix with the inmates without becoming infected by their depravity?"

"Yes, please trust me!" I had no idea what she had in mind, but any way to get me out of here sounded like heaven. "I am absolutely impervious to corruption, Miss Amity."

At this she let out a wisp of laughter. I was astounded that I had inspired a proper Quaker lady to laugh, and that she was permitted to laugh at all!

Whenever I had seen Quaker womenfolk walking on the street, they wore serious, pious expressions. They cast their eyes to the pavement and avoided direct gazes from strangers.

"Guard?" she called out. "Unlock this door and let me in. Evalina, please walk to the back of thy cell and remain there."

My knees nearly crumpled in shock. What on earth was she going to do? I hurried to the rear wall and stayed still to show her I was safe and reliable. At seeing an inquisitive mouse with flickering whiskers poke up through the hole in the corner near the door I panicked. Coaxing the creature down with urgent mental warnings, I breathed with relief when it ducked back under the floorboards.

Though I had a million questions I never asked one. The first: Who had given this innocent, god-fearing woman the permission to open the cell of a suspected witch? The second: Was she tricking me into trusting her only to get me hanged?

Grumbling, the guard turned the key in the lock and the heavy door squeaked open. He lowered the stuffy hood on me and tied it. Then he secured heavy iron cuffs around my ankles and locked them. I could walk but only in a shuffling manner.

Amity took me by the hand. It was a pleasant surprise to feel a warm hand clasping mine, and it almost brought me to tears. In another life, maybe we could have been friends. If I had been born to a genteel family. If my own hadn't perished and I'd never taken to the harsh ways of the streets. She led me out of the cell and down what seemed like four or five long hallways. It was hard not to trip in the iron cuffs and my hood was too big. It kept slipping down, so I couldn't always see out of the tiny eyeholes.

I wanted to ask her why the need for hoods, and where we were going but I could only hope she would tell me when she was ready. I knew we had ventured outside when I felt the sun on my back and a gust of balmy wind rustled my dress and pantaloons. The air smelled of August leaves, ever so slowly drying on their branches. It was heavenly.

She stopped me and straightened out my hood so the eyeholes were once again aligned. "Does thou see where thee is?"

I stood in front of a long wooden box filled with dirt. In the distance I saw more of the same, set at various angles on the brick courtyard. We were in a yard constrained all around by enormously high walls—I thought I counted eight sides. Were we in the central yard of the prison? It seemed so, because doors led out from each wall, but it was impossible to know for sure. At any rate, seedlings in small ceramic pots were lined up at intervals along the sprawling planters. Waiting for us. Lines of fellow prisoners stood next to, and across from me. An army of shrouded inmates, yet with eyes staring out like stunned owls. Under any other circumstance it would have been funny. In this one it was a chilling humiliation. Ah but the other sight!

"A garden. Yes, I see!"

"Can thee work a garden?" asked Amity. "Is thou good with thine hands?"

"A green thumb I have, Miss. Amity. To be sure."

This brought on some laughter. The guards shut the clamor down at once. "No outbursts, no chatter; nothing here but hard work, prisoners. You will toil to plant the food you will eat. To be out of your cell is a privilege. One wrong step and it will be over. Understand?" The big guard with the black beard was looking pointedly at me.

I turned my head to avoid his stare, and instead I glanced at the row of prisoners across from me. Was Dolly Rouge in this number? I did see some big-hipped, big-bosomed prisoners and a handful of short prisoners that might've been children. But how would I know if one of the former ones were Dolly since I'd never even seen her?

My eyes settled on a young man—maybe nineteen—who was tall and athletic and gazing directly at me. His gray eyes that glowed brightly from under the hood were full of curiosity. His stance was slightly stooped yet proud, defiant even. His hands were large and expressive with veins running over muscles as if from regular manual labor. Odd how one could drink in every detail in seconds even when one's vision was limited—*especially* when one's vision was limited. As if the seeing at these times was vital.

Other eyes landed on me—blue, brown and midnight black. Yet, none affected me like this one man's gaze. I felt a pull toward him of the likes I'd never known. On some ethereal plane, I knew the man already. Or was this a delusion from my time in isolation? Whatever the answer, I vowed I would talk to him. I was aware of his fast-pumping heart the same way I knew the soul of the wild beasts.

We planted cabbage seedlings. If planted in late summer for a second seeding it grew until hard frost. This I learned from the gardeners at Somerset Farm. The hooded man with gray eyes took a spot just across the container, close enough so that if we'd been allowed to speak, we could've heard each other with hushed whispers. But I didn't dare jeopardize this incredible opportunity. The mineral-rich scent of the leaves had me punch-drunk. I got to kneel, and paw into the soil with my bare hands. The feel of the peat in my palms was a revelation. It reminded me of jumping puddles with my brother, and of building houses with twigs in the yard. Of innocence and childhood before all the tragedy began.

When I tamped the dirt around each plant I swore it thanked me. Certainly, the leaves perked right up. It was a joy. Amity stood against the wall, her bonnet tipped up to allow the sun to warm her face. Her cheeks were tossed with pale freckles like my precious Speckle's belly. Her hair, escaping in wisps from either side of the bonnet was the color of caramel.

I stole many peeks at the gray-eyed man's hands. The way he scooped up large sections of the dirt, and inserted the seedling almost sideways. Then once the soil was scooped back in he pushed down and righted each plant with a flick of his nimble fingers. The crescents of the nails were blackened with dirt, which somehow made my heart flip in secret delight. Silly how a man's dirty hands could fill me with sensation. An impulsive giggle tickled my throat but I pressed it down because when I looked up I saw Blackbeard still staring. Why was he so intent on watching me? Hard panic rattled through me.

We planted two twenty-foot long containers of cabbage and one of broccoli. I knew this because we also stuck long, flat sticks by each seedling with their plant names written on them, and then tied the stems with twine to the wood. I was tempted to pocket some of the twine but Blackbeard's focus on me was too intense. Not that I had an exact plan for it. But tools of any kind seemed an obvious advantage in here. All too soon, the guards barked out an order to stand and line up. One last time, the tall, gray-eyed man met my gaze and held it. He seemed to be trying to memorize me. His focus slid from my eyes to my bodice and flare of the dress, to my hands, streaked in dirt. And then, like magic, without raising his whole arm, he lifted his fingers, and wagged them at me! A sly, secret wave. I copied his move the second Blackbeard looked away. It was rapturous, as if we'd gotten away with a jewel heist under a copper's nose! I swallowed down another giddy giggle.

As we marched off in separate lines I noticed his strange way of walking. It wasn't exactly a limp, more a listing from side to side, as if there were something horribly wrong with his feet. I shuddered. Life was so hard.

7

That night, Blackbeard came around with dinner—soggy lentils and a ball of stale rice. It made me grateful that we prisoners were granted the chance to plant a garden. How firm and sweet the cabbage and broccoli off the vine would be. Today's physical labor had sharpened my appetite. I wolfed down my dinner. After this, I must've passed out.

For when I awoke, it was dark as coal. I was in my boots with my jacket all twisted around me. I was about to get up and remove them when I heard a racket coming from Dolly's cell—of a chair being pushed or a tin cup being slapped against the table. I tried not to gasp as I eased back down on my mattress and tilted my ear to the hole in the bricks at the end of the bed.

There was another crash and a muffled curse—hard to determine if it was a man's or a woman's voice because of its rasp. It sounded like a heavy body had tumbled to the floor. I wanted to call out. But something told me to stay quiet a little longer to determine if it was, in fact, Dolly. I had forgotten to ask her how long her sentence was, or why she was even serving one. Maybe the guards had released Dolly and put in a new prisoner altogether. My ears were peeled for the sound of departing boots clacking out in the hall. None. No more crashing either.

I rolled toward the hole in the wall and spoke. "Dolly! Is that you? Are you all right?" When no one answered I called out again, louder. "Dolly! Answer me. Is it you?"

After more scrambling and crashing her voice rang out. "Who's calling me? Who are you?" It was definitely Dolly, but her voice was wobbly. "What do you want with me?"

"It's Eva. Where were you these last weeks?"

"Eva? Who's Eva?"

"Evalina Stowe. The prisoner in the next cell over."

A long pause. "Who are you, *really?*"

As if I had the luxury of a secret identity. I frowned. "I'm Dull Wit. Remember? That's what you called me."

"I know no Dull Wit."

"Why can't you remember? Where did they take you? Did you get my note?"

"Who are you? What do you want with me?" Her voice was clotted with fear. "I got no dratted note. Leave me alone!" After a weighted pause she said, "Don't let them take me away again."

I latched onto this. "Who took you, Dolly? Where did they take you?"

"I don't know," she wailed. "How am I supposed to know? Leave me alone!" With this, she burst into tears.

Her heartrending sobs frightened me even more than her forgetting me, because though I didn't know Dolly well I knew one thing for sure; she was no crybaby.

I was planning my next round of questions when I heard the dreaded footsteps clacking our way. It was Blackbeard, the one with the slower more determined step. He rapped on Dolly's door. No answer. He rapped again harder.

"Go away, Devil! Leave me alone," she yelled.

The key clinked in the lock and with a rat-like squeak of the hinges the door opened. Dolly released a bloodcurdling scream.

"Shut up, you crazy strumpet!" yelled Blackbeard. "D'ya wanna wake the dead?"

"Get out! Don't take me away again!" she pleaded.

"What're you talking about, woman? I never took you anywheres. Fact is, I was wondering where in blazes you disappeared to!"

With this she seemed to calm down. At least enough not to call him the devil again. "I don't remember," she cried. "Why can't I remember?"

"Beats me, Dolly!" replied Blackbeard. "Did some sly guard take you out and fill you with rotgut ale? Did you get blind soused on combustibles, or what?"

I couldn't hear her answer, only low mumbling.

"Who'd you drink with, foul woman? I thought you was loyal to this ole lad."

"Don't touch me!" she screeched.

I determined he'd attempted to calm her by caressing her hair or arm. Or...

"Lay off, man!" she ordered. "Can't you see when a poor gal is upset?"

"Don't you remember your bearded love? Here, some-thin' to put your spirits right."

I heard the clink of coins on a hard surface.

"I remember that, Whiskers. Well, now. This Madame welcomes you. I was having a lousy night until... " She released a trumpeting fart.

This launched Blackbeard into delighted peals of laugh-ter. "Woman, I know you're farin' better when you fire off one of your stenchy farts."

This must've aroused his ardor, because when I strained my ear I heard the juicy smacking of lips.

After a time, marked by murmurs and chuckles, Blackbeard and Dolly settled down. And that's when the conversation picked up again. I strove to hear as much as I could by pressing my ear right up against the cold brick.

"You remember none of it? And you wasn't all fired up on rum or homebrew?"

"That's right, mister. You got it."

"But that makes no sense."

"You're telling me! I could barely remember my name when I woke up in this dratted cell. Get me out of here and set me free. Can you do that?"

"I cannot, woman. I am under strict orders."

"Oh, bullocks!"

"They'll fire me." Blackbeard's voice became plaintive. "I need the money for rent and vittles."

"You randy set of trousers! I need coinage too. Lay it on me."

"Greedy wench. I gave you a pile already."

"Never enough, mister." More coins clattered onto the table. After this, the conversation was lost to me. They were mumbling too low to hear. Until Blackbeard spoke up.

"Did you ever speak to the girl next to you? Prisoner 113? Goes by Evalina Stowe?"

My skin prickled like fire. Why was he bringing me up?

"Funny you should say. The girl was yelling at me before you came," Dolly said. "Is Eva-line her name? She said it was Dull Wit."

What was wrong with Dolly? She'd seemed sharp as needles before! Now she was a blank slate with her brains scooped out like a ghoul from a Mary Shelley story. My insides did a horrified flip.

"Dull Wit. Stowe. The girl kept asking me where you was," Blackbeard said. "If she asked me once, she asked me a hundred times."

Highly exaggerated! I stewed to a boil.

"Why do you mention the girl?" Dolly asked with a tinge of suspicion. "Do you think she has answers as to where I was these last weeks?"

"Could be, could be," remarked Blackbeard.

Rubbish! I pictured the guard stroking his thick black beard in a philosophic manner unsuited to him. I was tempted to refute his utter nonsense. But I clamped my jaw shut. Better that I knew more of what he was truly thinking first.

"They say she's a witch," declared Blackbeard. "Maybe she put a spell on you, woman. Maybe she wants you to forget who you are."

"Why would she do that?" Dolly shrilled.

"Because it shows her power. Witches are devilish creatures. Do they need reasons to perform evil deeds?"

The neighboring cell was silent after that. I imagined Dolly stunned, motionless. Under my breath I cursed Blackbeard. He was the evil one, not I! What possible reason could he have to poison Dolly against me? The witches I'd read about didn't always need to prove their power. But a weakling man might.

"Well, wench," said Blackbeard, "I for one am glad to see you back again. I missed you. Don't let a soul in here but me and don't give that witch the time of day." I heard the squeak of the door hinges and then the turn of the key.

I needed allies in here. How dare he turn Dolly against me! I would curse Blackbeard if I had the power. Singe off his beard and melt his offending lips together for eternity. Yet I only had authority over the mice, the birds and insects.

This, I had learned was the scope of my talents. Shaking my head, I tried to loosen the knots of my fury. No time for hate or frustration. My wits needed to be clear to start afresh with Dolly and build trust brick by brick.

Amity came by every few days. She helped me lower and tie my hood and then led me to the garden. The second time, we planted butternut squash in a new container, and I wrangled my position so I again faced the tall, gray-eyed man. He grew bolder as did I. At least twice during our gardening sessions we whispered questions when the guards were busy with the inmates on the far side of the rows.

"Your name?" he asked under his breath.

"Evalina... Eva," I whispered, not daring to glance up for fear I would catch Blackbeard or Fast Step's eye. "Yours?"

"Bertram... Birdy." At this, my heart fluttered. Birds were so woven into the fabric of my being that this meeting seemed fated. *Don't be a lunatic, Eva.* I told myself. *Don't assume connections that don't exist.*

Not yet, my rebellious side countered. *But they might!*

The next time, planting a box of potatoes, I asked what happened to Birdy's foot.

"Explosion," he murmured. "Blasting rocks for the Pennsylvania Railroad."

"Where are you from?"

"Cardiff, Wales. Came here when I was fifteen. You?"

"Born on Brown Street not far from here."

"Ah. A hop, skip and jump away."

I nodded as much as I dared. He noticed because when I finally peeked his eyes were smiling, which delivered a heated charge.

We renewed our concentration on planting, for the guards were marching our way. The potatoes were a curious lot. No green seedling in sight; only the knobby, part-dry, part-rotten spud with its sprouting feelers covered by a solid six-inches of dirt. Concealed but growing, just like my budding friendship with Birdy.

When I returned to my cell, I tried to get Dolly to talk. The first time, she remained quiet as snow on a Sunday morning. The next time, she howled for me to stop my requests. "I don't converse with witches," she spat out.

"Who said I was a witch?"

She hemmed and hawed before finally admitting the guard had.

"You believe him? Why?" I persisted, not waiting for her answer. "He holds the entire ring of keys to this wretched jail, and he's not freeing you, is he now?"

Silence. Stumped. I could almost feel the broken gears of her brain cranking away before she creaked out a reply. "He's... not... allowed."

"How would you know what he's allowed or not? If he freed you who would know *he* did it? He's just keeping you in tow. Filling you with fear."

"Is not!" she said petulantly.

"Besides, when we first talked, before they took you away for the week you seemed to *like* the idea I might have powers. You told me we should work together to free ourselves. Come up with a clever plan. Perhaps involving magic," I added mischievously.

"Shut your trap!" Dolly bellowed. "Shut it now."

I didn't let this stop me. "It's good you're spitting mad, Dolly. It shows your mind is returning to you."

"My mind never went nowhere," she said unconvincingly. "And don't call me Dolly, witch."

"I was afraid they'd drugged or beaten out your spirit. When you came back in here you were a sad, confused rag doll."

"I'm warning you. Shut it, girl!"

"Ha! The Madame of Juniper Street is mad as the dickens!"

"How do you know where I worked?" Her voice quivered as if she'd seen a ghost.

"You told me, Dolly. You also told me about the Gentlemen's Directory that you store in your corset." I paused for dramatic effect. "Did they take it from you?"

"Huh?" She shuffled wildly around, knocking and scraping her chair or table against the floor. "Where is my booklet? Did you cast a spell and make it disappear?" The racket got louder. She threw something hard at the wall.

And then it grew oddly quiet.

"What's this?" she squeaked. "A devil's message scratched in blood?"

Embers sparked in me. Dolly had found the note I'd written. The mouse I'd trained had deposited it perfectly after all. "Read it, Madame Rouge."

Haltingly, she gasped out the line. "*D! Give a... sign you live! E.* What is this, witch?"

This woman was as stubborn as one of Somerset Farm's 500-pound hogs. "I was worried about you, Dolly, when I kept on calling you and you never answered. I wrote that with my own blood and pushed it through the crack in the wall, hoping you'd see it and answer me. I was praying they hadn't killed you."

She snorted. "Witches pray?"

"Why not? I care about people. I'm not a bad person." I sighed. "I'm not sure which is worse: killing a body or killing a mind. The death of one's spirit." Unexpectedly, I was on the verge of tears.

"You're a real Jenny Lind actress type. Did you perform tragic drama in the theater?" Her remark was meant to annoy me, yet there was warmth to her voice. It gave me hope. She was quiet for a time. "I live, witch," she finally said. "I'm here conversing ain't I? But don't expect me to trust you. I trust no one—not my regulars or my lovers. Not even my family, the rotten sons of… "

"That's a sad state of affairs. Not even your mother or father?"

"Ach, they were the worst! My mother beat me. My souse of a father left her with four squalling mouths to feed."

"I'm sorry."

"Don't be. Way of the world, witch."

"Name's Eva."

"Eva, eh?" With that, Dolly must've thrown herself on her bed, because the wooden frame gave a groan, and two boots clunked on the floor. "This old dame is tuckered out so you'd best be quiet."

"Sweet dreams, Dolly."

"Oh, bullocks!"

I lay on my bed grinning from ear to ear. It might take a while, but I'd coax her back to my side. And then we just might figure out an escape plan.

8

In the mornings the mice crept out for their meal. They were nocturnal creatures. But since I couldn't see them when it was dark I trained them to fend off sleep until the light streamed from the skylight. They detested the sun and mostly kept to the shady corners of the room. The biggest one was a glutton so I had to feed him first. Then I would place the other morsels far from where he sat in order to give the two others a running head start.

Afterwards, they'd sit on their haunches, raise their pink paws to their snouts, and lick off every crumb.

I would send them mental messages; direct them to do small tasks. *Bring my stockings to me, or run around the edges of the cell and listen under the door for the guard's approach.* Once I enticed the smallest one to scale my prison wall to the ceiling and back. I wasn't sure what this was leading to, but it was important to train them almost daily, so when the time came to give them an essential mission they would be loyal, sharp and understand my signals.

I looked for unspoken signs, too. The next time Amity came to prepare me for the yard work, she seemed terribly agitated. There was no warm hello and she avoided my eyes. I figured she was tired or sick.

"Why do we need to wear hoods?" I asked as she cinched my hood with a strange vehemence. The heavy cloth was stuffy enough, and made the air hot and stale. When tied so tightly I grew short of breath.

"The jailers don't want thee getting too familiar with one another," she answered.

"It might help morale if we became a little friendly," I protested. "These hoods scare me. The prisoners look like a ghost army."

"Pray tell, what does morale have to do with penitence?" Amity's sharp manner of speaking was unsettling for she had been an oasis of calm. My daydream of us being friends was just wishful thinking. Something unpleasant hung in the air but I couldn't name it. My mice sensed it, too. Just before we left, I saw them dart from their hole and run in frantic zigzags along the wall. There was no time to lure them back to their den but at least they didn't follow me.

Out in the yard we took our regular positions—long lines of prisoners on either side of the newest planter. The planters were all perhaps twenty feet long, and rose two feet tall and two feet wide. We stood at the ready with rounded trowels sanded dull as baby spoons so we couldn't use them as weapons. The long container was filled with soil, and the seedlings to be planted stood in clay pots at our feet. I snuck a look at Birdy, who was motionless and avoided my eyes. Glancing to my left at the arched entrance of the prison I saw why.

The shorter guard, Fast-Step wore an angular gritted jaw as he approached. I'd never gotten a good look at him before, only heard his rhythmic rapping on my cell door with his nightstick. As much as Blackbeard frightened me, this man was worse. For his yellow, wide-set eyes were cold stones against his reddish inflamed skin. He marched toward us and tapped on our end of the planter with his long metal stick.

"Prisoners, pay attention. Before you begin work today two important guests will join us in the courtyard. They are doctors from the new and esteemed Eclectic Medical College on Haines Street. They are here to tour our prison and interview the inmates."

Birdy sent me a puzzled look. I sent one back.

What do the doctors want with us prisoners?

When Fast Step turned and walked back toward the arched entrance to bring in the guests, I gave Birdy a saucy roll of my eyes. Even though he kept his arms glued to his sides, he relaxed enough to wriggle his fingers in a kind greeting. Delight skipped through me. It was so lonely in my cell that our small human interactions kept me cheerful until our next time together.

Though when I saw the two visitors who walked in on either side of Fast Step my entire being froze. One was a swarthy man with slicked back ebony hair. When I saw the second, a shocked wheeze escaped me before I could stop myself. Birdy looked over in concern.

"I present you with Dr. Horace Dowdrick and Dr. Condor Sumac," said Fast Step.

Dr. Dowdrick! How on Earth?

I remembered how upsetting it was to pry his filthy paws off my poor little Todd, and to plunge the scissors into Dowdrick's thick layers of fat.

Sickening, heartrending justice.

So, Dowdrick's wounds had not been fatal. But I had a clear picture of him spread out on the tailor's floor. His boots were splayed and his belly was like a swollen hillock, the long scissors I'd stabbed him with jutting from his side, his blood burbling into his fancy, tailored jacket. Horror invaded me like the fever of cholera, and the prison yard blurred before my eyes.

The three men drew closer. Their movement, at first indistinct sharpened to terrifying crispness. Fury roared up until my face heated and my heart throbbed in my ears. Dowdrick limped with a hand pressed to his side where I had stabbed him. One small satisfaction. If he came any closer I would be unable to stop myself from strangling him with my bare hands for the way he'd choked the life out of my brother. I gripped my trowel in a fisted hand. If need be, I could smash his face with the blunt end.

The three men stopped at our end of the planter and prepared to address us. As my rage boiled, I heard a swishing sound overhead and looked up. A rush of birds swooped toward us, dark against the cloudy sky. Crows and jays, gulls and robins as big as cats. They gathered as if they were of one tribe, and swirled overhead ever faster. The men weren't paying attention. Not yet. But some of the hooded prisoners noticed. A few faces turned upward.

My upset was agitating the birds. This sent me into a wilder panic.

Dowdrick knew how my power grew beyond my control when I was enraged. He had seen it first hand with the rampaging wasps. How they had stung me as well. Also, surely he'd read the evening papers describing how I'd sent my bird down Mr. Gaul's throat at Somerset to choke him. The birds could not continue like this. I would be dead if they did. I sent them desperate commands.

Stay up high, don't let them see you. Not yet!

One of the rebellious jays ignored me, and sailed low, right past my head. I willed myself to calm. Otherwise, the birds would keep swarming. Already, Amity was frowning at me.

"Prisoners, take off your hoods," Fast Step demanded. "Let the good doctors see you."

Good doctors, bah! Sawbones! Leeches. Murderers, my mind screamed.

"I said, off!" Fast Step smacked my knees with his dratted nightstick. It stung like hell.

As much as I hated the thick hood, it was the only barrier left between the safety of my anonymity and Dowdrick. Did he know I was in this lot? Would he kill me when he saw me? I had almost murdered him. Though he *had* murdered my brother.

"Inmates, get them off now!" yelled Fast Step. "These gentlemen don't have all day."

Why were they invited here? Were they donors to the prison?

I struggled to untie the laces that Amity had knotted. She stood against the wall, unmoving and stared at me sharply yet impassively.

As I loosened the last strap, Fast Step reached over and yanked off my hood. I quickly turned my back to him and let my long dark hair fall over my cheeks. Staring down the long line of prisoners my heart swelled and broke at the sight of their faces exposed like newborn babies, thrust into the world, pale-skinned with blue veins showing. They stared back at me as if a ghost army was unveiled.

Most were men as I expected. But there were a handful of women. The line of raggedy children surprised me most. One lad looked not more than six. Looking closer, I realized this was Lightning! He was the street urchin who had helped me steal food when I was starving. His pale, green eyes fixed on mine in recognition and horror for our situation. Rail thin with mussed blond hair, he had dirt streaks on his cheeks from the gardening. I looked away for my safety as well as his. Some dark-skinned Negroes and a Chinaman also stood in the lot.

And Birdy. Oh, my. If I weren't so terrified of Dowdrick seeing me I would have swooned. Without his mask, Birdy was ruggedly handsome with muscular arms as if he lifted heavy loads but also trekked up mountains and through forests with ease. He looked about my age, eighteen. His hair fountained down in dark waves, and his long, chiseled nose and jaw showed a stubborn, brave character. His kind gray eyes showed concern as he gazed at me. We were three feet away from each other, separated only by the tall wooden planter. If I leaned forward I could've touched him.

The birds retreated further into the sky. Some perched in trees, others meandered above the chimney-tops. I willed my heart to slow its pounding, for otherwise the birds would soon resume their hunt.

"Prisoners, if I point to you, state your name and crime." I knew that pompous voice without turning. It was Dowdrick's. I could only avoid his wrath for so long. I would need to face him and then...

For the moment I was spared for a trembling, high-pitched voice rang out. "Lewin Derr."

Now, I knew Lightning's full name. I snuck another peek. My heart bled, he was so close— in age and looks—to Todd. And we shared a history. He'd been my brother's friend, and then mine as well.

Dowdrick persisted. "Your crime? And address me as Sir!"

"Sir, jailed for stealing shirts from the market stall si—."

"That's not all," Fast Step cut in. "What else, Mudsill? Speak up."

Lewin dared to shrug instead of answering. Like the blue jay he exhibited a natural air of defiance.

Fast Step grunted from his position behind me. "You forgot your dirty thieving from the firehouses." Fast Step must have turned to address his guest for he spoke of the boy in the third person. "The ingrate stole bridles, reins, even a horse!"

"Faster than any thief is why they call me Lightning, *not* Mudsill," the boy stated flatly as he glared at Fast Step.

A ripple of surprised laughter rolled down the line of prisoners. I was terribly worried for him. Who dared talk back to a guard?

"Shut up, insolent boy!" A loud clap sounded as Fast Step slapped Lightning. "Shut up the lot of you!" I snuck looks from between my hanks of hair. My breath hitched at the guard staring at all of us. "Else I will handcuff you to chairs, seal your noses and pour water down your throats!" All chuckling ceased.

"Madame," Dowdrick said with oily interest from behind me. "We've seen you before but restate your name." Terror froze my heart. Was he calling me? I dared not spin around to see. Instead, I hunched over and kept my hair shrouding my face as if I hadn't heard him.

"Dolly Rouge," a woman answered. Daring another glimpse, I saw she stood at the far end of the planter. Regal and bosomy, she had a serious face and long hair, flaming red from henna except at the roots, which had begun to grow in gray. Not so different than how I imagined her—as a queen of sorts.

"Your crime?" Dowdrick's tone dripped with malicious pleasure. He had just admitted he had worked with Dolly before—or least *seen* her. Was he the one responsible for her amnesia? Or had he seen her on the street before her confinement?

"Being the head madam at a bawdy house," she hissed as if he was no bigger than a mongrel's flea under her heels. "Not that you could've afforded me," she added derisively.

Shush, Dolly! I wanted to say. If, as Dowdrick stated, she'd seen him before, then why didn't she recognize him?

"Madam thinks I can't afford her," Dowdrick bellowed. "Good one!"

Dowdrick's raven-haired henchman laughed heartily at this.

They moved their focus to the next victim. "You, Negro. Name and crime."

"Samuel Barton, suh." The dark-skinned man paused, and then resumed with a strained voice. "Imprisoned for the death of a Moyamensing gang member, suh."

Fast Step filled in the blanks. "This Negro had a straight razor in his pocket. The Irish man was found with his throat slit, murdered by Barton in cold blood."

I snuck a look at Samuel. He was gritting his teeth as if holding back quiet outrage. We all were. His frame was slim, his uniform neatly tucked. His boots had brown laces that had been broken and re-knotted many times. Two fingers on his left hand were chopped clear off. From his own razor? Most likely he'd been defending himself when he'd gotten injured.

And then Dowdrick tapped me on the shoulder with his walking stick. "You. Turn around and state your name."

My body was an ancient, twisted, unmoving tree; my heart a hard knot in its petrified trunk. Below me, a great skittering of insects arose—beetles, large crusty roaches and thousands of ants. They surged forth on the brick pavement, brought on by my fright, my sinking into a hopeless place. My breath came in shallow rasps. He whacked me on the backs of my knees. I doubled over in pain.

"You! Speak up!" He whacked them again. The insects swarmed around my boots, then moved in a stream behind me, to Dowdrick.

I willed them to stop, for myself to calm. But it was like trying to halt a hurricane. "Sir, my name is Evalina Stowe," I mumbled, my mouth barely able to move.

"Face me, Miss Stowe." Another vicious wallop, this time to the small of my back.

I winced as I turned. Dowdrick's bloated face, way too close to mine, quivered with rage. His eyes widened in obvious recognition and he pressed his palm into his side as if I was stabbing him anew. The vile image of him strangling my brother overpowered me. His castor oil and sweet powder stench hit my nose. Broken veins in his eyes were pink and glistening, the blemishes dotting his chubby cheeks a darker rose. "You," he hissed under his breath. "You. Tell everyone your crime," he roared.

"Choking a man," I sputtered.

"Murder then?"

"If you say so."

"*Murder sir.* Say it!"

"Murder, sir."

He must've seen movement below. For finally he looked down at his feet and noticed the frenzied insects, teeming onto his fancy shoes, and up his tailored pants. He did a startled kick and a jig to dislodge them. "Stop them, witch!" he yelled. "Get these vermin off me!"

I lowered my gaze and concentrated on calming them, my own rage and sorrow as well. I forced my mind to go blank and be filled with the thickness of cool river mud, and the humming sounds of a corn sheller I'd found soothing at Somerset Farms.

Twitching and jumping, Dowdrick succeeded in scattering only some of the bugs. In the corner of my eye, I saw Birdy approach—his wagging sort of walk. He carried something. *What on earth is he doing?* Despite his odd, birdlike gait he had a fast stride. When he reached Dowdrick, Birdy held out a seedling in a pot.

"Prisoner? What's the meaning of this?" Dowdrick demanded.

In a confusing flash of movement Birdy tripped over his feet and fell face first. The clay pot toppled onto Dowdrick. Dirt spilled down the front of his fancy jacket and the container smashed on the ground. Shards flew in all directions. Dowdrick's swarthy guest stepped back to avoid getting doused by the flying dirt.

"What in the devil's hell are you doing?" Dowdrick yelled. Fast Step grabbed Birdy by his arm. He clinked on an iron handcuff and barked out an order for Birdy to put his other hand behind his back, clicking on the second cuff as he did. Birdy flashed me a glance of fellowship. All that was missing was the actual wink. This was planned. Birdy was protecting me from harm.

In the midst of the day's icy horror my heart warmed.

Frantically, Dowdrick brushed the dirt and the rest of the beetles, ants, and roaches off his coat and pants. "Get the convicts gone!" he ordered Fast Step.

"Prisoners, line up!" yelled the guard, hauling Birdy behind him. "No more garden privileges for a while, if ever. Line up. Back to your cells."

Amity lowered my hood with the same gruff yanks and knotting of the laces she'd used before. There was no warmth in the grip of her hand.

The sadness of the human procession entering the dark hall hurt my heart. Where would they take Birdy? I had no way of knowing even where his regular cell was, and now I wondered if I would even see him again. I shook off my dread for if I allowed myself to dwell on it I might go mad. Perhaps there *could* be balm in the act of praying. In restoring a shaky faith.

Or perhaps not. On the walk to cell #113 Amity's mouth was set in a hard, thin line and she refused to speak to me. I dared not speak to her either. Because any penitence in this Cherry Hill prison involved truth telling, and Amity had seen with her own eyes what I did—how my fear agitated the beasts of earth and sky.

There would be no lying to her. I must find a way to tell her the truth. But most importantly, I must find a way to avenge my brother's death and put Dowdrick behind bars.

"Dolly! Hello? Madame Rouge!"

"What is it now, girl?"

I judged Dolly's mood on the tone of her voice, not on her words. Her tone held warmth, mixed with mild annoyance.

"You're interesting to talk to, Madame Rouge. Who can resist you?"

A delighted giggle escaped her. *Bullseye!* "So you were the girl that the priggish doctor was cursing. You were the one the guard was hitting with his nightstick. In the yard today I finally got to see the loudmouth who lives next to me." She snorted. "You're not so hard on the eyes despite your constant blathering."

"Thanks. You really let Dowdrick have it. Gloves off, full punch."

"That's what they say," she bragged. "I'm a fighter, all right."

"Did anything about the doctor seem familiar, Dolly? Anything at all?"

"Hmm. Nothing except his fancy jacket holding back his blubber. Once they get bushels of coins and a name for themselves they think we will fawn all over them," she said derisively.

"I've seen him before, Dolly. He's not a nice man. Not in the least." Had I already told her what he'd done to my brother? My head spun with angry confusion. No, I had only told Amity. Though I had told Dolly I'd been accused of murder.

"Where did you see this man?" Dolly asked. "In a gin mill? An opium den? A brothel? He looks high and mighty with his printed silks and all, but his type loafs in the foulest of watering holes."

"He was a client in the tailoring establishment I worked in. A brutal man."

"What in blazes did he do? Quit holding out on me, Dull Witt."

So, it was Dull Wit again? Irritating, still I took it as another hopeful sign her mind was returning to her. "He attacked my little brother. He's an angry storm of the worst stripe, beating on little children."

"What exactly did the depraved dandy do?"

"He killed my brother, Todd. He strangled him to death only because Todd had dropped his suits on the floor. Imagine."

Dolly's gasps resounded right through the chinks in the

whitewashed bricks. Then she got quiet. Her silence was most worrying because it was unlike her.

"Let me ask you again, Dolly, for your sake as much as mine. Was there anything familiar to you about Dowdrick? Aside from his type, or the style of his jacket? He seemed to know you. The time someone took you... do you recall his voice? His stink of castor oil and sweet powder?"

Another shocked gasp. Dolly pounded a fist on something hard. "Oh, lord, the stink of it," she echoed, gruff and ominous.

My heart raced. "Once you smell his stink, you cannot forget it."

I heard Dolly pacing. A long minute went by before she spoke again.

"It was all around me," she choked out. "I... I couldn't move; couldn't catch a good breath. And when I woke up... "

"Tell me."

"Someone, *something* had cut a deep line along my arms."

"What? Are you sure you didn't tear them on something? A loose piece of wood or a nail?"

"No, they were clean knife cuts. Each more than a finger's length."

"Who would do that?"

"Girl, I don't know who. My memory is gone. But someone sewed them up."

"You mean to tell me there are *stitches* in your arms?"

"That's what I said. Black turkey thread—twelve neat loops in each." She groaned. "My mind is a blank. What is wrong with me?"

My body erupted in goose bumps. " Dolly, your memory's returning. Surely, you will soon recall more."

"Why would they cut my arms?" she wailed plaintively.

"I don't know but we'll try to find out. Can you picture the room where they kept you, the rugs on the floor? Any people in the room?"

"Bottles," she intoned hypnotically. "Walking stick."

"What about bottles?"

"I don't know," she howled. "Don't even know why I said that."

"His brass walking stick. Did he—?"

"Hit me." She moaned. "He whacked me with it." She began to cry in jagged rasps.

"He's evil." The memory of Dowdrick strangling my brother was sharp. "His cane burns like fire."

Dolly keened louder. "He whacked me so hard I fell. Wicked monster!"

Sweat erupted on my back. I began to shake. "Dolly, what else? What did he do then? I'm not even sure he's a real doctor. Do you remember him giving you a potion, a pill, a—"

"Oh, heaven help me, girl. He held me down and pushed my face up by my jaw... he made me sniff..."

"What did he force up your nose?"

Silence. The air swelled with Dolly's fright, cold and dense. In it, I could feel an abrupt change as if a candle had been doused.

"Dolly? Talk to me."

"Leave off, girl!" Her voice was as cold as a corpse in a winter graveyard. "I don't dare speak to witches. You will poison me with the same venom."

"Never, Dolly! Believe it."

"Speak not, witch. Hold your tongue or I will yell for the guards."

I had delved too deeply. It was more than she could accept. She was too frightened. I didn't blame her. If

Dowdrick had trapped me in his quarters and drugged me I might've lost all trust. Dolly was so close to opening up to her memories. And in a wink she had slammed the gates shut. I sank onto my bed. Felt my bony shoulder blades poke against the mattress frame. Tears of fear and frustration rolled down my cheeks.

After some time, as I gazed up at a spray of stars through the skylight I brushed off my tears and devised a plan. "Dolly," I called into the weighty silence. "I'm getting out of here one way or another. And in the meantime, I'm going to find out why that bad doctor is creeping around here. I'm going to do my best to bring him down. If you refuse to tell me more, then I will find out myself without your help."

I could sense her mind asking *how? How would it even be possible?*

But she didn't ask it aloud, and I didn't volunteer it. Maybe if I disappeared from my cell she would panic as I had when she'd vanished. Maybe then she would help. Maybe then she would talk.

I silently called for my mice. They skittered forth in the darkening room. I let them scramble over me and poke their snouts in my armpits, under my chin, between my fingers. Marks to remember me by for if I disappeared they might be the only beasts to find me.

9

I saved a stew and a tumbler of milk from dinner and let it sit and rot for a week. Holding my nose so as not to inhale the stench, I mixed the foul concoction and forced it down my gullet.

By morning's light, I was deathly ill. In addition to this I bloodied my nose by smashing it against the wall and smearing some of the blood under my eyes and mouth. I vomited up my breakfast before Fast Step had time to walk down the hall and away.

"Help, Guard," I pleaded between gags as I rattled the bars. "I need to be seen by a doctor. Does your prison have a doctor? An infirmary?" I made great show of vomiting loudly and horribly a second time, scaring myself in the process. Perhaps my guts *were* liquefying.

Fast Step approached. "What is it Prisoner 113?"

I stumbled forward and leaned my head on the bars. "I am like to die. I need a doctor."

"Did you eat something bad?" he asked all-too leisurely.

"More than bad food, sir. Blood seeps from my nose, my

mouth, my eyes, and vomit from my mouth. I need a doctor. Have you no mercy?"

"Hmph."

My ears pricked at the sound of keys clinking on his ring. "Stand flat against the back wall, Prisoner 113."

I reeled around the puddles of sickness and pressed my back to the wall. "Done, sir."

The door creaked open. He strode in, keeping steady eye contact until he secured me with heavy iron cuffs. At least he thought not to put on my hood, rightly fearing I would soil it with sickness. He pulled me after him with a chain attached to the cuffs, making sure to steer clear of the mess on the floor. Dolly had been quiet since our last fateful talk. She said nothing now. Did she even care a fig about me?

Truly, I felt like death warmed over, no matter that I had brought the illness on myself. Perhaps I had gone too far with the rotted food. I was burning and shivering all at the same time.

As Fast Step led me down one hall and along another, I tried, despite my delirium, to note my surroundings. The numbers in the first hall were labeled 120 to 140. Along another they skipped to 250 to 270, and this hall was darker, with a stench of mildew. Along here, I heard a child's cry, which filled me with a sudden sorrow. Up a staircase—perhaps two flights—and down another hall. This one was lit with skylights all along it, and a balcony railing that looked down onto the floors below. These cell numbers jumped to the 400s.

A prisoner yelled, "Is it the beautiful witch he's got?" The shouting sure carried in this wing. So much for solitary confinement! Another prisoner called out, "Tell Birdy his lady friend is out of her cell."

"When he returns from his punishment, that is."

"Maybe she's going to see *him*," someone quipped.

"Witches have their ways!"

My heart jumped at this. First, how was it such public knowledge that Birdy and I had communicated? Had he told many prisoners about our private friendship? Secondly, where had the guards taken Birdy and for how long? These questions upset me so badly I curled in on myself and retched once more. My stomach was empty, so it was a painful, unproductive heave. Still, it elicited a disgusted grunt from Fast Step.

"Get along, Prisoner," he ordered sharply.

We reached the end of a long hallway. Fast Step rang a bell and another guard I hadn't seen before opened a heavy door with a label that read Infirmary. Fast Step hauled me into a windowless room with a metal examining table, illuminated by an overhead gas lantern. Its thin gleam showed an array of frighteningly sharp surgical tools arranged on an adjoining table. The guard retreated to the far left corner and toward a door just as a hunched man in a white coat and spectacles stepped from the shadows of the same door. "What have we here?" He peered at me with a look of concern.

"Prisoner #113 claims she is deathly ill." Fast Step's small eyes shone with animated distaste. "You will determine if the strumpet is lying through her teeth—"

"—Or not," finished the doctor, studying my bloody nose and dried cracked lips. The way I clasped my cramping belly. "Guard, please wait outside in the hall you came from whilst I examine her. There is a bench."

Fast Step grunted as he left. The doctor walked to a supply cabinet by the back door and reached inside it for supplies. This gave me precious seconds to glance around.

On the far right, along the wall I noticed something entirely unexpected.

Three connected holding pens of barred iron each about five feet wide, behind an opened curtain.

They were not all empty.

I strained my feverish eyes to make out their contents. Each held a narrow cot. In the cell on the left stood the Negro I had seen in the courtyard with his hands gripping the bars. Sam Barton it was. The whites of his eyes gleamed fearful yet fierce in the flickering light. He shook his head as if to warn me against staring too obviously. The cell on the right was empty except for a rolled up blanket. I had only a moment more to determine who was in the center one. A lanky figure was sprawled out on the cot, his leg in a bandage and arm in a sling. With some effort, the man raised his head to see who was there. My heart leapt to my throat. Birdy! He was wincing and groaning. Had they broken his limbs? God knows the quarry explosion had already damaged his feet. Fury shot through me. I thought I saw dark bruises on his jaw.

"Birdy," I mouthed. "Did they beat you?"

He rose on one elbow, wincing harder. His expression changed to worry when he saw my bloody face. Birdy shook his head as Sam Barton had.

"They will pay," I hissed under my breath. Under me, a vigorous, vibrating undertow started. I felt it shudder up from my feet to my leg bones. My sensitive ears heard scrabbling in the walls, under the floorboards. Hundreds of tiny paws hard at work running, surging forward. My turmoil was arousing the beasts.

The doctor, done with gathering supplies, took me by my iron wrist cuffs and instructed me to climb onto the examining table and lay down.

It wasn't easy with my bulky, stiff prison skirt. I was dizzy and the table was set too high for a woman. But I managed to balance myself on its metal edge and swing my legs around and up so I wouldn't topple over. The rapid movement gave me a bout of vertigo. Closing my eyes, I took a slow breath. The sickening swoon passed. What remained was dread.

"I am Doctor Shakesby," he said as he spread a thin blanket over me and then proceeded to draw dark curtains over the holding cells. "For a bit of privacy," he explained. "Now tell me what prompted your visit here."

"I have the shivers, sir. I am sick to my stomach. I was vomiting up everything."

"Let us see if you're running a fever. May I?" He held a thermometer above my mouth.

I nodded with surprise that he would ask a prisoner for permission.

He frowned as he read it. "Fever of 101 degrees." Next he took out a stethoscope and listened to my heart. With his thoughtful manner it almost seemed as if he was a regular physician and not a jail sawbones. There was a calm, respectful air about him, which tempted me to trust him. God knows! I had so many questions.

"Did you eat something foul?" Under his glasses his eyes were a milky blue. His hair was snowy white. He was surely someone's grandfather. Why would he work in a prison? Why would Amity or any normal person? My heart warmed at his small human kindness of conversation, and I sensed the beasts in the floorboards calming.

"Perhaps the stew was too ripe."

He nodded. "The food here can be tough on a stomach."

"Or perhaps I caught the cholera."

"Time will tell." Dr. Shakesby went to the cabinet and

brought over some bottles. "In the meantime, take this to calm your stomach." He doled out a tablespoonful and I swallowed it.

Heat radiated all the way down to my stomach. It tasted like rum mixed with something sour. "What is it Doctor, if you don't mind me asking?"

He held up the bottle. "Dr. Dowdrick's Digestive. An herbal mixture for the purification of the liver, spleen and kidneys, and for Malarial Fever."

Malaria! Alarm prickled through me. The first, at the thought I might have malaria. The second because the bottle said Dowdrick! This lunatic was making medicines? The label had an illustration of a winding plant and under it, a long list of herbs. I only recognized sarsaparilla. It said it was manufactured at the Eclectic Medical School.

Dare I trust Dr. Shakesby to answer my questions? This was why I'd made myself ill, why I'd come up here in the first place. I had to brave it. "Do you think I have malaria?"

Shakesby rubbed his white beard. "Most likely not. But we need to wait and see if your symptoms and fever continue." He slipped a pan to one side of me. I suppose it was just in case I had anything left in my stomach. It was still rolling and rolling. But the odd-tasting medicine had actually calmed it a bit.

"Do you know this Doctor Dowdrick?" I asked him.

"Why yes!" Shakesby gave me a look of surprise as if he never got questions from prisoners. "He practices downtown, near here." He capped the bottle, reached for another and doled out a teaspoonful of thick brownish syrup. He nodded for me to open my mouth and in anticipation of my next question he held up the vial. "Doctor Dowdrick's Miracle Clarify. It lowers fever, revives tired blood, soothes headaches and helps one sleep." Dr. Shakesby capped this vial and put it on the side table. "Why do you ask about Dr. Dowdrick?"

I had to be careful not to reveal much. Not act too upset or the rodents would come running. How exactly should I preface my interest? Trying to craft the right words made my head throb anew. "Dr. Dowdrick came to the yard while we prisoners were gardening. He had us take our hoods off. I just wondered... well... why?" A simple question. Innocent enough.

Dr. Shakesby appeared deep in thought before he answered. "Dr. Dowdrick is working on patents for his medicines. If prisoners can be helped in the process, well, all the better."

My mind reeled with the memory of Dolly's disappearance. Of her terrified outburst last night. The floorboards shuddered again. Tiny claws scratched below. I needed to steady my nerves. Ask another harmless question. Not bring up Dolly. I closed my eyes and brushed feverish sweat from my brow as I tried to act coy. "I would imagine Dr. Dowdrick is highly respected?"

"It would seem so. He is the president of the Eclectic Medical School."

"Lovely name," I murmured. "So quaint. Is it far from here?"

"It's on Haines Street, right here in center city. I suppose they call it thusly due to their work with botanicals and herbs. They often find new ones in their explorations."

"Oh? Fascinating. Where, might I ask?"

"For a sick lady you are brimming with questions." He shot me a suspicious look. "They are secretive regarding their sources."

My eyes ached and I longed for sleep yet I needed to prod him for as much information as I could manage. "Dr.

Shakesby, you're so knowledgeable. In your expert opinion, who *are* the best doctors in Philadelphia? And is the practice of trying their new medicines on prisoners commonplace?" I giggled so my interest might sound frothy, lighthearted.

"What prompts your curiosity?" Dr. Shakesby began to gingerly clean the blood off my face with cotton balls that he discarded in a receptacle under the table.

"I... I'm quite captivated by medicine. In fact," I improvised, "if I get out of here I should like very much to become a nurse, or even an animal doctor."

Dr. Shakesby broke into a crooked grin. At seeing his milky blue eyes brighten it was clear he valued outsiders' interest in the medical profession. "Yes," he said, "there are a few brilliant doctors in Philadelphia."

"Oh! Tell me about one, please!" I sighed. "I'd feel better just to hear it."

"Well, Dr. Thomas Mutter helps the burned. As you must know, the hair and faces of women oftentimes catch fire while cooking over open stoves. He rearranges their disfigured features almost back to their original order so perfectly one might think he was conjuring magic."

Magic? Had Shakesby heard folks calling me a witch? Was he mocking me? Testing me? I studied the look in his pale eyes. There appeared to be no irony there, no fear. "Does this Dr. Mutter also work with prisoners here?"

"No. His hands are full at the Jefferson Medical School. Patients line up to see him."

"Oh. I see. This Dr. Horace Dowdrick. Does he also have lines? Isn't he too busy with his own patients to uh... work on prisoners here?" I softened my tightening jaw.

Shakesby shrugged. "Apples and oysters."

"Pardon?"

"It's difficult to compare the two."

"Well, then, how does the doctor determine who will sample his newest medicines?"

"My, my this one is nosy!" The wry grin again. "Are you volunteering?"

Better me than Birdy. Better me than Dolly or Sam or Light-ning—especially Lightning.

"Tut, tut, you are shivering." Shakesby's tone had become hesitant. He took my temperature again. "No change yet. Still feverish."

I was suddenly afraid to return to my cell. My thoughts raced with visions of Todd being strangled, of Dolly's arms being sliced. Of what might happen if I were alone in the darkened cell tonight. Perhaps they were fever dreams, or perhaps my more sensible instincts for caution were finally alert. "Dr. Shakesby, might I stay here for observation? If left in my own cell no one would know if I fainted, even died. Just for one night, Doctor?"

Once again, the floorboards rumbled with the agitation of the furry and armored creatures that sensed my terror. If Shakesby hesitated much longer, they would swarm from the walls and teem up his trousers, his lab coat.

"That might be a wise idea." Finally he rose from his stool and helped me off the tall examining table. He led me to the unoccupied cell behind the curtain, gestured for me to enter and sit myself down on the cot. He brought in the tin bucket and put it on the floor by me. "In case you need it later," he explained. And then he locked me in.

"I will check on you and the others. Do sleep. Sleep will lower your fever." With that, Shakesby extinguished the lantern over the examining table and slid the curtains in front of our cells closed. Darkness engulfed us.

I held my breath until his footsteps grew faint and the latch on the door to his inner office clicked. Then I wrapped the threadbare blanket around myself and strained to see Birdy's form. Impossible. No windows in this section to draw light; not even a dim slice of moon. And with the curtains drawn the glimmer from under the infirmary door had vanished.

I might have panicked. Yet, next to me, within reach through the bars lay Birdy. If only his bones were healed enough for him to rise from his bed. My heart beat hard. There were no wardens glaring at us in the yard, ears pricked like foxes for forbidden talk.

I waited for what must have been twenty minutes before I whispered, "Birdy, can you hear me?"

"Yeah," came the answer. "I can."

10

"How badly are you injured? Did they break your arm?" I asked.

"My arm's terribly sprained, swelled up like a ripe watermelon it is. They kicked the ribs pretty good. But I'll survive. You, Evalina, how fare you?"

I hesitated. Who knew if Shakesby still hovered behind the door? It would be unwise to blurt everything out... not yet. Yet the low, caring timbre of Birdy's voice soothed me. "I must've eaten something that disagreed with me. Had a nasty stomach for a spell. Dr. Dowdrick's potion actually seemed to help. Did you swallow any?" I was eager to get Birdy's honest reactions to Dowdrick *and* his medicines.

"Hmph. No. That prissy clothes horse was horrid to you in the yard. I wouldn't give credence to his bottles of liquids. For all we know, fair Eva, they would poison you."

My cheeks heated at Birdy's unprompted use of my familiar name. And calling me fair! I wanted to waft through the bars like a freed spirit to kiss his bruised limbs until they knitted whole.

Perhaps Birdy was testing Shakesby in his own way. By

saying something provocative about Dowdrick he could see if Shakesby was eavesdropping by any sudden, surprised reaction. But there was no rustle, no gasp from behind the door. Still, we were quiet for some time. I breathed in the odor of stale urine and mildew and damp stone. And the particular scents of the medicines—a pinch of spearmint, sweet rum, and a sour, sharp medicinal tang that stung the nostrils. The chill from the dank walls seeped through the thin blanket. I sensed Birdy's ears pricked to the air for sounds as mine were. We heard nothing but Sam Barton's labored snores.

"Quiet as death, aside from Sammy's bellows, eh?"

I took Birdy's statement as a signal it was safe to talk—miraculous after time in my solitary cell ticking off hours, days, weeks.

"Thank you for defending me in the yard. I feel terribly guilty though. You paid such a high price for tossing that dirt at Dowdrick."

"Don't trouble yourself with guilt. It was my decision to get myself in hot water. A fine fix there, for the prickly fashion plate and his embroidered clothes!" We erupted in laughter, followed by a long groan from Birdy. "Ouch, the ribs. Laughter is treachery for bruised bones."

"Oh, Birdy! I apologize."

"Never you mind, love."

Love? Was that a figure of speech or...? My face flushed hot. I was relieved he couldn't see me well in this dark. Not more than I saw him—as a blurry outline of a figure. "What's wrong with Sam?" I asked. "Have you spoken to him?"

"Aye, a tad. He claimed he wasn't sick and wasn't sure why they had taken him here. They gave him a dose of

Dowdrick's tonic just before you arrived. When you were being examined he blacked out proper."

A sickening quiver passed through me. Did the doctors have designs on Sam too? Was it only Dowdrick or was Shakesby getting a share of the rewards? Shakesby had seemed so kind and mild mannered. Dare I tell Birdy about Dolly Rouge? If I didn't confide in Birdy now when would I have the chance? By tomorrow we'd be padlocked behind separate walls.

I heard shuffling, a groan, and a squeaking of bedsprings. Then Birdy's fingers were touching mine through the bars. I breathed in a stunned gasp. White lightning raced up my arm and into my heart. So many times I had imagined this— how our hands might reach for each other across the wooden planter, how we might escape our cells some night and share a long embrace in the dark. Never would I have guessed it could be more than a fairy tale.

Our fingers knit tightly around each other. Shocked delight rushed through me.

"Penny for your thoughts?" he whispered, warm breath wafting upon my face.

"Thank you, Birdy," was all I could utter.

"For what, Eva? I am doing what truly compels me. It is not out of choice."

"You are a wonder to me. And I confess... I am drawn to you as well. Though I never imagined we would get our chance to speak openly in a jailhouse infirmary."

We chuckled.

He began to stroke my hand with his thumb. "Sweet Eva, tell me the important things, the essentials for our time may only last for minutes..."

"Essentials?"

"What happened to you? Who and what is this Dowdrick? He glared at you as if he wanted to kill you right there in the yard."

I plunged in, Shakesby or no Shakesby. "I must tell you, Birdy, Dr. Dowdrick is even worse than you can imagine."

"How so?"

I told him what happened at Conklin's Tailor, what he'd done to my brother. Birdy gasped and gripped my hand harder. I said that Dowdrick had hurt Dolly Rouge, too. "She was taken out of Cherry Hill for over a week and came back with stitched up wounds on her arm she has no memory of getting. Dolly lives next to me in the jail. She was the tall madam with the red hair he spoke to in the yard. The one who dared insult him, remember?"

"Heavens yes, Eva, I remember Dolly Rouge! What does this doctor want with Dolly? Birdy sucked in air. "With *you?*"

"Surely he wants revenge for me stabbing him. Leaving him for dead after he strangled my brother." I decided to tell Birdy a newly forming idea. "I'm fixing to contact him, Birdy. I'm planning to pull the wool over his eyes."

"How's that, Eva? It sounds quite risky." Birdy loosened his grip on my hand.

In the dark, I imagined there was a wall of ears, all raised to hear my confessions. What if Dr. Shakesby was listening after all? What if he was a spy for Dowdrick? "Trust me, Birdy, I will reveal all soon. It's not safe to tell it all now. Answer me this. What is the number on your prison door? And on Sam's? And what of that fair-haired little boy, Lewin, convicted of horse thievery? What number cell is he in? My brother was a friend of his. If anything happens to him... I'd never forgive myself for letting another child fall into danger."

"I'm on the second tier in 407. Sammy is down the hall

in the 400s as well. I heard Lewin was in a hall with other children. The 200 halls have a row of young folk. And you?"

"Number 113. I received two years time here. But not for the incident with Dowdrick at Conklin's Tailor."

"No?"

"For a later event at Somerset Farms. The owner drove my pet bird to frenzy when he destroyed my birds' houses and beat me. My bird flew down his throat and choked him."

"My word, Eva! How was this your fault?"

"It is a mystery, Birdy. I never touched the dreadful tyrant. I never spoke a charm or incantation."

"Eva, your tribulations were brutal. I am sorry you suffered so! Perhaps we'll be freed at the same time at least. I received a two-year's term as well. So, freed at twenty, I'll be. You?"

"Me as well! I'm eighteen. Your crime?"

"The dynamite I set off while working on the railroad injured a dozen workers... and killed one. I was beside myself with guilt, though I was also badly injured."

"Accidents happen—tragic ones, too. Your feet."

"Aye. The one is worse than the other."

"If we ever get out you can get them fixed."

"Aw, such a lovely thought. I'm afraid, though, it would cost the bank. To fix my mangled limbs would take a bloody miracle! And who would do it, sweet Eva?"

Birdy was making me swoon. His low voice was soothing and enticing all at once. Was calling me fair and Eva and *sweet* simply the Welsh way? I struggled for a believable way of telling him I could make animals do things. That this was not quite the mystery I claimed. But if my wording were clumsy it would sound frightening, even demonic. Precise wording was such a difficult task. I had only gone to school in my early years. "Birdy?"

"Yes, love?"

Holy mother of god, he was saying *love* again. Suddenly, I forgot everything I meant to say. I strained to recall. "Um, Birdy, I have mice in my cell."

"We'll need to get you a ferocious alley cat."

"No, Birdy. I *like* these mice. They're my friends."

He laughed at this. "I've heard it all. Your friends! Next you'll be telling me you take high tea with them and share jailhouse gossip." He gave my hand a reassuring squeeze.

"No, but I can send them messages, I can give them tasks. They work for me. And if I'm truly honest, I suspect I did have an influence on my pet bird back at Somerset. I simply did not know it then. He felt my upset, my desperation."

"Eva, you're having fever visions."

"I'm telling you something real, Birdy. I know it sounds highly unusual. But I have a way with wild beasts. You saw those birds in the courtyard flock to me."

"I did but—"

"You saw the insects swarm up Dowdrick's trousers."

"You're telling me you did that?" He let out a snort that rivaled Sammy's racket. This was going badly. How could I make him understand?

"Birdy, if you see a mouse running toward you with a paper or bit of fabric in his snout, don't be afraid. Don't kill him or throw out the paper. It is likely a message from me. And Birdy, will you give it a piece of fabric or something from you to take back to me, that it can ground a scent to? That way it can find you wherever you may be."

At this, Birdy let go of my hand and fell silent. Had I deeply troubled him as I had done with Dolly? Now neither would speak to me! Fear rattled my bones. I needed allies. I had known that from the very first night here in this stinking place. If I didn't gather allies, I would perish. Plus I would never again hear Birdy utter his sweet words to me. "Birdy?" I asked unsteadily. "Did I offend you?"

"I'm thinking, Eva."

"Penny for your thoughts?"

Just as Birdy gave me a lock of his hair that he had just yanked out, Sammy released a deafening shout that made us both gasp. His body flailed against the hard mattress. "Where am I? It's dark in this tunnel! Help!"

With groans of agony, Birdy struggled back to his bed.

Footsteps approached hurriedly and a door swung open. I heard the pop of the lantern going on and the swish of the curtains parting.

Dr. Shakesby peered through them at the line of holding cells, his white hair tinged by the greenish gaslight. "Who's that making a ruckus?"

Again Sam wailed as if he were being whipped. Dr. Shakesby called for an orderly. I quickly pocketed Birdy's lock of hair and feigned sleep. Though I watched through the bars with narrowed eyes as the orderly held Sam down. I kept on watching as Dr. Shakesby drove a needle full of liquid into his neck. Sam let out a wail, a whimper and went limp. "For his own good. Poor man. He's having nightmares," Dr. Shakesby muttered to the orderly. "This should tide him over until he's transported in the morning."

Transported to where?

The men left Sam's enclosure and locked it. Then they proceeded to peer at Birdy through the bars. "Slumbering peacefully," stated the orderly.

Not a chance. I prayed Birdy could hold stock still until they left.

After this, they unlocked my cell and Shakesby strode in. Leaning over, he held a flat, dry palm to my head. "Fever's down," he reported. "Miss Stowe? Are you awake?" I must've wrinkled my brow because he asked me again more pointedly. "Miss Stowe!"

"Uh, yes?" I feigned a groggy confusion and made a show of rubbing my eyes.

"Your fever's down. No malaria, no cholera. Just a bit of putrid food I suspect." Shakesby grinned amiably. "The guard will help return you to your cell." Fast Step appeared at the door and glowered at me. He looked tired from being called back to the infirmary so late.

Panic set in, partly at the reality of being alone again, but also at leaving Birdy. No use protesting though, it would only make it harder if I needed to visit here again. I rose carefully to make sure I had no lingering dizziness or nausea. My vision was clear, my feet steady. After Fast Step put me in chains, I risked a furtive nod at Birdy as I followed Fast Step out.

Blackbeard let Amity in my cell with a muttered, "The witch gets her dose of God today, eh? Will it make her less eager to dance with the devil?" Fast Step might despise me, but at least he didn't make sly remarks like Blackbeard.

Amity marched in with nary a greeting or glance my way. She sat stiffly at my wooden table and opened her prayer book with her finger marking a passage. Gone was her playful ruffled bonnet. In its place was a plain black one, along with a somber black dress and shawl. With her head already bent to her book she said, "Time to pray."

After my fever and my alarm at hearing Shakesby's plan

to transport Sam Barton, I could've used a comforting word or look. "Yes, Miss Amity, I will try."

"Thee will repeat these lines," she ordered. "'Tis the message we have heard from Him and declare unto thee: God is light; in Him there is no darkness. If we claim to have fellowship and yet walk in the darkness, we lie and do not live out the truth. But if we walk in the light, as He is in the light, then thee and thine have fellowship with the Holy Spirit."

I looked down at my hands and concentrated, repeating the lines a few times to get them right. Inside, I bristled. Was Amity suggesting I was a filthy liar reveling in darkness? Dancing with the devil himself as Blackbeard had accused me? I dared not ask. I had lost my pluck.

"Evalina, are thou listening?"

"Pardon?" I raised my head. She was staring at me with a hardened look. My cheeks scorched with shame. Perhaps my sin was fear itself—to be cowed by my fear.

"I shall begin the next passage. Thou shall repeat: And in those days cometh John the Baptist, preaching in the desert of Judea. And saying: Do penance: for the kingdom of heaven is at hand. For this is he that was spoken of by Isaiah the prophet, saying: A voice of one crying in the desert. Prepare ye the way of the Lord, make straight his paths."

I tried valiantly to parrot the verses, but on my tongue they grew hopelessly tangled. I was distraught by Amity's coldness, by her unwillingness to help me along. Soon, my fear turned to hurt and then to outrage. "You saw what I did in the yard with the insects, the birds, didn't you? I called them forth, not by my will, but in a natural way."

"Natural!" Amity's eyes widened as if this subject vexed her.

"Yes, an instinctual way! Clearly you consider me a

sinner of some sort. But is it a sin, Miss Amity, to commune with animals? Don't you have warmth and compassion for the cuddling lapdog, the soft purring cat? Why then, should wild birds and insects be seen as second rate? As beasts of the devil?"

"Indeed! Thine impudence astounds me." Amity leapt up and marched to the door, soundly knocking on it. "Guard, please let me out. Guard, make haste."

"Miss Amity. I am not trying to frighten you," I said as the guard worked to unlock the heavy door. "Please listen. I am simply asking you questions about the verses to best see how they apply to my situation." Desperate for her to understand me properly, I was tempted to run after her and tug at her shawl as she was led out into the hall.

I had my dignity though. I had just scolded myself for being led around by clammy fear. Why should I be ashamed of my own questions, however difficult? With a rusty squeak the guard locked the door. My blood boiled and I felt feverish once again. So much strong emotion could not be good for a recovering body.

I reclined on my bed. A flurry of squeaks rang out from the corner as the mice scurried out of their hole. They scaled my bed then my shoulders as they sniffed at the air of injury.

I took in long breaths that slowed my pulse, cooled my blood. I sent the mice focused messages while my sense of Birdy and Sam was still acute. I sent them smells – the sharp, queer tang of medicines, the rank stench of urine in the holding cells, the sick buckets. I sent an image of Samuel in his neatly tucked shirt and broken brown bootlaces that he'd fixed over and over. I took the lock of Birdy's hair from the bottom of my pocket and let them sniff it. I concentrated on the numbers as well—the children's hall,

200—and images of Lewin as he looked in the yard. Thin, defiant yet delicate as a seedling, and fair as the sun.

Mice, go find Birdy. Find Sam and little Lewin, too. Collect things from them. Go. Treats upon your return!

After this, I must've fallen asleep. For when my eyes opened a delicate blue dawn was breaking through the Eye of God. I thought of Birdy and his smiling gray eyes. I thought of Sam's wails and of Amity's glare. Eyes all looking back at me. Lines of Amity's verses floated up and I whispered a part of it, twisting it 'round to make more sense:

If we walk in the light then thee and thine have fellowship.

Fellowship was a good thing. This meant friends and family. A new family to fill my terrible loss. It would be something wonderful to find, to build.

If I ever got out of here.

Or was I already building it, bit by bit, here and now?

11

My peace of mind was short-lived. By mid morn, an angry clamor broke out between two men in the hallway. I recognized Blackbeard's sandpaper shouts. The other voice oozed with high-pitched scorn. *Dr. Dowdrick!*

"She don't fancy going with you, Doc," Blackbeard declared. "So, I ain't taking her out of her cell."

Was he talking about me? Why would Blackbeard protect *me?*

"You're no one, Mudsill. I'll get you thrown in this very same jail that you patrol!"

"Miss Rouge stays right here! Warden's orders," Blackbeard retorted.

Dowdrick yelled, "Take the haggard wench to the infirmary then. Treat her with cloves or lye or pour strong rum over her. She's surely got the scabies! Just get her gone."

"For a sawbones you speak as crass as a sailor," Bluebeard muttered.

"Is that so? You speak rather crassly yourself, guard! Shall I tell the warden to put you in an iron gag? Eh? That would teach your tongue to wag."

"No need, Doctor, no need." Blackbeard said with muted fury. His keys clinked in the search for the proper one. No doubt he was as relieved as I that Dolly would not be riding out of Cherry Hill in Dowdrick's carriage.

The rusty lock turned with a squeal next door. No protests from Dolly Rouge. It was highly unusual for her to stay silent but she had good reason to be terrified of Dowdrick. Their footsteps grew fainter and then silent as they walked down the hall and turned off to one side.

I sat on the bed, my hands thrust under my legs, hunching to make myself small. Was Dowdrick still here or had he gone with them? Was he aware I lived in the next cell? Why exactly had he come down here if he wasn't hell bent on taking Dolly?

It only took a minute to find out.

"You, guard, unlock cell number 113," Dowdrick bellowed from the silence.

Soon, Fast Step and Dowdrick both stood in my chamber.

"Cuff this girl. Then go. Leave us be 'til the half hour is up."

Fast Step complied, only glaring at me once with his yellow, red-rimmed eyes. He reminded me of a rat with rabies, foaming about the snout. Yet I wasn't as scared of Fast Step as this new intruder. Not by a long shot. I leaned against the cold stones of the back wall, my chained hands in tight fists pressing into the small of my back.

Dowdrick dusted the table and chair for germs and then sat. Frowning, he set his beady eyes on me and looked me up and down. Why was it that ghastly men often had teensy eyes? Pinholes let in only the dimmest light—pinholes could close quickly to wallow in darkness of the soul. This thought would've given me a laugh, but now... it was a puny respite between heart-pounding frights.

"Well, well, well. We meet again, Witch." His voice oozed with scornful confidence.

"So we do. What do you want with me?"

"Ah! The query of the century! I want to know how much you understand of my business." He stood and walked my way. As he did he ran a hand through his powdered hair, sending waves of castor oil and sickeningly sweet talcum my way. I held my breath until the stench passed.

"I'll tell you. But first... why did you kill my brother?"

"Why did you stab me and leave me for dead?" he shot back as he leaned in.

"You were beating him."

"Poppycock!" Crimson veins in his eyes seemed ready to burst and bleed. He lunged but stopped short of grabbing *my* neck. Instead, he shook his fists at me.

"No poppycock; stark truth," I braved. "I caught you strangling him."

"Oh that." He loosened his fists and waved at me dismissively. "Your clumsy brother had wrinkled my suits. He dropped them on the floor, the careless twit! I was simply scolding him."

"Horse dung!" I blurted. "I'll believe that when pigs fly. You have a murderous temper! You didn't have to strangle him. He was only a boy."

"Quite a nasty mouth on you!" He scolded. "Unfitting for a woman. Oh, I forgot. You are the devil's mate." Dowdrick's nostrils flared. "You set those wasps on me with your devil's magic," he accused. "I was trying to shake them off. Hundreds stinging me! They nearly killed me! I was frantic.

Not myself. Who knows what I did?" Dowdrick's laugh was high-pitched, nervous.

No wonder he wanted Dolly out of her cell and Fast Step away. He wanted no witnesses to any admissions. My spirits sank knowing it would be only his word against mine. Under my feet, the floor shivered. Rats, mice, insects, all were readying for battle. Birds began to settle on the skylight and scratch at the panes.

"I'll tell you what I know, but..." The floor trembled and the pecking on the skylight increased in volume. "My beasts, they—"

"Witch, don't send your familiars my way. Don't you dare!" Dowdrick's voice wobbled.

I wanted to frighten him. He richly deserved it! Besides, I wasn't sure I was able to contain the beasts once rankled. "What will you do for me in return?"

"What makes you think I am amenable to deal-making? It is not me who is behind bars." He raised his haughty chin and snickered. "Tell me all you know before I even consider it."

If I told him nothing, he would find me safe, but he would have no need to speak to me again. On the other hand, if I told him what I knew, it would be a risk, yet I might wield more influence over him. I decided on the latter —and to play even that to the hilt. "Pay heed, I know what you did to Dolly Rouge; what you're doing with your medicines," I improvised. "You have no patents for them." That one Shakesby had revealed. "Who knows how poisonous they are? You could kill prisoners with them. No legal patents and dosing prisoners! This is surely a crime. Shall I tell the wardens? The police? I shall!"

At this, the birds began a frantic pecking at the skylight. Their clamor sounded like a torrent of hailstones.

"Who would believe a witch? And who would be your character witness? The German farmhand?" Dowdrick erupted in derisive giggles. "I read the damning reports in all the Philadelphia broadsides."

So, my hunches were right. Yet, this gave me pause. Who *would* vouch for my character? Birdy was accused of injuring the miners. Dolly mistrusted me. Amity despised me. My mother, father and brother had all perished.

"I have an idea," I whispered. "Let me describe it to you. If not, I send my beasts who will—"

"I am not open to bribery. You are nobody—a dirty street vixen. Your sense of importance is ludicrous."

"Oh? Then why did you want to speak with me if not to see how much I knew of your hideous behavior and to bribe me to stay silent—?"

"Enough! I could seal your mouth permanently, order you killed." He approached me again with his fists raised just as a distraught pigeon broke through a gap in the skylight it had pried open. Glass shards rained on us, nicking my arms and cheeks. The bird swooped down and tore at Dowdrick's scalp while he frantically batted it away. "Ahh!" he screeched in pain. "Leave me be!"

"Doctor, I venture to say you need me," I contrived.

"Get them off!"

"Take me for your next experiment. Promise not to take any of the others for your cutting and I will immediately tell the bird to cease its attack."

"Guard!" Dowdrick ran for the door and pounded on it. "Guard! Now!"

"Wait!" I pleaded. "I have a unique idea guaranteed to make you *famous!*"

But Fast Step had, in one fierce motion, unlocked the cell, un-cuffed me and pulled Dowdrick out to safety. Who knows if Dowdrick had heard me at all? The pigeon soared out, unseen. In its beak was a bloody scruff of Dowdrick's talcum-powdered hair.

The whole ordeal happened so fast that Fast Step must not have noticed the shattered glass by my feet. After he locked me in, I collapsed on my bed and fell asleep for hours.

When I awoke, a deep purple dusk cloaked the skylight. They had not yet extinguished the gas lanterns. In their glow I saw my trencher of supper uneaten on the shelf that the guard had skated through the door slot. I drank the cold soup and pocketed the bread heel. Absentmindedly, I stroked my cheek, where it stung. My hand came away with dried blood flecks. I remembered the enraged bird hammering a jagged hole in the skylight with its beak and leaving a storm of shattered glass. I shivered from the stream of chilled air rushing in.

Autumn was already rushing toward winter. The air smelled of wood smoke. Looking up, I saw a smattering of red oak leaves stuck to the pane like pointed rubies.

Dowdrick had seen the glass shatter. But the guards seemed oblivious and I dared not report it. For how would I explain it? I wondered how the garden was doing. Was the cabbage green and thick? Had the pumpkins transformed from puckered white blossoms into fat orange gourds? It had been three or four weeks since we'd been allowed out for yard work. Surely the vegetables were ready for harvest. Perhaps it was too late and they were overripe, already rotting. This thought saddened me immensely.

The memory of carving a Jack-o-Lantern as a child with my brother Todd comforted and distracted me from my failures with Dowdrick. My mother would help us set a candle in the gourd's spicy core and we would stare in awe at its lopsided, one-toothed grin. It made the kitchen glimmer with mischief and delight. On All-Hallows Eve we would collect taffy and hazelnuts from our mother's favorite shop-keepers. Then we'd hurry home already nostalgic for Pumpkin Jack's departure and spread out our sugary bounty by his glow.

I lay back down and wrapped the threadbare blanket tighter. My conjuring of beasts was exhausting, for it was brought on by extreme emotion. Its magic drained me. My limbs were weak, my head aching.

I turned on my side and stared at the jailhouse door. In the dimming light I saw movement along the bottom. Tiny creatures were worming their way under! Squealing triumphantly, they wriggled in and raced toward me. In their jaws they carried things.

My spirits leapt at seeing this. The largest one dropped his prize. A broken brown shoelace—surely Sammy's! The next mouse bore a tuft of white blonde hair—Lewin's. The mice had found their cells and if need be could find them again. The third mouse nudged a wedge of dirty bedding fabric toward me. I opened it up. It was torn into a heart shape. Scrawled inside the heart with swaths of dried blood was the initial B.

"Birdy," I murmured. "My Birdy." I pressed the bit of fabric to my chest and then remembered the mice, still sitting by my face with their whiskers quivering. "I promised you treasures, didn't I?" I pulled one of the bread heels from my pocket and tore it into three large pieces. "For you, I will-ingly go hungry tonight!"

The mice scurried off the bed and down into the corner hole to savor the treats.

⁂

I couldn't have been resting more than forty-five minutes, hands behind my head, before I heard the now familiar pounding on the walls followed by the crowing of Dolly Rouge. "Dull Wit! I know you're in there."

"Dolly! How nice of you to greet me once again," I replied in my cheeriest voice, truly shocked she was speaking to me again.

"This ain't a social call, Dull Wit! Dolly here ain't feelin' so very *nice*."

"Oh? Whatever's the matter?"

"You were wagging your jaw to that pompous toad of a doctor. First you said how villainous he was. You got me all riled and recalling nightmarish happenings with the bastard. And now? Now you're chums?"

I was suddenly teeming with jitters. Why hadn't I heard her footsteps returning or the squeak of the lock opening and shutting? "How did you know this?" I asked her. "I thought Blackbeard hauled you up to the infirmary."

"You think me a dunce? I've got my eyes and ears in here. Remember, the guards creep around in socks. They can be quiet as thieves when they want."

"Fair enough. Well, the truth is that Dowdrick entered my cell uninvited. I had no choice but to speak with him. He had Fast Step chain me to the back wall. It was no spring picnic." As thrilled as I was to hear Dolly loudly call for me, even using the insulting Dull Wit—I was horrified word had spread so rapidly about my dealings with Dowdrick.

"What all did you discuss then?" Her tone leeched suspicion.

"The incident at Conklin's Taylor I told you about. Dowdrick said it was justified because my brother dropped his pressed suits on the dirty floor." I sighed. "I tried to gain information, Dolly. One must play games to win prizes! You of all folks know that."

"I believe nothing that flies from a liar's lips! You told the man you could make him famous. What else did you promise him—my pound of flesh? Another prime cut on my arm?"

Dolly's screeching was maddening, when I'd promised her I would help get to the bottom of her injury. "I'm doing this for *you!* For all of the prisoners this charlatan might seize in order to harm."

"Oh, bullocks! Witches speak lies as easily as breathing. Don't tell me you're not one."

I sighed deeper. "So what if I am?" I thought of the misunderstood man in *House of the Seven Gables,* and fairy-tales my mother told me about women in forests mixing herbs for healing. "Witches also do worthy deeds," I reasoned. "Charms that heal and incantations for love and good luck."

"Bah! Then chant a spell to fly me out of these bars."

"I can't. My powers lie with animals."

"Tell your filthy rodents to steal the warden's keys or gnaw an escape tunnel to Market Street."

"I am working on plans, Dolly. How are your arms?"

"One tore open the worse," she whined. "Caught it on a long splinter."

"I'm sorry to hear."

"I'll wager you're not," she grumbled.

I ignored her denunciation. "Is that why they took you up to the infirmary?"

"Don't you worry your witchy head over it."

"I care, Dolly, I do."

"Oh, bullocks!" With that, she kicked her boots across that room.

When I first made Dolly's acquaintance this would have had me grinning. But now there were many concerns. I had to prove to Dolly and whoever my allies were, even to Birdy that I had no real partnership with Dowdrick. Yet wasn't that exactly my hope in order to implement my plan? *A worrisome conundrum.* I tossed and turned as cold air streamed in like bitter ire from the Eye of God.

12

The days dragged on, each indistinguishable from the last. No yard work, infrequent exercise time in my tiny outside pen. No visit from Amity. No more talking to Dolly Rouge. The sheer boredom would've killed me if my constant worry did not get to me first. I had thought my mysterious offer of fame an irresistible tidbit, yet Dowdrick had not returned to inquire how I would do this. And more worry about the vegetable garden sank my spirits. Surely by now it had perished in a punishing frostbite. The early darkness of impending winter was setting in.

How was I to get to know Birdy if I could not speak with him again? How was I to save us all from Dowdrick if he ignored my offer? How would I convince Amity of my good intentions if she refused to visit? How would I find out how Sam fared if I could not see him working in the yard? The grim reality of prison weighed on me.

I persisted against the heaviness, the gloom. I made Birdy a fabric heart with a bloody E scrawled inside it and sent it out with a mouse. As my tiny messenger scurried along the prison halls, I helped to navigate it with pictures of Birdy's gray eyes, his bruised limbs, and the shapes of his long feet tangled inward.

I was thankful my mice kept me warm at night. We formed a protective ring. And I fed them generously with breadcrumbs and soup.

I startled awake with a gasp. My rodent tribe scattered, anxiously squealing.

Someone yanked on my arm, "Up with ya!" Blackbeard's voice rang out. "The fancy leecher wants to examine the devil's dam in his own office. Up and out, I say!"

After all of these weeks? I had hoped for Dowdrick's return. But now, sheer terror was all I felt.

Blackbeard lowered my prison hood, momentarily suffocating me as the small openings for nose and mouth were set crookedly to one side. When I yelped, he slid it to the proper position and then tied it firmly. He also fastened a wide band around my eyes so I could not see out. He handed me my boots and I sensed him hovering over me while I struggled to put them on without the benefit of sight. "Hurry, we ain't got all day."

This isn't day, I was tempted to retort.

Chains were secured around my feet and hands so I was forced to shuffle down the halls instead of properly walking. A few prisoners yelled out, "Which poor sod they got?" or "Is this one riding out on a rail or heading to the gallows?" or "At this time of night! Must be feeding 'im to the man in the moon!"

"Shut your traps," Blackbeard shot back, "or I'll douse

you all in freezing water down in the hole. Celebrate the winter 'n all that." The prisoners instantly fell silent.

I could tell we were outside from the rusty squeal of the door hinges and the blast of frigid air, which swept right through the roughshod wool of my hood, up my skirt and thin coat and set my teeth to chattering. Someone smelling of hay, manure and garden lime hoisted me into a carriage. With the snap of the reins he gave a sharp command to "Git!"

Horses, large and steady carried us into the night. Judging from the volume of the *clip clops* and the deep snorts of the beasts, not to mention how high the carriage rode, I determined they were probably enormous Clydesdales.

I tried to sense another human presence but could not. If we were heading to Dowdrick's he was not in this carriage. Of that I was sure. My acute senses helped me attune to beasts yet they sometimes helped me read people as well.

I strove to align my vision to the large draft horses. Beasts thought in pictures. I'm not sure how I knew this for I had not learned it in any school. There were *two* sets of snorts and a regular side-to-side *clip clop, jig-jag*.

The Clydesdales sent me colorful pictures of things that pleased them: carrots, sugar cubes and apples. Next, they sent a clear glimpse of their watering hole, with its mounted granite basin. The basin was chipped and dripping on one side from a horse's high kick.

What's behind the basin? I pictured the horses drinking and resting beside it.

A wide gray building protected by a gate. I strained to see what style of gate it was. *Tri-leaf patterns atop each bar, very pretty, very posh.*

My pulse raced. This was a nervy exercise, like the sleuths solving cases in the penny dreadful thrillers Mama had read aloud to me years ago. How danger ticked off precious minutes from the clock; how some clues led nowhere while other ones fit perfectly into a larger whole. I always liked puzzles. If only real lives were not in the balance.

After about fifteen minutes the horses hastened from a trot to a bracing gallop that echoed off the cobblestones. They were rushing to get back to the comfort of their water and hay. The previous images rushed into sharper focus: the stone basin, the gate with leaf designs and a gray building with a sign splashed across it. I could not make out more than its E. I assumed the rest: Eclectic Medical School.

"Whoa, Nelly!" The porter snapped the reins. The carriage rocked with his jumping off, and then his hand reached for mine and coaxed me down. One rather gentlemanly arm steadied me to make sure I didn't fall. I was grateful for it, because my eyes were still bound and my ankles still chained.

The wind whistled through my thin muslin clothes as the porter led me down what seemed a narrow pathway to the back of the establishment. "Stairs ahead," he warned.

I stumbled up one, two, then three steps and through what seemed like two sets of doors. They slammed behind us.

"Is this Dr. Dowdrick's establishment?" I ventured.

"Patience. They'll speak to you when they're ready," was his cryptic reply.

They?

He led me to a sturdy chair and eased me onto it. Then he stretched my arms tightly behind the chair and secured them with chains. "They'll see you shortly," he said. With that, he was gone.

It was terribly disorienting to not have the use of sight. My arms throbbed. If I did not move them shortly, they would turn numb and bloodless. "Please, Porter, come back!" I begged.

"He is gone. I deign to speak with you now." This petulant voice was none other than Dowdrick's.

"Take my hood off, if you please."

"Perhaps, perhaps not. Do not rush me. So, you requested a visit to my office and here you are. Happy now?" He sniggered.

I resisted my rising panic. "As I said over in Cherry Hill, I know what you did to Dolly."

"What might that be?"

"You drugged her with a foul concoction that banished her memory."

"Ah, not foul. I'd call it miraculous. But, yes, correct. I could do the very same to you."

"I have told other prisoners about your experiments. Why, I even spoke to Dr. Shakesby about your testing without patents. If prisoners start to sicken or die while under the influence of your elixirs, people at Cherry Hill will know who was responsible."

Dowdrick let out a malicious chuckle. "Who will believe your word over mine? Who will care that a thief or a madam or a filthy witch went into a stupor, even died? Most would find it pure relief. Benjamin Franklin and William Penn's Philadelphia has a thin sheen of civility and reason. But we both know one need not dig far beneath its surface to find rampant superstition and chaos lurking there."

He was right. People claimed to be God-fearing Christians but oftentimes they prescribed to the old ways—hexes and curses and calling up night sprites to keep their households safe.

"Look, I am not here to blame or report on you," I told him. "Let's put that aside. I am here to discuss a business proposal. What exactly was it you gave Madame Rouge?"

"Ha! You're beside yourself with curiosity."

I pushed on. "What did you gain from cutting her and stitching her up?"

"I had my reasons."

"I am riveted. Please, tell me..."

Dowdrick broke into peals of laughter. It disgusted me he was so thoroughly enjoying this. "You are a mere street mongrel. Your elevated sense of importance is a joke."

"I must be the smartest of street mongrels then! For I know more than you can imagine about you and your dubious activities."

"If nothing else, you entertain me," he said jovially. "Do go on!"

I needed to stoke his explosive rage, his rivalries. I used every tidbit of what Shakesby had relayed and made up the rest. "You are in savage competition with the finest doctors in Philadelphia. There is a frantic race to find cures and obtain landmark patents. The first to succeed in these will be graced with having their discoveries in the medical books; they will be the toast of the prime medical establishments."

"The only frantic thing is the fairytale you weave," Dowdrick said. But his next question revealed his jealous interest. "If you are so wise, which famous doctors do you know of?"

"Thomas Mutter for one. Already famed for his revolutionary work with burn victims. They say he conjures practical magic with facial restoration."

"Ha!" Dowdrick was clearly taken aback. "He is no one to me."

"Surely you've read of him. Why, I hear tell folk are lined up for blocks around Jefferson Medical Hospital waiting eagerly to be helped by Dr. Mutter."

"From where, pray tell, did you receive these faulty rumors?" Dowdrick's tone gave it away. He was seething with envy. I had hit the mark. If I could see him now, no doubt his nostrils would be flared, his pudgy cheeks red with fury.

"Ah! I must hold some cards close to my vest until you listen to my offer. And if you please, before we conduct business, remove my hood."

"All hell-fired up you are, Miss Almighty! I could take you down a peg or two; administer the same powder I gave to Madame Rouge. It would make you forget everything. If I give you enough, it could easily kill you…"

At this, my pulse began to beat in terror, but I forced myself to calm. "And then? You would never gain fame through my method. My *foolproof* method."

"No need. I already have the powders I gave Madame Rouge. I will be the star of the spring Discovery Symposium. Dr. Mutter will be astonished. They will *all* be astonished."

Discovery Symposium! This was better news than expected—a tool to gain leverage. "Then your powders and vials must be quite magical to astound the best doctors in Philadelphia! Do tell what the mixtures are intended for."

"Surgery without pain," he exclaimed. "We are all racing to perfect the medication that can do this. With it, patients will not have to get blind drunk, or scream in agony as we cut off limbs and stitch their raw nubs."

His earnest answer caught me off-guard. It was a worthy

quest, which forced me to admit that villains as well as heroes had missions they believed in. People contained both good and bad; the truth and the light could, indeed be hard to discern through the many gray layers. This made me think of Amity and her spiritual verses. Still, life wasn't only about moral perfection, but striving to be better, to do better. I had my own mission, however winding and I needed to stay the course. "Your powder so perfectly put Dolly into a painless state of being," I gushed. "Why, she had no memory of even being under the blade. How utterly impressive, Doctor! I misread you. I underestimated you and your talents. Let me ask again with a more open mind, where did this impressive mixture come from?"

"My partner, Dr. Sumac procures it from Peru," Dowdrick revealed with fervent glee. "A lovely white flower. They call it Angel's Trumpet, though it has a pinch of the devil in it, too."

I laughed with him, all the while, my innards crawled in loathing. The impertinence, the criminality of experimenting on a woman, or any person—without their consent! It was Dowdrick who should be behind bars in Cherry Hill Penitentiary, not I. Not Dolly, who was helping desperate women earn a day's wage—albeit in a questionable trade—yet with their full consent. "I suppose we all have a bit of the devil in us," I said, "mixed in with pure genius."

"My concoction *is* rather genius," he agreed.

The fact was, this Peruvian powder could kill. It could scrub someone's mind. Make them a zombie as in one of Poe's horror stories. But I dared not say this.

Because I had him.

Dowdrick had already said too much. His overweening pride was the glue that would bind him. I only had to lure him in slowly so he would not see my web. Prideful men had an insatiable appetite for flattery, adulation, shiny medals and coinage. I would do my best to supply these if it kept my friends at Cherry Hill Prison safe from harm. If it brought him to justice.

We were quiet for a time. Silence was dangerous though, for I sensed Dowdrick also knew he had confided too much.

"We are done here for now," he said coldly as he began to pace, leaning to one side.

"My mysterious offer still awaits," I tempted. This heavy hood was stifling. I needed to hurry before I fainted from its wooly confines. "Are you not curious? It will propel you to the highest of heights. Make you far more famous than Dr. Mutter."

"What is it then? Hurry! Out with it! I must get to work. I run an entire medical college here." He groaned. "My ribs pain me where you plunged in those infernal scissors. At night, I can hardly walk. I brought you here to interrogate you where I have total control, to find out how much you know. Perhaps also to give you a taste of your own medicine," he finished sharply.

The powder. I must avoid him dosing me. "Look, we have both been hurt. My brother no longer lives. Please, remove my hood so we can see eye to eye. Let me discuss the offer, which shall help us both."

He limped faster. "Why should I trust you?"

"I could ask the same of you. As I said, we have badly harmed each other. Let us steer this boat around and help one another. What's to say we can't?"

The air bustled with his unexpected motion toward me. He yanked off the eye binding and then my hood. Greedily, I gulped in air and brushed itchy fibers from my face. Furtive glances showed glassed-in wall cabinets lined with bottles and test-tube vials. In the center of the room stood two long wooden tables piled with beakers, vines, dried leaves and a microscope. Three windows were set along one wall, though the blinds were all drawn. Gas lanterns glowed from each table. They illuminated the lines of stools alongside them. For the students?

Dowdrick pulled over an armchair and sat facing me. With a sick flicker of recognition I took in the outfit I'd pressed for him many times at Conklin's Taylor—a red damask vest bordered with black ribbon, a waistcoat of silver silk with ivory buttons. High-waisted gray plaid trousers perched atop his egg-shaped belly. I shuddered as his over-sweet odor hit my nose.

Business, Evalina, business.

"You've seen me conjure beasts," I began, "the wasps and the insects crawling up your trousers in the prison yard. Before I was imprisoned at Cherry Hill I was a Bird Girl, rousing birds from the cornfields—"

"What on earth does this have to do with a momentous deal?" Wincing, Dowdrick began to massage his left side where I'd stuck in the scissors. He pulled out a pocket watch and checked the time with his other hand. "I am a very busy man."

"Look, every household has common pests. Mice, rats, roaches, and the mosquito who carries deadly disease."

"So?" For a supposedly brainy doctor this prick was not adding up the score.

"So! You make a potion that claims to lure house pests— or field pests in the case of the farmer—and once they are gathered, a second dose claims to kill them for good!" This idea went against everything in me that adored animals. Even beetles with their glittering green coats of arms and wafer-thin wings were wondrous in my estimation. But I only needed to lure him.

He looked befuddled. "Where exactly do you come in?"

I sighed. This doctor's brains were mush. "*I* am the conduit! *I* lure them in. The potion only pretends to do the trick of rendering me a Pied Piper. You'll need *me* to do the work. I, alone, have this power." I smiled in a show of warmth at him. "I will generously help your endeavor if you help me."

He stroked his aching side as he pondered this. Clearly, I needed to hasten this along.

"Now wouldn't this miraculous elixir top any little flowery powder meant to loll patients to sleep?" I asked him. "As you stated yourself, many doctors are already hard at work on a surgical aid, so who knows how soon someone would upstage you? God forbid, you should work for months and have a competitor with the same product before you even mount the stage? What humiliation! Wouldn't you prefer a completely revolutionary potion? A wildly unique one no one has thought of in any way, shape or form?"

Dowdrick's eyes gleamed and he forgot to keep nursing his badly healed rib wound.

I went on, my heart pattering a hopeful beat. "Name it something witty like your other potions I saw in the infirmary. And of course, the label would have only *your* name on it!" I mentioned pleasing headings I had already devised. "What about *Dowdrick's Hypno Beast Rid, Dowdrick's Pest Destruct* or *Dowdrick's Monster Mesmer*?"

The twinkle in his eye grew shinier. He approved! In the next instant, though, he frowned. "What would you ask from the bargain?"

"I ask that my sentence be reduced. A letter of recommendation from you to the warden would be excellent. More importantly, I would want a solemn promise you would conduct no more cutting experiments on my friends. They are not Thanksgiving turkeys."

"Who might your friends be? Ah, let me guess! That over-tall Welshman with the lame feet? The hussy, Dolly Rouge…" His eyes narrowed to pinholes. "Who else, pray tell?"

"Samuel Barton."

"The runaway slave accused of attacking a man with a razor?"

"Yes. Samuel was framed by the Moyamensing Killer Gang. I heard from a fellow prisoner that Samuel was not the first to attack. Have you *transported* him here?" I used Shakesby's term and then leaned back to see if Dowdrick flinched.

No visible flinch but his pale cheeks flushed. "Who knows and who cares? One of my colleagues at Eclectic Medical College may have." Dowdrick dabbed his moist forehead with a handkerchief and then returned it to his waistcoat pocket.

"So, *Samuel* is not being held by you?" If Amity ever visited me again I would mention Sammy to her. The Quakers, known for their underground railroad to help carry slaves north to freedom, would not take lightly to Dowdrick's careless attitude toward Sammy.

Dowdrick shrugged. "I told you, I don't recall. I've seen too many a patient. Any other so-called friends you care to mention?"

Dare I mention Lewin? This tender sapling needed the most protection. Yet if I called attention to him… "No, no one."

"I can try to keep an eye out for prisoners from Cherry

Hill. Yet I cannot guarantee anyone's total safety," he scoffed. "And why should I?"

"Because if you don't I shall make a deal with say, Dr. Mutter himself! And... because of the beasts," I whispered ominously. "They have a mind to harm."

I sensed many creatures under the floor—not just dainty mice. My mind's eye filled with pictures of snarling snouts lined with needle teeth. I pictured these wily beings dining in the cellar on roots and herbs, bursting from burlap sacks. But now, their snouts sniffed at the malice above the ceiling. Now their paws began to tear up through dirt and stone channels toward Dr. Dowdrick's lab. Their quivering was my quivering. My sprinting heartbeat matched theirs.

Dowdrick's eyes darted around in fear. "If you send them to me I will have you swiftly killed. You are the one in chains, not I."

"It is not simply I who sent them, so killing me will not end this. It is in large part your hatred, your own sickness of spirit," I dared.

"Hatred, sickness of spirit, bah! It is *you* who are full of evil, Witch."

"No sense in arguing. This pact is for your own safety, Doctor. Hurry! If we do not form a pact they will maul you, rip you apart with their claws. Remember the wasps— " was as far as I got before the ravenous rats teemed out of the holes in the walls and over to Dowdrick.

They tore at his boots with ferocity. Slavering, drooling, they gnawed ragged holes in the leather. A storm of teeth and hair and claws they were. I jerked back as well, with my heart racing. I lifted my own boots above the floor because the rodents swarmed everywhere, tipping their raw, quivering snouts upward as they went.

"Off! Off, vermin!" he screeched, batting at them with his

cane. It stunned a few of the rats, and brained others, who lay splayed and bloody. Yet many more came squealing from the crevices. "Wicked conjurer! You swore you could control these things. What good would a deal be if you do not control them?" As soon as he smashed the guts from a rat or two, a fresh grouping went to mauling and shredding his nearly destroyed boots.

Of one thing Dowdrick was right. I had no idea if I could stop this rampage. I had never tested it. But if we were to go forth, I would have to prove myself. "I do control them. I can!" Shutting my eyes I sent desperate pictures. Frantic pleas:

Stop this carnage! Back off! Retreat to the edges of the room! Off, now!

As with my mice, I promised these rats a reward. But Lord, could I deliver? Despite my iron cuffs I was able to dig down in a pocket of my prison dress. I gulped in relief that I had stashed a heel of bread in there, saved for my own rodent tribe. Was it enough? It had to be.

Treats! Lovely treats for you straightway.

By the time the rats retreated, my brain beat against my skull in a blinding headache. I had sweated through my pantaloons, camisole and prison dress and my hair was soaked as well. Dowdrick's boots were in tatters, pieces scattered amongst the red slime, rat carcasses and hairless tails all in a ghastly swirl. The room reeked of the rusty iron of fresh blood.

Stunned, I leaned back in my chair. Dowdrick was blurry in my gaze. This terrified me as much as anything, for I had never lost my sight before in the effort of corralling a beast. I could only pray that my full sight would be restored in time. I took a wobbly breath and spoke. "This is how we will do it. See what theater for the ages we could put on?"

Dowdrick shook his head as if to clear the fog. Then he stared, wild-eyed, at his boots. Three or four of his toes in their black stockings poked out from uneven holes. At least the roughshod beasts hadn't bitten his toes clear off. "You owe me for this, Witch!"

"We will make a fortune. I will buy you dozens of fine leather boots! Oh, the spectacle!" I erupted in exhausted laughter. "You will be in all the broadsides, Doctor! Think on it."

At this, Dowdrick's beady eyes sparkled with intrigue. I saw *that* despite my half-blinded state. "*I* will make the fortune, Witch! *I* will pocket the money. You will make nothing."

I glared at him. "I must earn a ticket out of Cherry Hill. Promise me it."

"We shall see."

My voice sharpened. "Shall I call in a second army of rodents?"

"No need," he was quick to say. I watched with amusement as he rose and stumbled, almost falling face-first into the gory mess before steadying himself on a table corner. He skated to the other side of the room, cracked open a door and called for the porter. Then, he said the words I waited for. "Yes, yes, we shall do this."

"Promise it!"

"Promises, promises. What good are they?"

"Promise it! Or I shall call more rodents to eat you alive in your sleep."

"Oh, I promise it." He rolled his eyes and then bent

toward the keyhole in the door and called out, "Porter, do not enter. I will bring the girl forth."

Dowdrick returned with the dreadful wool hood and eyepiece. He took malicious revenge, binding it extra tightly. Completely blind once more, it was my turn to stay aloft as I slid across the slick floor.

Just before I left the office to board the carriage, Dowdrick murmured, "We will need to practice. The performance at the March symposium must be perfect in every way. *Dowdrick's Monster Mesmer* sounds like the best choice of label."

"Yes, of course. Quite theatrical." He had taken the bait! My heart leapt. "How will we communicate?"

"I will send notes under your food trencher. Your warden will do my bidding."

"Ah, Blackbeard."

"Heh. He does resemble the infamous pirate!" The cretin had a sense of humor after all.

Outside, the cold air cleared my head and helped cleanse me of the greasy guilt I felt in forming a secret pact with Dowdrick.

Back in my cell with my hood and blinders removed, I lay on my back gawping at the skylight as dawn floated in. I appreciated every tiny wonder: flattened maple leaves like flaming stars, the chink in the glass a portal hinting at life outside, water drops like transparent pearls, and even the beige dots of pigeon droppings.

I trembled at a sudden, fierce blast of wind. November chills—where frosty sprites and imps seeped through the very brick and mortar to freeze noses and fingertips. My earlier bravado was stunning to me now. Perilous, a fool's game. It was a miracle Dowdrick hadn't given me a killing dose of the Trumpet Flower's powder. I wasn't very religious, though I mumbled prayers Amity had taught me. During these hours my sight returned.

And I wished for the dour Quaker matron's return.

13

Had my prayers worked? Impossible to know, yet Amity did come calling. She was still dressed in severe black. I was so very lonely I imagined a smile where there was none. At least she looked over at me before sitting and cracking open her prayer book. I wondered if she missed seeing me? Or whether I was simply a burden to her? I knew Quakers undertook social work others scorned. Feeding the poor, educating young women, preaching against the wages of intoxication and violence and working to free the slaves.

Was I another task? Somehow I hoped that for Amity, I was more than a job well done or a guilt-clearing good deed.

"Pray tell, what bothers thee?" She gazed directly my way.

This kindness startled me. A million concerns flew across my mind. I thought of Sammy being transported by force from the infirmary. Did Amity know where he'd been taken? I thought of Dowdrick seizing me and taking me to his office—our secret pact and my plan to double cross him. This was a forbidden topic. I thought of Birdy and my constant ache to see him, speak to him; to hold hands and make sure he wasn't afraid of me now that he knew I spoke to animals. I had so many concerns, I didn't know which to pick.

"I... I missed seeing you. I thought I'd angered you, and you had abandoned me."

Amity did not smile, but flecks of gold sparked in her hazel eyes. Then, her gaze fell to her prayer book on the table. "No person shall be deemed a failure, Evalina. Every person is worthy of redemption."

"Is this why you chose prison work? To try to redeem us sinners?"

"I was led to it."

"I hope you see me as more than a task. More than a leading." It was above my station to wish she be my friend.

"There is no sin in following a leading from God."

"I am led to work with animals. Who's to say mine is not God showing me *my* path?"

She sighed wearily, but did not call me impudent, and march out. This was also an improvement. "Has thou been praying?"

"Yes, Amity."

"Does thou remember the verses I taught thee?"

I recited my version. "'If we walk in the light then thee and thine have fellowship.' I lie in bed at night and recite this to the skylight."

"Words are missing and others twisted." Amity seemed to think my scrambled adaptation absurd. Yet she did not stomp out. Another improvement. "What might provide balm to thy soul, Evalina? Which prayers shall I teach thee?"

"I miss the garden. I miss the yard work. We did not get to harvest the crop. I worry that it was ruined by frost. We missed the pumpkins and squash. Will we ever be trusted to do yard work again?" I was suddenly on the verge of tears. "Do you have a prayer about plants? About gardens?"

Her eyes lit up again and she *did* smile. It wasn't just my wishful thinking. "Yes, there is one. The parable of the mustard seed."

"Oh! Teach it to me, please!"

"I shall. Jesus was speaking to his flock." Amity closed her book. She knew this parable well enough to recite it by heart. "Again he said, 'What shall we say the kingdom of God is like, or what parable shall we use to describe it? It is like a mustard seed, which is the smallest of all seeds on earth. Yet when planted, it grows and becomes the largest of all garden plants, with such big branches that the birds can perch in its shade.' Can thou repeat the verse?"

This one came easily to me. I repeated it five times with no mistake.

"What does thee make of the verse?" Amity asked, ever the teacher.

"From the smallest, most humble of creatures can come great gifts, abundant harvests."

"Truly," she whispered. "Anything else?"

"Yes," I whispered. "It reminds me of planting a garden with my mother when I was small. Of working by her side and her showing me how to gently push the seed in and tamp it down." My voice faded as emotions gripped me.

"Does thine mother live nearby? Perhaps she could visit thee sometime."

"No. She died when I was young of the cholera. My father, too."

"My sympathies, Evalina. It is hard to lose loved ones." When Amity looked up her eyes were glistening. "Bring forth therefore fruit worthy of penance. Keep this message in thine heart."

"I shall try."

With that she arose, her face mottled with pink, and rapped for the guard to release her.

The parable was beautiful, and about growing things, and I didn't feel critical of it, or hateful toward Amity. I had to insure my efforts with Dowdrick brought forth healthful not rotten fruit. Her whispered plea played in my mind all day as I went about my tasks.

The next morning, I was granted a second wish. Fast Step came by after breakfast and barked out an order for us prisoners to don our coats. He chained my feet and put on my hood, but left my hands to dangle free. Then he led us, single file with chains clanging, to the yard.

The wind was gusting but the sun was shining, giving us gilded reprieve from the dank cells. It was sweet relief to see the long planters we'd spent so many hours working on, brimming with cabbage and broccoli. Some plants had mounds of half-melted snow upon them. It was a miracle the frost hadn't decimated the crop. The pumpkins and gourds had all been lopped off their stalks though. Had the wardens divided the bounty or had they been sold at market for All-Hallows Eve?

While the wardens organized the prisoners into rows and counted them, I searched for my friends and acquaintances. Hoods were on, but having seen at least some folks without them, I was able to identify a few from height and shape; from the way they held themselves and their eyes. That woman with one hip cocked was Dolly Rouge. The tallest man across from me with a lopsided stance was Birdy. He winked and the warmth of his kind eyes sailed right into me. I made sure no one was looking and then I winked back. This set his eyes to smiling—pebble gray, bright with feeling, wisdom and patience. One could see so much in a simple gaze when other ways of seeing were forbidden. Birdy was tired, too. Sallow half circles sat under his eyes. His body had healed from the beating and sprains but it was clear the toll this place took.

I scanned the rows for a brown-skinned hand missing two fingers, and boots with broken laces. There were eight or nine Negroes but none with Sammy's identifying features. My heart sank. Dr. Shakesby's ominous words rang out: *transported*. Where was Sammy?

My terms had been clear to Dr. Dowdrick. He was not to haul off prisoners and carve them up to experiment with surgical drugs. Or, drat, had my demands been too narrow in scope, too easy for Dowdrick to skirt around?

Next, I studied the children from the 200 halls. I counted seven of them in a choppy line. Some were so short they couldn't have been more than six years old. I struggled to imagine a crime someone that young might commit— stealing a rabbit so his family could eat, or filching bags of sugar from a Market Street vendor to sell for double the price by the piers. The older, taller children sprouted up like weeds in a meadow—all ungainly elbows and knock-knees.

Panic arose in my throat. How would I identify Lewin aside from his white-blond hair? I almost wished Dowdrick were here demanding the removal of the hoods again so I could be absolutely sure Lewin was still safe.

Fast Step was done counting the prisoners. He joined Blackbeard at the end of a long planter. They made a strange pair—one tall and bearded, the other short and red-faced—in their dark prison garb and the thick socks they wore over their boots to muffle their footsteps.

Blackbeard surveyed the prisoners with his coal black eyes. "Today you pick the harvest. Twist and crack the cabbage and broccoli from the stalks and drop them in the baskets." To demonstrate, he leaned over the end of a planter, curled his hand around the underside of a cabbage and snapped the green gem clean off as he twisted it. In his mammoth hands, the crunch echoed throughout the yard. Mitts like his were terrifying. They could break stalks or necks with equal ease.

"No dillydallying," Fast Step chimed in, corralling us with a spiked truncheon, which was even more frightening than Blackbeard's huge fists.

The work was fulfilling, knowing that we'd planted these vegetables, watched them grow from seedlings, and now were harvesting them. They were ours even if the guards didn't see it this way. I could only hope the cooks would allow us to fill our bellies with these wonders. It was only fair.

Bending over the planter was bracing work, what with one hand balancing on the container as my other hand twisted and snapped the stalks. The cabbage was easier to pull than the broccoli, which grew tall and took every ounce of strength and two hands to yank out. My knees bruised from scraping them on the cobblestones and my back ached. More than anything though, I ached from not being able to speak to Birdy, just across the planter from me. I could have reached out to him if only Fast Step wasn't eying me with truncheon in hand.

When we got up to work on the next sections, it alarmed me to see Birdy limp and grab his elbow in pain. It hadn't healed well.

By the time we were done, we had filled fifteen baskets and the dusk was nigh. Early winter winds had picked up and with them, a dusting of snow. Still, I was sad to leave the yard, for it meant saying a silent goodbye to Birdy. I needed to ask him about Sammy and Lewin. Other things too. I would have to figure out a way to communicate soon because with prisoners disappearing, this place was dangerous. I felt the heavy drain of time, and even the footfalls of death creeping ever closer.

That evening, a rare delight slid in with the dinner trencher. Steaming cabbage! Butternut squash dotted with raisins! My mouth watered like a leaky bucket even before the first bite. The fruits of our hard labor dribbled with butter were veritable slices of heaven. I tried my best to eat slowly and savor the meal, but it was a losing proposition.

Even Dolly called out jovially, "These here are the best victuals I've had since a customer of mine took me out for fruit-cup and hand-whipped cream at Strawberry Mansion."

"It's from the vegetables we planted. Isn't it exciting? We grew all of this!"

"I'm aware, Dull Wit," Dolly said in a droll tone. "Tell me something I don't know."

Ah, back to Dolly's curmudgeonly self. I'll take it over her silence.

"Do you think they'll let us garden again?"

"If we don't pull any more witchy stunts like that man who's sweet on you shoveling dirt at the doctor's suit." Dolly laughed. "Say, what did you talk about with that squab's ass?"

"I'm trying to trick him."

"Into what?"

"Into proving his own guilt. Into landing him in prison and getting us out!"

"I'd like to see that hornswoggling rat fry in hell. But how on this green earth do you plan to do it?"

I hesitated. Dolly didn't trust me; that much was clear. But did I trust *her?* She often spoke to Blackbeard. They had some type of friendship. Or possibly they were lovers. I might trust Dolly but from all I'd seen I did not trust Blackbeard. Though if I didn't reply, she would doubt my motives again and clam up.

"I will expose his medical crimes and trickery."

"But how?"

"I haven't planned it down to the stitches and hems yet, Dolly, but I promise to keep you informed." I spooned in the last bite of squash and chewed slowly, savoring it. "Have you seen Samuel Barton? You know, the Negro barber accused of slicing up the Moyamensing thug?"

"Oh, sure, I got me a hair trim and a red henna rinse from him just the other day. No charge. Cherry Hill special." Dolly paused. "What do you think, Dull Witt? That I can stroll up and down the halls of this dungeon making sociable chit chat?"

I sighed deeply. "'Course not. I know you converse with Blackbeard though." I needed to take a risk and mention him. "Perhaps he told you scuttlebutt regarding Sammy. You see, Sammy was in the infirmary. He was drugged—I mean, utterly knocked out—and there was talk about him being transported." I let that land. "I was hoping he didn't get transported to where you went. To the nasty sawbones *for cutting up.*"

Even through the wall, I heard Dolly's sharp gasp. "Good God, the evil bastard is taking more of us?"

"I'm not certain, Dolly, but I vow to find out. If he

snatches any of the children here I'll never forgive myself for not trying everything to stop it."

"If I see Blackbeard I'll work the conversation around to it." She paused. "Only if I can mention it without him getting suspicious."

"Yes, mention it as light chit chat." I snickered. "We must get to the bottom of this for our own sakes."

"Light chit chat," she echoed darkly. "Just a bit of scuttlebutt is all."

Two days later we were allowed out in the yard again, this time to yank up the harvested roots, toss them in a discard heap on the cobblestones and turn the soil one last time. Then, we were instructed to cover the planters with pine boughs to winter them over. The boughs were in four brimming piles, two at the end of each planter. I wondered whether they were the castoffs from people's Christmas trees, and it made me sad to think my brother, Todd and I would never spend another holiday together decorating a tree of our own.

Putting a garden to bed was hard work. The air was so frigid we could see our own breaths billowing out like white clouds. The guards watched us closely yet there were two distinct times they looked away to speak to a third warden who I did not recognize. Birdy and I strove to work close. So, during the first of these, he was able to reach out and give my hand a squeeze.

Hot fire charged through me and his broad smile was mirrored in the light of his handsome eyes. I gave his hand a stealthy squeeze after which we bent to our tasks as innocently and fervently as monks and nuns.

The second moment was one I took. In the process of leaning forward to spread the fragrant boughs I moved my mouth close to his ear and whispered, "Have you seen Sammy since the infirmary? I didn't see his hands and broken boot straps during the last lineup. Also, any word on little Lewin?"

Birdy shifted his head ever so slightly as he bent to place the branches and his hood brushed my cheek. "Word is, Sammy has not returned. Sammy's welfare worries me greatly. I know nothing of Lewin."

Our eyes met in a solemn stare of dismay.

"I will find a way to send notes. Keep an eye out," was all I managed before Blackbeard and Fast Step finished their conversation with the third warden, and they all walked our way.

"Line up, prisoners," barked Fast Step. His eyes were even more ringed with crimson than usual, and they watered from the cold. Blackbeard looked my way, and I swore he spent extra moments staring to see how I would react to his attention. Had Dolly Rouge spoken to him of Sammy? Blood pounded in my ears. But this was just the start of it.

For next, Blackbeard shouted, "Remove their masks, warden. All of them! The prisoners must be counted and examined."

Hoods were untied and yanked off. Blackbeard paced down the line as the third warden barked at us to state our names and mark us off on a clipboard.

I barely heard the names because my eyes landed on the children and with dawning horror I realized Lewin was not among them. My breath seized up as I recalled the dreadful scene at Conklin's—my brother's pleas, the swarm of wasps, the nauseating odor of talcum and my hand thrusting in the long scissors. And finally, I saw in my mind's eye clear as day my brother splayed out on the floor, cold and blue.

Another child. Over my dead body.

The birds circled overhead. A scream pressed on my throat. I wasn't sure which might come first: the scream or my collapse. Dazed, I forced myself to look down the line for the Negroes. No Samuel Barton.

My knees trembled, and graced with a sudden idea, I pretended to faint.

14

I opened my eyes. The guards had carried me to the place I hoped they would. Dr. Shakesby was now leaning over me, administering smelling salts. Sharp ammonia burned the inside of my nose and I sneezed. My hood was off.

"I see you're awake," he said.

I tried to sit up but faltered halfway when I discovered he had secured me to his examining table. "Doctor, I am much better. Will you loosen my cuffs, please?" After my time over at Dr. Dowdrick's I was as nervous as a young filly.

"Tell me, what prompted you to faint?" he asked. There was mildness in his milky eyes.

My breath hitched. *Little Lewin is gone. Sammy is gone.* Shakesby's mild look might be deceptive, for there was ample reason not to trust this doctor any more than Dowdrick. Shakesby had approved the transport of Sammy to an unknown place that could have been Dowdrick's lab as easily as a ticket north to freedom. Therefore, how did I know whether Shakesby intended to help or hurt me?

Watch my words. Parse them carefully.

"I may have fainted from the fear we were about to be scolded once again."

"They said you screamed. What did you imagine you'd be scolded for?"

"One never knows in Cherry Hill," I said vaguely.

"The guards told me something unusual happened when you were unconscious," he said, staring at me. When I said nothing, he went on. "Pigeons flew down and encircled you, clucking and fretting." Again, he seemed to be waiting for my reaction. I gave none, but I recalled the fluttering of wings. "They were fierce," he added. "When I arrived, the birds were still pecking at anyone who got close. It was a challenge to push through their throng and carry you from the yard. What do you make of this?"

"Who knows? Perhaps they felt sorry for me."

Dr. Shakesby laughed. Good, he took it as a joke. "Are you quite sure you are faring better?"

Now that the burning from the smelling salts had eased, I breathed in the room's off-putting alcohol and musty vapors. Looking to the side, I saw the bottles of Dr. Dowdrick's supposed cure-alls lined up behind Shakesby on the medical cart. I was consumed with the need to hurry along the plan with Dowdrick, yet he hadn't passed any more notes under my food trencher. Had he forgotten? Gone back on his word? "Dr. Shakesby, there is one thing."

"Yes?" He held a thermometer.

"Remember our chat about Dr. Dowdrick's medicines and his need to test them?"

"Yes." Shakesby paused from shaking out the thermometer to look at me.

"If you speak to him, please let him know I'd be willing to have him test one of his medicines on me."

"Oh?" He put the thermometer down on his medical cart. "Why this sudden interest?"

"You spoke of his need to obtain patents. I could help him achieve one. If he would like to take me to his laboratory over on Haines Street . . ."

Shakesby exhaled in laughter. "Ah, I see! Anything to get out of prison for a day."

"No, sir. It is only that I am fascinated by medicine. It would be an honor."

"I will consider it, if I see him. Now please open your mouth. I must take your temperature." His tone was neutral with no hint of whether he would truly consider it.

I had no fever. I knew I wouldn't. Dr. Shakesby went out to the hall and called for Blackbeard to walk me to my cell. As he did, I craned my neck to see if anyone was being held in the corner holding pens. No Lewin or Sammy. No one. When Shakesby returned I thanked him, and Blackbeard walked me downstairs. Once again breathing in the stale hood air I clanked along in my leg irons. "Sir, Guard," I said awkwardly, realizing I did not know Blackbeard's actual name.

"What is it, girl?"

"Might you be willing to let Miss Amity know I'm in need of prayer?"

"I reckon you are," Blackbeard said. "You need to pray that witchy darkness right out of you. I saw how those devil's familiars flocked around you in the yard. Pretty soon, you'll gather enough to fly you right up and out. But I'll be here to beat 'em away before that happens."

I lurched to one side as he swung the club at a pretend monster.

When we came to cell number 113, he unlocked the door, pushed me inside, unhinged my leg irons and stomped out.

The clink of the door lock was a weighty brick in my heart. I sank down on my bed, undid my hood and recited the mustard seed prayer over and over again.

A light knock on the door woke me. "Evalina, it is Amity. Would thee like a visit or are thou sleeping?"

My eyes blinked open. Above, the skylight displayed a shimmering, violet dusk. "Yes! A visit, please." I sat bolt upright as if I'd gulped a coffee dark as midnight.

"Stand against the back wall, Evalina."

I obeyed immediately, plastering my arms against the cold surface.

The sight of Amity entering my cell was pure relief—a human being with a listening ear, and a willing heart, albeit narrowly conscribed. She was dressed not in her usual severe black but in a pigeon gray muslin with a matching ruffled bonnet, which set off her dewy face. The guard locked the door behind her and she requested he give them ten extra minutes over their usual time. "Come, sit," she advised me, pulling out my chair and sitting delicately in the other as she gathered her skirts. "It is cold in here." She wrapped her shawl tightly about her and then placed a satchel on the table. "Thee requested my presence?"

"Yes, I did." My pulse galloped like a wild mustang's as relief turned to sadness and my tears could not be stopped.

"What ails thee?" She reached into her canvas carryall, pulled out a neat square of unbleached cotton and handed it to me.

"Thank you." I wiped my eyes. "Have you heard? A child prisoner named Lewin is gone. Samuel Barton, a Negro former slave as well. Lewin is a petty thief but only six or so. He has no family. I am worried for their welfare."

She raised her brows but did not seem unduly alarmed. "How does thee know of this?"

"When we were working in the yard, putting pine boughs on the garden beds, the guards asked us to remove our hoods and be counted. Lewin and Sammy were gone. Gone! I know Sammy well by his face, and also by his hand that's missing two fingers. I know Lewin . . ." The shaking in my voice forced me to pause and gasp in air. "I knew Lewin from the streets before I came to Cherry Hill. They called him Lightning. He helped me get food when I was wandering, penniless. I owe him a debt of protection for this." I sobbed into the handkerchief, and I was grateful that Amity sat patiently waiting for me to collect myself. "The guards spoke as if we prisoners knew of the disappearances. As if we had anything—"

"Hush! Watch what comes out of thy mouth." Amity's eyes were gleaming under her bonnet. "Best make sure it is civil and nothing the guards cannot hear."

"Yes, ma'am." With that, I brushed away more tears and tilted my ear toward the door for any stirring of Blackbeard or Fast Step. Then, I whispered an impassioned plea. "If anything happens to Lewin it would be as if my brother was murdered all over again. And if they find Sammy? I know that Quakers help to procure protection for former slaves—send them to safe houses. Sammy is innocent of the crimes he is accused of."

"Tis true there are certain safe houses ... but are thou sure this is the gospel truth?"

I held her gaze and nodded. "I sense things. You must know this? As I come into my own, these strong senses lead me to truths, not just with the wild beasts but also with people. As a Quaker woman who follows the word of God you know leadings. I have leadings not so different from yours. Sammy has a good heart. I believe his story of being brutally attacked by a Moyamensing gang member, who took the razor he used to cut people's hair and—"

"Shhh! Thou have uttered enough!" Amity hissed.

Startled, I jerked in my chair. Strange, how this polite Quaker lady could be almost as terrifying as Fast Step.

"Thee should recite the Mustard Seed parable, loudly and with spirit," she commanded in a booming voice quite unlike hers.

Something was wrong but I dared not disobey. As I launched into the parable, she rose from her chair, padded softly my way and leaned boldly near me. She whispered, "The Samuel thee speaks of has indeed, been transported. The guards will not say where." She paused to cock her head toward the door before proceeding. Then, she murmured words I could barely believe. "This Lewin lad is indeed lightning fast because . . . he escaped from this prison four days ago."

I continued to loudly chant the Mustard Seed parable as I stared at her in shock. How could she know this? I dared not ask. My heart galloped again. This time, not from fear but wild, wild hope.

Dinner came soon after Amity left and with it, another wild hope. For under the trencher was a note from Dr. Dowdrick.

The guard will call for you at midnight. Be awake and ready to ride in the carriage. Practice makes perfect. Dr. D

I tried to sleep for a while, knowing I needed my strength and wits about me. But my legs seized up in cramps and my stomach churned not from the watery rice and chicken but from nerves. Two birds squeezed through the hole in the skylight and perched on the end of my bed, clucking like a mama fretting over her baby. I hated the cold that blew in from the hole but the birds warmed my heart.

Finally, I got up and paced.

"What was the blasted ruckus?" came Dolly's voice, grumbling through the cracks in the bricks. "First you're bawling like a lunatic then you're singing like a drunken fool. Has your mind cracked?"

"No Dolly," I said as loudly as I dared. "The Quaker matron paid me a visit. She told me Sammy has indeed, been taken. She told me that—"

"Stand against the back wall, witch," Blackbeard hollered from just outside my door. Lord! I almost fainted, for he was the last person I wanted to get an earful of my revelations. If he heard what I knew all hell might ensue. At least Dolly had the sense to shut her mouth for the time being. The birds startled and squeezed up and out of the skylight.

Blackbeard turned the key in the lock and barreled in. "You're in demand today—a real Queen Victoria, ain't ya?" he teased as he secured my leg irons for the third time in one day.

"What's that you say, Whiskers?" Dolly yelled through the walls.

"I was talking to the witch, mind you!" Blackbeard bellowed back at Dolly. "Are ya jealous, wench?"

"Bullocks, old whiskers! You flatter yourself!" she retorted. Though once he had me out in the halls, and had pushed the cell door closed with a bang, Dolly's voice squeaked with alarm. "Where are you taking her?"

"Don't you worry your head with it!"

"Where to?" Dolly cawed.

"Not your business, woman!"

As Blackbeard hauled me up and into Dowdrick's carriage, and then gave the driver the signal to proceed, my thoughts went to Dolly. What must she think? And what if things went horribly wrong?

"The hour is late. You must be exhausted," Dr. Dowdrick said when I arrived and was ferreted by his porter into a spacious drawing room I'd never seen. My hood was still secured and my legs still in irons. But I could see enough to know he was in a fine mood and a fancy outfit: navy jacket with pink pinstripes and gold, engraved buttons, all over a salmon pink vest. A gold pocket watch chain dangled over his rounded belly and down into his trousers pocket. His cheeks looked unusually rosy—from whiskey or excitement? "Why don't you rest for a bit before we practice?" he suggested. "We'll fetch you a cup of tea made with a soothing mix of mints."

We? "I'm fine. I've already napped as you suggested. I'm ready to work." Through the eye holes in my hood I caught glimpses of landscape paintings in gold frames gracing the walls, two crimson velvet settees that faced each other, elegant wooden side tables on either ends of the settees and a thick oriental rug spread across the plank floor. This doctor, and his Eclectic Medical School certainly enjoyed deep pockets.

My plea to practice was ignored. Dowdrick clearly had another agenda. He led me to one of the settees and bade me sit. The swarthy man with slicked back hair that I had seen in the prison yard stepped into the room holding a silver tray. He set down three china cups and poured steamy tea in one from a pretty china pitcher with roses on it.

"Meet Dr. Condor Sumac," Dowdrick said with a flourish of his hand.

"Estoy encantado," said Sumac. His deep-set ebony eyes were piercing.

"Pardon? I only understand English."

"He is saying he is enchanted, in Spanish," explained Dowdrick. He unfastened my hood and put it on the back of the settee. "So, drink up and I will show you to a couch you can rest on . . . until my lab is ready."

"I'd rather not. I'm not thirsty or sleepy."

"Don't be silly. It would be insulting to Dr. Sumac if you turn down his lovely tea. He brewed this blend just for you."

I glanced again at Sumac, who was grinning. He was handsome, but in the way of a worrisome stranger in a Poe novel who crept around in cobwebbed attics and infested cellars. His grin indicated he likely understood our conversation. I tried him. "What herbs did you use?"

"A pinch of Coco and muña. Also, other healing Peruvian mints," he answered in heavily accented English.

"Ah, so you do speak our language."

Dr. Dowdrick gestured to the two remaining empty cups. "Let's *all* have a spot of tea. Please, Dr. Sumac, pour more. It is so soothing and *gentle* to the stomach." With his emphasis on the word gentle it was clear he knew I was suspicious. He took a long draw of it and smacked his lips. "Wonderful blend," he said to Sumac, who nodded and drank his tea as well.

"Miss Evalina, do tell me your opinion of its flavor," Dr. Sumac said with a smile.

I watched the man pour it. They both sampled it. It's probably safe. I'll only drink a little.

After three sips a ghastly blackness drew over my eyes.

❄

I woke up in a cell, much smaller than the one at Cherry Hill. It had bars on all sides and the narrow metal plank I lay on took up almost the whole space. My mask was still off. I was in my prison garb and my hands were cuffed. Condor Sumac was nowhere to be found, nor was Dowdrick. The room outside of my cell was dark except for a thin sliver of light from a narrow transom on the far wall. Dim outlines of baskets brimming with plants lined the floor. The place stank of mushrooms, and the exposed roots one might find by a muddy creek. I released a blood-curdling scream.

I did not stop until Dowdrick came running. "Let me out, you scoundrel!" I screeched. "This is not part of our agreement!"

He stood four yards from the cell door leaning on his walking stick and studying me.

"How long have I been in here? What did you do to me?" Rising, I gripped the bars and shook them. "Say something!"

"You needed rest. You slept. That is all."

His dismissive answer made my blood boil. My legs throbbed. Something was very wrong with the backs of my legs. I reached around to feel my calves but my handcuffs prevented access. "Uncuff me, you brute!"

"Be careful what you call me. I am in charge. This is my laboratory," he growled.

"We struck a deal!"

"Yes, yes. But I needed to put the fear of *God* in you." He snorted. "Being a witch, you clearly have no fear of the devil." He called out to Dr. Sumac, who entered through a side door. "Unlock Miss Evalina's cell and keep the cuffs on."

From far-off corners, I heard the chittering of rats. I could summon them if need be. "No cuffs or no deal!" I demanded.

"Very well," Dowdrick said crossly. "Release her."

Sumac wore his sardonic grin as he unlocked the cell and cuffs and walked with me just behind Dowdrick toward the cellar stairs. I spun around at the sight of two more holding pens but it was too dark to see more than a dim outline of bars.

Turning, Dowdrick said, "Your friends are not in there."

"Which ones?" I snapped. "Might you know of Samuel Barton's whereabouts?" A scrabbling of tiny claws from nearby was a worrying refrain to the rodent chitters for if I called them forth, I might lose control of them.

"I have no interest in your Samuel Barton. He would be too hard to find in the dark," Dowdrick teased.

Filthy Negro hater! I bit my tongue. I had to keep the big picture in my sights. I only said, "I've heard more amusing jokes than this."

We had reached the first floor, which led to his laboratory. On his long, tall table he had arranged a shiny new display of potion bottles. The labels read Dowdrick's Monster Mesmer, and there was a clever illustration of a dragon breathing fire and bucking on its hind legs, with a man behind it securing a chain around its long neck. I was impressed despite my utter fury. Dr. Sumac went to the display and adjusted the bottles to a more perfect order.

"So, can you conjure and release at will?" asked Dowdrick. "Let us see you do it on cue. We will need to ensure you have much greater command over the . . . beasts. Can you do this?"

Dr. Sumac, too, observed me with keen curiosity.

"Yes. But first . . ." I reached around to feel my leg. My fingers ran over a raised wound roughly stitched up with course poultry thread. At the touch, my leg burned. My other calf had a matching wound. "What the devil!" I twisted around to get a glimpse of the damage. Sure enough, the two bloody scars were as real as the boots on my feet. "What did you do? How dare you? You promised me no more cutting and experimenting on—"

"Ah, ah, ah! You said no experimenting on your fellow *inmates*. You never included yourself in that number." Dowdrick narrowed his eyes in a superior squint, as if he had won five hundred dollars in the horse races. He shrugged. "After all, if you cannot produce, I must keep working to perfect my sleep elixir. As even you pointed out, there is quite a contest for doctors to perfect a drug to induce sleep in patients so they do not have to stay awake during surgery."

It was true. I had not included myself. I would never have thought of it. I took long, deep breaths in order not to explode, because the other problem with giving my emotions free reign was losing control of the beasts. They rumbled under the floorboards, buzzed by the windows, fluttered and pecked at the roof in a ferocious fugue.

I took labored breaths. I remembered, in those clarifying moments what exactly I wanted to get from all of this. Amity's voice rang in my mind: 'From the smallest, most humble of creatures can come great gifts, abundant harvests.'

I wanted to bring forth fruit worthy of penance. I was fighting for Lewin, to honor the memory of my murdered brother Todd, for Birdy and Sammy and Dolly and all of the inmates at Cherry Hill who might be damaged next. I was working for our dignity, for our freedom, and most of all to expose this ogre and slap him behind bars. Monster Mesmer was meant to trap Dr. Dowdrick, not my beautiful, wondrous wild beasts. The joke would be on him—*if* I could stay the course and pull off my plan.

"Well?" Dr. Dowdrick "What is the verdict? Shall we forget about our plan? Shall I call for the porter to take you back to prison?" Dr. Sumac broke into a hoarse giggle at this. I suppressed a string of curse words.

The universe was testing my temper as much as anything.

"No. Let's get started." Standing, I planted my feet firmly apart in a warrior's mode. I ignored the burning pain of the wounds.

"That's the spirit." Dowdrick turned to Sumac. "Do you have the iron canes? We'll need firearms and weaponry to kill the dirty rodents, should this woman prove unable to be a Pied Piper."

Sumac pointed to a long leather satchel perched on two chairs, pushed against the wall. "We are armed, Doctor."

"No!" I insisted. "No guns, no knives, no poisons."

"What then, wench?" Dowdrick snorted. "I will not have another hideous episode where the filthy rodents are teeming around me, biting my boots to shreds."

"I told you, I control them all with my mind. Nothing else is necessary."

"Like last time, eh?" Dowdrick took a few steps toward the outer door. "You are suffering from delusions. I shall call for the porter to remove you."

"Wait!" I shouted. He stopped but did not turn toward me. I had to think fast. Under no circumstances would I let the animals be harmed. It would be like cutting off my own arms or being shot in my own belly. "No killing the beasts.

The audience must see that the mesmerizing is complete and absolute. That the creatures scurry into the cages of their own accord."

At this, Dr. Sumac nodded and rubbed at his chin, already shadowy with stubble. "The lady makes a good point," he admitted.

"I will be the judge of that," Dowdrick snapped. He spun around and glared at me. "How can you guarantee your power? I refuse to be bitten."

As if refusal will be granted if the beasts hate you, or are ravenous for your flesh.

"I am a mage, Dr. Dowdrick. This is what I do." A flame of pride and wonder shot through me at my very first admission of what I had become, what I suppose I always was. What my granny had likely passed down to me, unbeknownst. My bravado seemed to placate him. Sweat trickled down my back. The scratching of rodents pressing in on the room frayed my nerves.

"Very well," sighed Dowdrick. "Sumac, fetch two large cages from the laboratory closet. Line them up against the far wall. Go!"

The grin left Sumac's face as he marched off to grant his boss's request.

An awkward silence followed. The thought of Dowdrick and I now being partners was as ghoulish to me as it must be to him.

When Sumac returned he set the cages along the wall opposite the chairs as I requested. I made sure the doors were cocked open. And as politely as I could, I asked the men to sit in the chairs on the other side of the room, and nowhere near the bulging leather satchel.

Then, I pawed in my pockets for the bits of saved bread. It would have to be enough for I could not trust these hooligans to give me untainted food. I closed my eyes and silently called to the animals. *Beautiful beasts, wild and free beasts, spring forth! Run to me, not to the human evil sitting along the wall. Only to me! We will play a game. We will fool these dreadful men.*

I sensed the critters sniffing at the air, making sure they were safe, inching forward from their tunnels and dens.

"What are you doing?" whined Dowdrick from his chair by the wall. "You are saying nothing. I see nothing. How dare you waste our time!"

"Shh!" I hissed. "Stay quiet, unless you want the rodents teeming to you in confusion."

I opened my eyes just long enough to see Dowdrick's pasty features contort. He pressed back against the chair and wrung his hands. Dr. Sumac, fascination livening his face, sat two chairs from Dowdrick. I closed my eyes again and pleaded to my beasts in a style not unlike Amity's preaching. *Come! Don't be afraid. No need to bite or gnaw or pay the foolish men by the wall any attention. Gather round me, friends. I will give you treats.*

My cheeks grew hot. As I repeated the message I heard a pattering across the floor. My eyes shot open to see a steady drove of rats, not mice—maybe twenty—driving forward, their meaty tails switching.

Dowdrick gasped and uttered low curses. "Filthy, damned vermin!"

I did not care for my heart was fluttering, joyous.

Come close, come close! Leaning over, I held out the crumbs and let them nibble. I tamped down a momentary fear they would rebel and bite, dissatisfied by my meager supply. When they finished, some rose on their hind legs and cocked their heads at me, sniffing.

Play along, dear beasts. Run to the cages. The doors are open.

I promise never to lock you in. Just enter the structure. You only need stay a short time. This is all the game entails. When I give you the cue, you may return to your dens.

I had to simmer down joy and fear alike, reassure myself that Dowdrick would not dare leap up and slam the cage doors on the beasts. The rats seemed confused as they lowered again on all fours. They sniffed at the floor and began to shuffle off in different directions. I gathered all of my strength to send the commands again. The effort made me dizzy. My legs were hollow logs and I teetered on my feet. *Hold on,* I told myself, *Hold on!*

Dowdrick and Sumac scraped their chairs against the wall. This startled the rats into greater confusion for a few ran toward the noise while others ran toward the cages. I was a hair's breadth from fainting when the rats that had wandered off turned to rejoin the rest. They all raced into the cages and clambered over each other in an excited mound.

Well done, my red-eyed beauties! Next time we practice my pockets will be brimming with bread for you. Well done!

"Girl, lock the cage!" muttered Dowdrick.

"I told you no. You must be quiet, Dr. Dowdrick! Can't you follow directions?" At my stern admonishment, Sumac let out a dry chuckle.

"Return to your dens, my wild beasts," I whispered. "Go free. Return to your homes, and I thank you."

The rats rose again and sniffed. As if my very words had a scent, and maybe they did! Silently, I repeated the command. After another tense moment, they streaked from the cage off to crevices in the molding so tiny that Dowdrick had surely never noticed them before.

It was as if the strain of communicating had drained my

life force, for it was all I could do to stumble to one of the settees and collapse upon it.

"The lady has fainted," said Sumac. From the corner of my eye I saw him rise from his chair and gesture to Dowdrick.

I tried to speak. No words came out.

Dowdrick stood. "Do you think the girl has had a heart attack? Is she dead?" he asked with a rising edge. "Do something, Condor! Don't just stand there like a bump on a log!"

Fool. Can't you see I'm breathing? It's good you don't want me to perish. Now it's clear how valuable I am to you alive. My thoughts were lucid but I was unable to even wiggle my toes.

Condor Sumac dashed off somewhere. When he returned, he threw an icy, dripping cloth over my face. At this, I jerked.

"The girl is alive, she moved," Sumac reported. He picked up the cloth and tossed it onto my shoulders this time. I flinched again as freezing water dripped into my armpits.

"Cold!" I squeaked. "Stop!"

Dowdrick kept his distance until I was propped up on the settee, my hair sopping and my prison dress dampened. His eyes darted, studying the floor by my feet. Perhaps he feared that some rats were lying in wait for him.

Finally, he stood over me and glared. "So, this ... act of yours will not work if you collapse during the symposium. Are you able to work, or are you too ill? Tell us now so we can avoid wasting our precious time!"

I *was* ill, from the colossal effort of communing with the animals. I recalled other times of stress—training my own mice, trying to stop the horde of birds from attacking Dowdrick in the prison yard. The supernatural energy required wore a body out. Truth be told, I had no idea if I was capable of lasting through a daylong symposium in front of a skeptical audience. "I'm fine, Dr. Dowdrick," I lied.

He snickered. "Oh, Tommy-rot! You look like death warmed over."

"Well, I may have a lingering malaise from that poison you put in my tea! How did you do it?" I looked at Dowdrick and then over at Sumac, who was sipping a cup.

"Whatever are you talking about?" A wounded look spread on Dowdrick's pouty face.

"You know. How did you get that poison in my tea without me seeing it? After all, I saw you both drink it."

"Oh, that." Dowdrick rolled his eyes. "Dr. Sumac lined the teacup with powder before he brought it in."

"So, it was never in the tea, but in the cup," Sumac needlessly elaborated.

"Regarding the show," Dowdrick said. "You are sure you are up to it?"

"I will get lots of sleep before our next practice. Don't worry. When shall it be?"

"Next week, and every two weeks after. Until you perform like the ace in a deck of cards. Everything must be perfectly timed and choreographed."

I nodded sagely, even though I didn't know what "choreographed" meant. I was well read but I would not reveal my lack of formal schooling. He needed to think I was a strange genius in order to keep his begrudging admiration keen. "Fine. May I go back now?" I feigned a yawn. "I am quite tired."

"Very well." Dowdrick turned and called for the porter, who did not answer so Dowdrick ordered Sumac to fetch him. Sumac's face curled into a resentful frown as he ran off. I almost felt sorry for the man. Here he was a doctor, yet his colleague was ordering him about like a servant. I shook off my sympathy. Sumac was as guilty of poisoning me as Dowdrick.

Dowdrick cuffed my hands again, lowered my hood and led me out to the carriage. Once I was seated, he locked me in and disappeared back inside. As I waited for the porter, I heard a sudden knocking on the carriage. This startled me even more than the villains inside the medical School. I twisted around to peer out of the side window. The knock sounded again, this time on the floor. Looking down, I spotted a small square of grating. Two large green eyes peered up at me. "Evalina!" came the high-pitched whisper.

"Yes?" My heart began to pound. "Who are you?"

"It's me, Lewin!" came the familiar boyish voice.

Relief flooded me at finally knowing where he was, followed by worry. "Lewin! I'm glad you're alive. How did you get out? How did you know where I was? It's not safe for you here!"

"Miss Stowe, don't fret on my account. I can outrun the devil. I see the doctor's been taking folks from Cherry Hill so I came to see why."

"I've no idea how you escaped prison, but if you get caught and sent back to—"

"I keep to the shadows." Lewin interrupted. "I've been snooping in Dowdrick's lab. We both know he's a very bad man, not just a silly goosecap. Why are you talking to him?"

"He does merciless things to prisoners, Lewin. I'm trying, in my own way, to stop him. Even though it may look odd, please trust me."

"You fainted on his couch. I saw it through the vent. I was worried."

"I'll endure. But you stay safe! You hear?"

Just then, the porter exited the building. I felt the dip of the cab as he hopped onto the front, and sensed the horses' reluctance to leave the comforts of their water and salt lick. I was terrified Lewin would be seen, or worse, crushed by the abrupt turning of the carriage wheels when the porter snapped his whip.

I took a long, desperate breath and prayed as Amity had taught me. Maybe there was wisdom in prayer after all if it could help keep a young boy from harm.

Lewin lived. The wonder of the world touched my heart.

15

Blackbeard escorted me back to my cell in the dead of night. The city was dark and spooky. If there was a God, it seemed that he had long since risen up from the grimy alleyways where beggars slept in garbage and murderers stalked their victims.

The guard kept a good three feet away from me as we walked. Did he fear I'd cast a spell on him? The idea was comical for I was only a witch to put things right again, not spread evil. After all, I had not turned him into a warty toad or magically procured my freedom from the keys that hung from his trousers! The only thing he said after removing my irons and hood, was, "Did the witch amuse herself at the doctor's?"

Why bother to answer? I'd let him continue to fear me. At some point it might grant me the advantage.

Dolly's loud snoring penetrated even the thick wall. I clambered to my bed hungry for sleep. The weather had turned especially frigid. My mice pattered over and leapt up, cuddling around me like a living quilt as I drifted off.

✳

The next morning as I ate watery prison gruel dotted with stale raisins, I thought of Lewin. Why would he risk recapture in order to spy on Dowdrick? Did he have a stink with the doctor, too? If only I'd had more time to talk with him!

I needed to find a way to communicate with my fellow prisoners, especially with Birdy. I wouldn't always be able to feign sickness in order to visit Dr. Shakesby, and since the December chill there was no more yard work.

At dawn, my mice retreated to their dens. They now returned, expecting treats. I had to be stingy. Some bread must be saved for the sessions at Dowdrick's for I had promised those rats larger quantities. I had to keep true to my word so they would trust me. Funny, how animals knew human talk through my voice and pictures I sent in my mind. Funny, too, how keeping my word was important to them. In ways, the wild beasts were sometimes more human than men, with their bestial urges.

As I sat at my table I noticed the mice were skittering behind the flush toilet. Peering back there, I spied a high vent leading to the pipes. The prison sewage was only flushed twice a week, on Monday and Friday. Between these times, the pipes became dry and malodorous.

Yet, they formed a natural roadway for rodents! I had already trained them to track Birdy, Dolly, Sammy and Lewin. If only I had something to write upon, my mice could deliver messages, protected from view.

Later that day, when Amity visited I made my plea. "I have dreams and nightmares. Sometimes poems float into my head. I would dearly love to write them down."

Amity primly nodded. "What would this accomplish? And to whom might thee show thy writing to?"

I gave her a heartfelt smile. "Why, I could read to you! Perhaps you could interpret them. Beyond this, the act of writing would help my mind gain peace."

"More peace than the prayers I provide thee?" Amity looked hurt, and in the narrowing of her eyes, a tad suspicious.

"Why, no, Amity! The mustard seed parable has provided me hours of peace. Writing would simply provide a *different* type of peace, that's all. Writing and speaking are two peas in one pod."

"Thee would only use the pencils for writing?"

So she *was* suspicious. "Of course. For what else would they be useful?"

She did not answer. But she did notice the dark splotches on my dress, still damp from Sumac's dousing. "How did thy dress become wet, and ..." She drew her shawl around her. "And... why is it so cold in this cell?"

"Frigid air and icy water seep in from the crack in the skylight." I pointed to it.

Her pleasant, freckled face wrinkled in concern. "Thee cannot live in a freezing cell. This must be fixed. The Eye of God must be whole." She rose and headed toward the cell door.

I had almost gotten used to the wintery air, and I rather liked the birds having free passage. But her care touched me. "Thank you, Amity. Have you seen or heard from Sammy Barton?"

She turned back to me. "Nothing. I will keep thee informed if I hear word. He is lucky to have someone worrying after his welfare in this cold, damp place." With that, she asked me to stand against the wall and called for the guard.

✳

Amity visited me two days later, which surprised me because her visits were normally at least a week apart. She wasn't in her somber black, but in a navy dress and blue bonnet. These colors of undiluted sky were uplifting against the prison grays and sooty floors. Her hazel eyes were almost mischievous as she pulled from her satchel a sharpened pencil and a diary with a floral border. "For the organization of thine thoughts and increased peace of mind." She handed them to me.

"Oh! Amity! How can I ever thank you?" Grateful tears pricked me as I took the diary and thumbed through its bounty of creamy pages, waiting for entries.

"No need. Just use it for the greater good. Perhaps write a prayer should thee be led to."

"That sounds splendid!" I surged forward with a natural urge to hug her, as I would have my own mother or brother, rest their souls. But I caught myself because she was a Plain woman. Clearly, she sensed my awkwardness, for she took a step forward and crisply patted my shoulder three times.

"Sit for a minute," she said with a sweep of her hand.

She moved her chair directly next to me, also unlike her. We normally sat at either end of the table facing each other, with plenty of space between us.

She gestured for me to lean in and whispered, "Samuel Barton has returned. No one knows where the carriage took him, not even Samuel himself." With that she gave me a concerned stare. "I will do what I can. I intend to examine his case."

Again, I wanted to hug her but held back. Her way of showing affection was to administer three crisp pats on my shoulder. Thus, in the manner of the Quakers, restraint was key to gaining her trust and keeping it. Yet, I had my own news about Lewin. Wasn't it betraying her trust to withhold it? Maybe not, if I told her later when I knew more. For now, the thought of telling Amity I had seen him on the outside felt wrong. For what if she was led to tell the guards who would hunt him down and recapture him? I hoped there would be a time in the near future where I could lay all of my cards on the table with Amity.

"Thank you for telling me about Samuel," was all I said.

In her austere way, she nodded. "One more thing, Evalina. Apparently, Mr. Charles Dickens' treatise against solitary confinement has had an impact."

"How so?" My heart was already pattering.

"The directors of the prison are implementing an experimental work program. Thee will be a part of it, starting tomorrow. Thee will work on gluing shoe soles with other prisoners in the workroom since it is still too cold for work in the yard."

This news was as shocking as one of Birdy's explosive charges blasting rock for the railroad. My heart banged against my ribs and I was unable to contain myself from leaping up in celebration. I swallowed back a cheer. She sternly waved me back to my seat, and soon after, called for the guard and was gone.

Another wondrous gift she had granted! I might see Birdy tomorrow and see for myself that Sammy was safe.

When Amity left I thought it would be good luck to first compose a prayer before writing notes. Out of practice with handwriting, it looked more like a chicken's scrawl, but to be able to write was freeing.

The sojourner gazes upward through the Eye of God to a place beyond words.

The stars tell tales of soaring, skipping light.

The birds create poetry in their circular flight.
Even here, in this bleak prison, the night is illuminated.

After this, I was distracted by my pressing need to write notes. I neatly tore out a sheet from the back of the diary, and tore it into tiny bits.

I composed two, hoping these men could both read:

Dearest B! Hope to see you tomorrow. Much to tell! I will brush by you and whisper news.

Samuel, are you well? Where did you go? From the girl who draws birds to her. (If you work on shoes tomorrow I will somehow say hello.)

I thought of writing Dolly a note, but the idea that Blackbeard might seize it during a nighttime visit vexed me. Noiselessly, I called to my mice. When they scurried forth, I gave two of them a folded note and let them sniff the leads for Birdy and Sammy—Birdy's lock of hair, Sam's knotted shoelace. Then I directed them toward the sewage pipes. They went with no confusion. The idea that my messages would find their marks made me positively giddy. I added a protection spell to hopefully keep the notes from being seen by the guards. This involved me closing my eyes and surrounding the objects with violet light. I'm not sure why I chose light except it felt right. With this type of magic I was less certain. Worry ate at me until I forced it out by repeating a line from my new parable: *Even here, in this bleak prison, the night is illuminated. Even here, in this bleak prison, the night is illuminated. Even here, in this bleak prison, the night is illuminated...*

Later, I lay upon my bed, hands cradling my head and imagined what freedom might look like—a room in a house, a brimming pantry, a modest job that paid, friends whom I could visit.

Birdy near me.

I pictured what justice might look like for Sammy—him working in his own barbershop, safely up north. And I pictured a warm, welcoming home for little Lewin—a life where he no longer needed to rely on thievery to fill his belly.

My hopeful daydreams must've called the birds to me, for a few of them squeezed through the jagged hole in the skylight. Hopeful thoughts were blue, like the sky and the sea. They contained the same gentle movement as clouds and waves. The pigeons floated down gracefully, perched by my feet on the mattress and began to coo. I would miss their company when the skylight was patched. Though in this jailhouse, who knew how long one might wait for a handyman?

I slept, waking only at the grating sound of the dinner trencher sliding through the rough slot. I jumped up then, to see if Dowdrick had left a note. He had, in a sealed envelope with a scroll border. Blackbeard must have wondered at this. How many folks would he tell about my strange bond with the sawbones? How many people, having heard the gossip, would misinterpret my dealings as trading favors for favors or even an odd love affair? This last idea had me laughing until I gasped for air.

"What the dickens is the big, stinking joke?" called Dolly from next door.

"The outlandish image of Dr. Dowdrick courting me," I rasped before launching into another fit of the giggles.

She joined in the snorting. "And why, pray tell, would you be thinking of this? Has he written his name on your dance card?"

"Oh, Dolly, you make me laugh even harder," I said between gales. "It's just that, well, if word gets around that I visit and speak with Dowdrick..." I stopped, remembering I had decided to leave her in the dark about the exact details of my plan; she was too much of a gossipmonger.

"What do you do to you lure him to your side? Is it working thus far?" Her tone was tinged with lurid interest.

"I think so, Dolly. I will reveal more soon. Promise not to gossip to Blackbeard – to any of the guards or—"

"Or what? What do you take me for, Dull Wit? Dolly Rouge ain't no gossip!"

"Settle down, settle down! We are friends, remember?"

"Who says? Bullocks, girl!" At this, she tossed her boots across the room and they hit the wall with a booming *thwack*.

I had no more words for Dolly. Instead, I opened the envelope as quietly as I could and read Dowdrick's note.

Practice Makes Perfect. Tomorrow at midnight.

Relief pooled into my legs. It would not interfere with my day work gluing shoe soles.

Or more precisely, my longed-for rendezvous with Birdy.

16

Blackbeard led me to a large public chamber and directed me to a chair. "Hood can come off, witch," was all he said. I had leg irons on, so there was no possibility of my running.

It was a shock to remove my airless hood and stand in the largest room I had seen at Cherry Hill, as vast as Independence Hall. An entire line of castle-like domed windows graced one wall, which let in wide swaths of lemony winter sun.

Most beautiful of all were the prisoners, sitting in chairs without hoods.

All together.

There were four tables parallel to each other and one on each side that stood perpendicular. At each of the six tables were barrels of shoe soles and boots. Fat glue pots with brushes stuck in them were at evenly spaced intervals along the tables, along with rectangles of cardboard.

I sat in a high-backed wooden chair Blackbeard led me to.

Dolly sat at the table in front of me. Even from the back, her tall physique and long red hair with graying roots were unmistakable. She was regally fanning herself with one of the pieces of cardboard. I looked around for Birdy and Sammy.

Sammy was at the right side table. His eyes darted my way with an unmistakable shine of recognition. I smiled faintly, not enough to draw attention but to signal he was a friend.

Looking to my left, I spotted Birdy at the other side table. He towered over everyone. His bruises had healed, and it looked like he had scrubbed his face and hair, for his dark curls were buoyant and his long, handsome face shone. Our eyes met and my whole being caught fire. Funny that we had such a strong bond with so few words exchanged. Perhaps sharing dire circumstances moved people to unite. I longed to talk to him. But Blackbeard stood at one door, Fast Step at the second, and other guards stood at attention around the hall.

Had Birdy gotten my note? He held up his thumb and index finger, and pressed them together as if holding the tiny note my mouse had delivered. I grinned, he winked and shivers of delight rushed through me.

Then a man began to speak. He stood under the line of windows, the light turning his brown hair auburn. "Prisoners, as you are aware, you have been called together to work, and your hoods have been removed," he said in a heavy British accent. "This was due to a treatise I wrote, insisting that prisoners of this penitentiary be treated in humane fashion, and removed from isolation for a certain amount of time during the week." He paused to look around at us and stare deeply in our eyes as if he actually cared for our souls. This was quite remarkable, for even Amity, as friendly as she had become, rarely looked at me for any length of time.

The man was balding slightly, with shaggy hair on the

sides, a moustache and beard. He wore a black coat trimmed at the collar with soft, ebony felt. And he had on a white shirt and bowtie. He did not smile and seemed the quiet type. Perhaps a teacher, I thought, noting a rumpling of his trousers and coat, as if he did not care about his appearance. This was in stark contrast to Dowdrick, ever the clotheshorse.

The man went on. "Let me introduce myself. I am Charles Dickens, the author of *Oliver Twist* and other tales..."

Charles Dickens! Now I remembered. Amity had told me Dickens had written a treatise regarding Cherry Hill. Incredible that this famous man had trekked to this dank prison to address us deplorable convicts.

I was utterly awe struck. His stories made us common folk seem as noble as the highborn. The line I had memorized from *Oliver* played in my mind: "We need be careful how we deal with those about us, when every death carries to some small circle of survivors, thoughts of so much omitted, and so little done- of so many things forgotten, and so many more which might have been repaired."

"I live in London," Dickens announced, "far across the Atlantic Ocean. Since I had to stop by Philadelphia for a visit to my American publisher I thought I'd take a carriage ride over to see if this great penitentiary had paid mind to my treatise. I fancied letting you good brethren spend a moment outside your pens, in communion."

Good people. *In pens.* The irony made my stomach twist.

Wild cheers erupted. The guards struck their truncheons against the floor. "Order!" and "Shut it!" they cried.

"I see my presence causes the guards concern," Dickens noted, his brows raised. "Shall we prove together that you are worthy of leaving your cramped cells to spend a bit of time with your fellow prisoners? Shall we show them you can conduct yourselves properly, without violence and mayhem? This way, the great experiment of fellowship can continue. Do you agree?"

A more civil cheer rose up. The guards shared worried looks, but they held off from striking their truncheons on the floor.

"Dearest prisoners, would you fancy me reading a chapter from *Oliver*?"

"Yes!" called the inmates, with my assent among the loudest.

Dickens began, and these lines stuck out to me: "'But even if he has been wicked,' pursed Rose, 'think how young he is, think that he may never have known a mother's love, or the comfort of a home; and that ill-usage and blows, or the want of bread, may have driven him to herd with men who have forced him to guilt. Aunt, dear aunt, for mercy's sake, think of this, before you let them drag this sick child to a prison, which in any case must be the grave of all his chances of amendment.'"

When he had finished and shut the book, a pall settled over the room. Dickens smiled for the first time. "I'm sure you are paying penance for your various crimes," he said. "But keep in mind that you are not bad people. You have decent lives ahead of you. You need not make this your entire legacy. Think of this prison as a workplace from which you can gain skills, not as a festering pit of despair. Think on your garden work, and this honest labor making boots. Keep hold to your dignity. With that, I bid you all adieu."

Cheers went up as he exited the room. Then, at the sweep of the guards' hands our appreciations died down. A second man entered the room. He was in a plain gray jacket and dark trousers, with a brimmed gray hat. Tall and potbellied, he had an imposing, lumbering walk. "Prisoners, I am the director of this penitentiary," he boomed. "You witnessed a rare visit from a famous author. Pay heed to his words and make an effort while you are at Eastern State. Today, you are lucky to work on the construction of boots. If you do a good job and behave, this experiment shall continue. If not, you shall return to solitary confinement... or worse, the irons in the hole, where it is so dark one cannot see at all." He surveyed the room with a ferocious glare. "Understand me?"

"Yes!" came the rallying cry from most though I heard muttered gripes. "He should spend time in a filthy pen" and "I want what he's stuffing his belly with" and "Ornery turnkey!"

I stole a peek at Birdy, and caught him looking at me. We traded grins. All grew bright with him in the room, however menacing the prison director's threats.

The director brought out a boot maker, a gaunt man in a black apron. He demonstrated how to glue the soles to the boots with three swipes of the brush and then how to press the sole and hold it. And finally, he pointed to where we would go and place the finished boots in pairs on the drying racks, set up behind me.

The task was surprisingly absorbing. It felt good to be put to work, and God knows any poor soul could use a sturdy pair of boots. I was fast with the glue brush and quick to sop up sticky spillovers with a rag set by the pot for this purpose. After two pairs of boots I was ready to put them on the drying rack. I glanced over at Birdy to time my approach. Sure enough, he was already staring at me with a gleam in his eye. He cocked his head ever so subtly, inviting me to set out first.

I balanced the boots on a plank of wood as I walked to the rack. Blackbeard looked my way and narrowed his eyes, but a loud ruckus by the windows distracted him. Someone had dropped the boots they'd glued, which clattered to the floor.

One of the guards began to yell. "You clumsy fool! What the Blazes!"

Another guard ran over to inspect. "You tore the soles from the boots. They're stuck to the floor! What a foul mess!"

A blessed mess, indeed!

I had just put the last boot on the rack when I felt a sigh by my left ear. "Fair Eva, I cannot believe you are here. So many days I've spent daydreaming of you. What bliss it would be to be out of here, walking down Market Street with my arm wrapped around you."

My knees nearly caved I was so overcome. I needed to right myself or one of the guards would surely know I was swooning.

Besides, I had important news to tell and I needed to convey it at breakneck speed. Bending down, I readjusted the boots and whispered back, "Dear Birdy, it is wonderful to see you as well. I have news!" I grinned. "I saw Lewin outside! He broke free. We spoke."

"Lewin?" Startled, Birdy jerked his head upward at the news and my front teeth almost hit him. This sudden motion made it clear that we were speaking. Luckily, the guards were still distracted by the gluey mess under the windows. "How did he escape?" he asked.

"No idea. Have you spoken to Samuel? He is back."

"Aye. With no memory of where they took him."

"Did they cut him?"

"Cut him? His old wounds were already healed from his beating."

"No new cuts that required stitching then?"

"None I heard of. Why would you think this?"

I gave a slight shake of my head. Our time was fast running out. "So, you got the note my mouse delivered?"

"Aye," he whispered. "I could barely believe it."

"Believe it! Soon you will no longer doubt my abilities with animals." I snuck a look at the guards to make sure they were still preoccupied. "I have begun work with Dowdrick, to trick him; expose his crimes. Of this, I beg you trust me. For I hope to get us out of prison after my plan is implemented."

I sensed Birdy's energy cool. Shift to doubtful. "Be careful, love. Please?" was all he said, as he straightened the line of newly soled boots.

Love, oh my. "I shall try."

The racket by the windows had settled down, and when I stood upright again I was horrified to see Fast Step marching my way.

"Step it up, prisoners! No lazing about! There are more boots to be soled." He glared at me with his small, redlined eyes.

Luck was with us. He had missed our whole exchange. Birdy had already walked with his lopsided gait back to the table. I hurried back to mine.

During the next two weeks I returned to Dowdrick's laboratory twice to practice my performance. For the most part the rats behaved, with only a few mishaps. One rebellious young rat kept scurrying around the cages instead of going in, before racing back to his den. Another one chewed on Dowdrick's oriental carpet, which sent him into apoplexy. A starling got in the window and circled as we worked. I lured him onto my finger and sent him on his way.

There was a compelling discovery unrelated to the animals. It became obvious that Dowdrick and Sumac were at odds. Dr. Dowdrick took malicious pleasure in ordering Dr. Sumac to do trivial tasks, such as washing the lab beakers, carting trash to the alley and scrubbing dung from the rat cages.

It was also clear that Sumac thought he was above these menial tasks. He grimaced at Dowdrick when his back was turned and even cursed at him in Spanish under his breath.

"I am much too busy to scrub out beakers," Sumac insisted one evening after my arrival.

"Busy doing what, pray tell?" Dowdrick retorted.

"Busy printing *our* tonic labels," Sumac shot back. "Certainly you have a moment to wash out your own beakers." Dowdrick opened his mouth to argue but with me staring at him he must have thought better of it.

One small victory for Sumac who rarely got his way. For I witnessed him hauling heavy cartons of tonics up and down the cellar stairs, and he was constantly running to the vendors on Market Street for raspberry cookies. Dowdrick had an unhealthy passion for them. No wonder he was the perfect likeness of a round pink, dough ball!

But the tension ran deeper than Sumac's resentment of performing menial labor while Dowdrick lolled about in his silks. When Sumac spoke of Peruvian herbs his eyes lit up, his voice took on a jittery excitement like a child imagining his presents under the Christmas tree. Dr. Sumac demanded respect as an authority on wild plants. I could imagine his students at the Eclectic School hanging on his every word. It was clear Sumac expected Dowdrick to be a willing apprentice, learning happily and taking notes while Sumac lectured and demonstrated the uses of South American botanicals.

This was not to be. In fact, after practice the second week, I witnessed a nasty argument while the two men fussed over a new batch of Monster Mesmer bottles.

"My name should be on these labels," Sumac growled. "My contribution of Peruvian Muña and Maca root is what gives the drink strength. The sharp burst that convinces a person they can conjure magic."

"That's rich," Dowdrick scoffed. "It is my expensive brandy that gives the real punch."

"To the contrary, every tonic contains brandy or rum. Common as dirt." Sumac glared at Dowdrick. "So, tell me, why is your name the only one that appears?"

The name Evalina Stowe should appear, for I thought up this entire idea!

Dowdrick's nostrils flared as he spoke. "I am the leading doctor for Monster Mesmer. Dr. Dowdrick's Tonic is my long-held brand name." He began to pack a crate. "Besides, Condor, you are not even a citizen of this country, thus the patent cannot be jointly filed. This is my lab. I am the director of the Eclectic Medical School. You simply *teach* here." He said this as if teaching was as despicable as thievery.

Dowdrick snickered and looked haughtily over Sumac's head. Sumac only came up to Dowdrick's chin, though Sumac was built like a wrestler with legs like solid oaks. Again, I felt sorry for the Peruvian doctor. I had a natural sympathy for the vulnerable—street urchins like Lewin, destitute women like Dolly forced to work their wares at night, Negro escapees from the south like Sammy, regularly pounded by the Moyamensing gang.

After the practice, when Dowdrick excused himself to go to the powder room, I saw my chance to speak with Sumac alone. "You must be an absolute wizard at botanicals, Dr. Sumac," I cooed. "Pray, tell me more about them. Let's say... the Angel's Trumpet that many call the Devil's Trumpet," I rolled out slowly.

His dark eyes widened in obvious surprise that I knew the plant's name. "The powder from this one has many possibilities in the surgical ward. And yes, I am considered a famous authority down in Peru. I have studied these special, em... *flowers* for many years."

"Why not stay in Peru where you are already highly esteemed?"

"Teaching in Philadelphia offers new recognition. New opportunities. It is the home of many famous medical centers such as Penn's Medical School, Jefferson Medical College and the Philadelphia College of Medicine."

"So! The Eclectic Medical College is not even in the top tier. I see why you need to be seen and heard, in order to move up the ladder. Yet, I hear that Dr. Dowdrick will not share the limelight." I cast him a shrewd look. "Perhaps you could take some of his light and let it shine on *you* during the symposium."

Sumac cocked his head and gazed off into the distance, as if considering his career from a new vantage point. "How would I do this?"

"Take what is rightfully yours! Seize your moment!" was all I had time to say before Dr. Dowdrick returned, clutching his belly.

"Blasted indigestion," he groaned.

"No wonder. You have stuffed a carton of muffins down,

muffins that drip with butter," Sumac chided with a cluck. He glanced at me and we shared a momentary grin.

"Cookies! In English, we call them *cookies*," Dowdrick grumbled and then bellowed for the porter to take me away. The games were over. My cell awaited me.

During this time we had two more work sessions gluing boot soles in the great prison hall. The guards assigned us the same seats as before. This time, the winter sun did not grace us. Instead, the skies unleashed a brutal rain shot through with hailstones, which battered the line of cathedral windows. The noise served us well, though. It blocked out our murmurs and distracted the guards from the movement of my fellow prisoners. As before, I was determined to speak to Birdy. But first, I needed to pass by Sammy. I saw him rise to bring boots to the rack and I hurried to grab my finished ones. When thunder boomed I leaned close and whispered, "Are you well? What happened to you?"

"I don't recall, Ma'am. I ain't hurt though."

"You remember nothing?"

"Only the morning I woke up, back in my cell, flat on my back on the floor."

"Oh, no!"

"But I ain't complainin'. I got no beating."

I gave him a slight nod. What a harsh world it was where a person was thankful merely for *not* receiving a bloody beating? I returned, my temper boiling, to my seat. Sammy's memory loss must be the work of Sumac's Angel's Trumpet. If the plant's name was interchangeable than the better name was Devil's Trumpet! My sympathy for Sumac shriveled like a violet caught in a brush fire.

Abruptly, there was another commotion. Guards began yelling and smacking their truncheons on the hardwood floors. "Clumsy ox!" someone roared. "You think it funny to make a sticky mess, do you? I should glue your head to the floor!"

Over on the far right near Sammy's table, someone had dropped a whole plank of boots. "Throw him in the hole! Give him the water treatment!" I recognized Fast Step's angry voice. The guards grabbed a man with dark skin, and for a terrible moment I thought it was Sammy. But as I continued to stare, I saw Sammy in his regular seat with a look of horror spreading over his face.

Warm breath tickled my ear. "Sweet Eva, how can I help in your efforts to trick Dowdrick?"

"Birdy! You want to help?" Boldly, I touched his arm. It was pleasing, strong.

He brushed his hand along mine, which gave me exquisite shivers. "Can I organize anything in here whilst you work your magic out there?" he whispered.

This gave me a novel idea, but we couldn't talk much with guards milling about. "Perhaps! Look for my mice within the week."

Birdy snuck in another quick stroke along my hand. "I'll await your miniature herald," he whispered. Then he hurried off in his lopsided way as the guards dragged the Negro prisoner out a side door. It surprised me that I was able to forget about the sadness of others for fleeting moments of happiness. A part of imprisonment, I supposed.

The next time at Dowdrick's I was more confident, knowing I

had lured an unwitting Sumac to my side. I would need this soon, perhaps even tonight if the opportunity presented itself. While Sumac was still giving instructions to the porter I had to settle a score with Dowdrick. "May I talk to you about a matter?" I said as soon as he removed my hood and cuffs.

"What is so pressing that it cannot wait until after practice?"

"There will be no practice tonight or *any* night unless we straighten this out."

"Watch the barbs that fly off your tongue, for I can give you another punishment at any time." With an impatient wag of his hand, Dowdrick gestured for me to sit on a settee, while he sat on the one facing me. "Proceed, proceed," he grumbled.

"You promised you would not haul over more of my friends from Cherry Hill."

"Right." He studied me coolly.

"Yet, you took Samuel Barton over here and forced your demonic Devil's Trumpet on him," I fumed. "You gave him such an enormous dose he recalls nothing!"

"Oh, that." Dowdrick snorted.

"Is this all you have to say for breaking your promise? I should have known better than to forge a deal with a no account sawbones!" I used the most insulting term I could think of as I glared at him. "This deal is null and void since you have broken your part of it."

"Witch, not so fast." Dowdrick held up a hand. "I never broke my word."

"How is that?"

"I did not cut into the Negro. No knife, no stitches. I left him whole. I simply put him to sleep—a long, peaceful nap to test the levels of the powder one last time. Afterward, I sent him home, unharmed." Dowdrick's face spread into a smug grin.

I thought back to our original pact as I ran my hand along my own scars. Had I only warned him not to inflict more surgical wounds? Had I forgotten to insist he never take more prisoners for *any* reason? Dowdrick was correct. Drat! My warning had been too broad. "Our agreement must be amended!" I snapped. "Never take a prisoner unless I request it!" My ire had roused the beasts underfoot. Their coiled, predatory energy was profound. "Else I will set a whole horde of beasts on you," I added.

Dowdrick raised his arms as if to ward me off. Then he proceeded to clap. "Good Heavens, witch! You are as over dramatic as one of the actresses in the Walnut Street Theater. Brava!"

"Promise me no more prisoners!" I persisted.

"Very well," he said wearily. "I promise."

Despite myself, wry amusement at his absurd clapping trumped fury. My beasts quieted themselves.

At this point, Condor Sumac strode in with a steaming pot of tea. It smelled of fragrant mints. But I held back. We launched into another practice.

During our sessions we had developed a demonstration worthy of the most colorful Market Street busker. The long lab table brimmed with Monster Mesmer tonics, arranged fetchingly in groups—blue labels for small, easily lured pests, green labels for mid-sized bugs like moths, orange extra strength labels for fierce, wily critters like rodents and bats.

Dr. Dowdrick would hold up a bottle while launching into the wonders it wrought. "One large swallow and you will have almost magical power over your worst household pests," he would boast. I cringed at the word *pests*.

"Granted, the tonic is a tad sour," he would admit, "but oh, what talents you'll have to lure any and all filthy insects, disease-carrying vermin, and silk-chomping moths into the cage of your choice. No more need for the rat catcher, or for poisonous chemical compounds such as nicotine and arsenic! Then, at your leisure you may carry them out and release them. Or kill them on the spot." At this, he would glance at me and smirk knowing how strongly I disapproved. "Don't just take my word for it. I will show you! Oh, miss?" He would point to me as I stood in a make believe crowd. "Yes, you!" I would gesture to myself as if I couldn't believe he'd asked me. "Step up!" Dowdrick would say. "Want to test your talents? It is easier than you imagine."

I then nodded eagerly and stepped forward. He pretended to dole out a capful of the tangy tonic and pour it down my throat. I pretended to swallow.

I made a radiant face as if I could feel the wondrous luring tonic spreading through me. After this, I made a show of holding out my arms and wiggling my fingers, and coaxed my wild beasts forth with no actual help from the Monster Mesmer. But no one at the symposium would be the wiser... at least at first!

This night, as the last two, went quite well. Each time, we heightened the drama as if we were experienced Shakespearean actors. I even rolled my eyes back in my head as if transfixed.

After the rodents had run into the cages on cue and were safely back in their dens, I seized my moment. "There is one grave concern," I said to Dowdrick. "What if the crowd wants a second test subject, or even a third? The medical establishment is full of intelligent folks such as you fine gentlemen." I turned to Sumac and grinned. "Wouldn't you agree, Dr. Sumac?" He nodded, a mix of worry and pride on his face.

"Your point, Miss Stowe?" whined Dowdrick, ever impatient if it wasn't about his cookies, his fashions, or the size of his billfold.

"They are bound to be skeptical."

"So?" Dowdrick asked.

"So, I think we need more plants in the audience."

"Plants?" Sumac frowned.

I giggled. "Ah! Not botanicals, doctor. I am referring to *human* plants, which means others in the know who are in on our act, who willingly participate. So when they are called onstage, they act on prompt."

"But you are the only one with the luring talent," Dowdrick said.

"True. I will still be the one mesmerizing the beasts, from wherever I stand. I can entice them from across an entire room. One catch..." I stopped to see how completely I had convinced these gullible doctors. Their mouths were slack, their eyes wide. A thrill rippled through me. If I couldn't mesmerize humans I was at least good at my powers of reasoning.

"What is the catch?" Dowdrick asked.

"It shall have to be someone I know and trust," I explained. "Someone I can give orders to who will loyally follow them."

Dowdrick frowned. "But if you do the luring, then it could be any doctor who steps up, none the wiser."

"Not exactly. They could call it all malarkey. They are not in our full control."

"The lady is right," Sumac said.

"Oh, quiet, Condor, you sound like an echo," Dowdrick grumbled.

"One more thing," I ventured. "You will have to compensate the players."

"Piss off! No damn payout!" Dowdrick shouted. "I collect money not dole it out."

I ignored his shockingly foul mouth. "These folks will not require much. Any coinage will be appreciated. But you do owe them. At least two of them."

"Spit it out! What is your dratted plan?"

Sumac, to his credit, remained mum, listening intently.

I said, "On the day of the Discovery Symposium you shall send for Dolly Rouge, Samuel Barton and Birdy Castell."

"Bullpucky!" Dowdrick shouted. "Have you lost your godforsaken mind?"

"Not at all! They trust me, and know me. They will play along ... for a modest fee. No one will recognize them. Whereas, any other person you pull from the street might trick you or be too dense to follow instructions, while as I say, my friends are loyal to me and—"

"The lady has a point," Sumac repeated. I offered him a broad smile. It was nice to be called a lady. And his hatred of Dowdrick was as glaring as the bald spot on Dowdrick's flushed head. He would do any thing to contradict his rival who might cast a pall over his part of the sun.

Dowdrick grimaced, yet said, "I will consider it."

It had been a gamble, but I had him. I sensed this as I sensed the wild beasts.

Later, outside, the horses were in a strange lather, while I waited, cuffed and hooded inside the carriage for the porter. Dowdrick had taken to securing me and then scurrying back to his lab, as the snows had been falling hard these last weeks of February.

I did not mind. Even a glimpse through my hood was

heavenly. Such feathery beauty proved that God must be somewhere up in His Kingdom, bestowing white confection on his citizenries.

"Pssst! Miss!" a boyish cry rose up through the floor grate.

The horses, excited by the boy's arrival, snorted and pawed at the snow.

"Take a care, Lewin! Don't get caught here!"

"The porter won't be out for some minutes, Miss. He's in the shitter a' grunting."

"Lewin!" I couldn't help but chuckle. "Why do you lurk here, putting your safety at risk? What is it you seek?"

"I knew this leecher from when I was almost a baby. My mum sold turnips she grew. The doctor argued with her about the price. I told you about his rotten tempers. He grew red in the face, kicked her hard in the belly and she fell."

I gasped. "Then what?"

"He got her sent to the slammer. I had to walk the streets after."

"Is she still in prison? Is she in Cherry Hill?"

"Naw. She perished in the Walnut Street Jail." Lewin's voice grew wistful. I wondered if he was crying beneath the carriage. But then he rallied. "So, Miss, let me help you throw him in prison. That's where he belongs. Or six feet under."

There was a loud rumble at the door and the horses snorted again.

"Run! We shall work together—just hurry now! Run!"

Lewin was gone in an instant and I saw no footprints. The porter leapt in the carriage, which dipped and jerked to action.

"Lightning," I mumbled, "Godspeed."

17

I wrote notes that my furry messengers ferreted to their
marks through the sewage pipes.

*Dear B, Date is set. March 15 – The Ides! – The doctor will collect
you at my request. Your role: after a drink of the tonic, pretend to
be a Pied Piper and lure the rodents to the cages while I actually
do the luring. Destroy this paper! Your Eva*

I wrote a similar note to Sammy and I thought of writing
Dolly a note, but there was the problem of Blackbeard
finding it. I had to wait for the right moment to speak with
her through the walls.

I composed prayers and recited them as I gazed up at the
newly patched skylight. The handymen had finally come
when I was soling boots in the great room. I dearly missed
the visits from my bird friends, and I yearned for them to
perch by my feet as they cooed. But I had to admit my cell
was warmer. No longer did I awake shivering under a frosty
sheet of snow. Snow was only lovely from afar.

Amity visited, this time wearing a dark gray dress and bonnet under a gray wool coat to bear the last gusting blizzard. I read her my newest prayer, more like a poem.

Winter shall pass into spring.
With it, the blossoms shall open to the sun.
In Cherry Hill, prisoners too, shall unfurl their hearts,
And nourish their souls with the nectar of their futures.

"It's an odd prayer, yet rather beautiful," Amity said.

As I gazed at Amity I felt the same of her. The paradox of her innocent modesty mixed in with her old crone's wisdom at only twenty-one. Her wild-rose cheeks and caramel freckles in contrast to her long prim skirts and tucked up hair.

"Has thou been content with the work in the great room?" she asked me.

"Yes! It is sweet relief to escape my chamber, even for an hour. Thank you, Amity for helping."

"Oh. I cannot take the credit. That would go to the director of the prison ... or rather Master Dickens." She paused. "Has thee seen thy friends? If so, this must provide comfort."

"Yes, I was glad to see Sammy again; and of course, Birdy. We did exchange some words during the fall garden work. I hope you will not judge me for that. I'm not sure how we became friends with so few words between us. But ..." At this, my cheeks heated up.

"It is natural to want friends," Amity said quietly. "To seek out a partner."

I could hardly believe my ears! This proper Plain lady had said something almost as racy as wearing lace pantalettes on the street. I was at a loss for words. But then, in my own immodesty they soon tumbled out. "Do you have a partner, Amity?"

It was her turn to blush. "I met my husband, John at Meeting. My father brought him over to say hello. He makes furniture, and he is a trustworthy, kind man. I could not ask for more." She folded her hands on the table and stared at them as if she had said too much.

"That is wonderful, Amity. My parents also had a good marriage, yet they were gone way too soon."

"I'm so sorry, Evalina. How did they pass?'

"Of the cholera. My brother and I fended for ourselves as best we could. I left school and grew what I could in our family garden. Many nights we went to bed hungry when the winter came. I knocked on many a door, and finally found tailoring work. I convinced them to hire Todd, until… well."

"Thee's had sad tribulations." Amity's eyes were brimming as she gazed at me. "No one can guess the depth of another's trials." After a pause she said, "I hope I have not been too harsh with thee. If so, please forgive me."

"You have helped me endure the loneliness, Amity."

"Of that I am glad."

"So, I hope I have a good husband someday," I began, but could not help falling into a deeper place. "If you have a strong family, why are you compelled to visit us at Cherry Hill?"

"I have much to be thankful for and I want others to feel as hopeful."

She cleared her throat and readjusted herself in the chair. "Regarding another matter Evalina, I have looked into the various court papers. Thy trial comes up next year; Birdy's as well. But Samuel Barton … well, he is slated to remain in the penitentiary for three more years."

"They have no evidence on Sammy, do they?"

Amity sighed. "It is one man's word over the other's. Unfortunately, even in the City of Brotherly Love an Irishman's word is taken over a Negro's."

"How maddening!"

She nodded. "Precisely why I minister to the prisoners here."

I was tempted to reveal my plan to trick Dowdrick and try to unearth his criminal acts. Also, to tell her I'd seen Lewin, but the words stuck in my throat. It must wait until the bitter end. As bold as I was, I was terrified of losing Amity's trust and affection. She was practically all I had that connected me to the outside world. And the impossible was beginning to seem possible—perhaps we understood each other more than I'd thought. Perhaps, we could be friends after all. We were lost in a heavy silence. Then Amity spoke once more.

"They say the prison work is a big success. Hundreds upon hundreds of boots have been soled and shipped. As soon as the snows melt the director plans to start the yard work again. Spring is not so far off. Pine boughs must be cleared from the planters. Soil must be fertilized and seeds sown. As nice as it has been to spend time in the great hall, it will be even better to be out in nature's own air once again. Do thee agree, Evalina?"

"Oh, yes!" In fact, my heart thundered in anticipation of it. I only wondered if our first day in the yard would occur before or after the Ides of March. For if it was after the Discovery Symposium, the world might well have shifted on its axis.

❄

That night, a note from Dowdrick waited for me under the trencher. I snapped it up before Blackbeard might be tempted to steam it open. Though the doctor must be slipping Blackbeard much coinage for him to even agree to deliver envelopes to "the witch" in the first place. I set my dinner of beef broth, baked beans and brown bread on my table and ripped open the seal.

Miss Stowe,

The symposium ticks closer. Our presentation will be in the afternoon of March 15, the grand finale. Only one more practice session (tomorrow eve) before I hoodwink all and secure my fame! Inform your actors of every detail of the Pied Piper scheme. Tomorrow night expect the porter at half-past midnight.

H. Dowdrick

I slipped his note through a tear in the mattress and sat for dinner. In his excitement, Dowdrick was getting sloppy. Even his signature graced the paper! Clearly, he now saw me as more of a co-conspirator than foe. Had he forgotten he'd killed my brother in cold blood? That he was my sworn enemy? I hadn't. That ghastly day was forever etched in my ever-bleeding heart. It would drive me to justice.

"Dull Wit! What are you up to?" yelled Dolly at the top of her lungs when I was scarce through my beans. "You skulk around in there, praying and mumbling to the crotchety Quaker bat and never talk to poor Dolly Rouge anymore. Have you forgotten me?" She gave the wall a hard bang with her boot sole for emphasis.

"'Course not, Dolly," I called back through the gap in the bricks. "How are you faring?"

"Like stinking horse dung! My back is all but crippled from sleeping on this hard mattress and to pile on the agony, my lovely red hair has grown out gray and ugly."

"I'm so sorry, Dolly."

"What are you sorry for?" She began to cackle. "I've seen you whispering and touching that tall, gimpy Welshman in the great room. Not a bad looker—all dark curls and long angles. You think I didn't see it? Dolly Rouge has eyes in the back of her head!" She chuckled again. I had to admit, the image of her with eyes behind her head was comical.

"Well, isn't it nice to get out of our cells and breathe in the great hall?" I asked. "It is true I am friendly with the Welsh man. His name is Birdy Castell. He injured his feet from his dangerous railroad work. I pray they can be fixed. Don't you also have a friendship of sorts with Blackbeard? Or don't you see him any more? Is this why you're cross?"

"Oh, him." She snorted. "Whiskers got a grand raise from the director, and he now has a swelled head. He is too busy for me."

"I'm sorry, Dolly, I—"

"Oh, shut up about being sorry, Dull Wit! You'd think you was the sorriest gal in this here prison. Never be sorry. Never be sorry for anything, girl! Always stand behind anything you choose to do. You hear?"

"Yes, Dolly. I do." I was touched she was giving me heartfelt advice. I supposed it was the softest way she knew to deliver it. A timely reminder, for it was essential I stand by my convictions—to protect Lewin, to free the innocent and have the guilty locked behind bars.

"So, where is Blackbeard?" I ventured.

"I don't carry his schedule on me." She was quiet for a time. Perhaps she thought she'd been too harsh for she softened her tone. "Why is it you ask?"

"I want to impart something. Without him hearing," I said in a lower voice.

"He ain't here now. I know his footsteps even though he pads 'em with his silly socklets. What's on your mind?" she asked.

"Do you still want to get Dowdrick put in prison?"

"You bet the devil I do."

"Well, then, do you want to take part in a trick I devised? This performance will not only embarrass him in front of his esteemed peers, but also alert the authorities to his vile criminality. You'd have to travel back to his lab, which might scare you. But you'd be paid a modest—"

"Hoo-eee!" Dolly let out a piercing guffaw the likes of which could have peeled whitewash off a wall. "You just hell-fired up this strumpet! That leech needs to pony up to the penitentiary! Tell me what day the theater opens, which part I'm playing and what my lines are."

After I finished explaining, she paid me an enormous compliment. "Girl, is it Eva? Eva, you have a mind as smart as a steel trap and as sharp as a meat axe. I underestimated you!"

"Thanks, Dolly. That means a lot to me."

"Now don't get all teary on me. Stay sharp, Eva. Stay sharp."

"Promise."

Later, as darkness swathed the skylight I slid on my night-gown and settled under my thin blanket. For once Dolly did not throw her boots against the wall. Instead, she sang songs, mostly in key.

"Wait for the wagon, and we'll all take a ride!" she bellowed, and "Bold is my warrior good, the love of Alfarata,

Proud waves his snowy plume, along the Juniata." Then came some lines I recognized: "Camptown ladies sing this song, doodah, doodah! Ah, the Camptown race track's five miles long, oh doo dah day."

Her spirited voice soothed me almost as much as the cooing of my birds before the skylight repair blocked their passage. Just as I was floating off to sleep, my mice padded up by my sides to warm me. One nudged me on my cheek, with what felt like folded paper.

I jumped up. It was my note returned and refolded, I was sure of it. Drat it all! There was no light to read it by. I fell asleep with the note curled in my hand.

The day brought sun, and the melting of the last clumps of snow on the glass above. Recalling the folded note in my fist, I unfurled it.

The Ides have it! I am Welsh not Irish but can play a convincing Pied Piper. How fun with fair E as fellow conspirator. Eat this note! Yours, B

My mood soared at the anticipation of not only seeing Birdy, but the both of us pulling the wool over Dowdrick. I had allies. I would hopefully have my day in court as Birdy would.

As Dowdrick would.

Yet doubt ate at me. It was long gambling odds that everything would go smoothly at the Discovery Symposium. And if it went horribly wrong we would either spend our entire lives rotting in prison or be snuffed out in seconds by the snap of a noose. The thought chilled me to the bone. Perhaps it was fortunate that I scarce had time to worry for Blackbeard came to collect me. I thrust Birdy's note in my boots.

"Against the wall, witch. Hood on."

"Where are we going?" I asked as he led me gruffly down the hall by a chain connected to my cuffs. He still did not like to walk near me. It was a surprise he was so full of superstition.

"Yard work," he replied curtly.

My heart stirred and burbled as sweetly as warm butter. My dread was eased for now. Yard work, Birdy, sun and fresh air! Digging in the dirt like a child. What could be better?

Out in the yard, I inhaled the brisk air still infused with melted snows and wood fires, yet with the tang of sap-sharp leaf buds. Blackbeard pulled me by the chain into position and yanked off my hood. I was delighted to see Birdy standing across from me as before, with only the long planter dividing us. His untamed hair formed a wavy, pleasing counterpoint to his long, serious face and sturdy jaw. His eyes glowed with intelligent light and something like hunger.

"Remove the pine boughs from the planters," barked a guard. He pointed to the far end of the yard. "Place them in a pile in that corner. Go back for more until you see the dirt beneath." He eyed the lot of us. "No fast moves! Understand?"

"Yes, sir!" the prisoners shouted in unison.

Sammy was in the same row as Birdy, but ten men down. Dolly was in front, two planters ahead, her back to me. Everyone was safe. Lewin was still free. I breathed easier knowing this.

The evergreen pile grew wider and higher and took the shape of a Christmas tree almost as tall as a man.

A good hiding place.

When this occurred to me, I grew fidgety with the desire to speak to Birdy alone. It might actually be possible! For with orders already given and time on their hands, the guards rested their truncheons against the walls and began to chat amongst themselves.

Birdy must've gotten the same idea because he crooked his head toward the piney mountain and grinned. I hesitated, my heart thudding wildly. Then I plodded over first with my arms loaded with browning branches. Creeping behind the towering stack I tossed down my bunch. Then I waited.

It didn't take long for Birdy to appear. After a furtive peek through the boughs to make sure we were safe, he spun around, his eyes gleaming with glad mischief. He gently dropped his branches. "What will you need me to do at the evil doctor's?" he whispered.

"We'll need a doubting Thomas," I said under my breath. "State your suspicion that Monster Mesmer is so much snake oil. I will call on you to volunteer. You will be my astonished convert!"

"Sounds like a lark! I shall be thoroughly convincing as a country doctor with clients from farms plagued with country mice and weasels. I shall be quite the cynic and—"

"—after you drink the tonic and make a show of shaking your arms, the critters shall teem forth into the cages. You shall be fully, convincingly astonished." Jovially I poked Birdy in the ribs and we softly chortled. "Wait until you see my talents! You will no longer be a true-to-life doubting Thomas."

"Anything for my darling," he murmured, leaning close. "May I?"

"You may," I whispered, as my legs shook.

He kissed me. His lips were bliss, firm and tangy as the leaf buds, and demanding in their need. I kissed him back. Dolly had said not to apologize for anything. No regrets. To take what one needed. I did. Unabashedly. His long arms pulled me in. My body lit on fire.

"Eva, fair Eva," he murmured when we finally took a breath.

Unexpectedly, brutally a guard yanked me away. "Caught red-handed, Witch," Fast Step snarled. He dragged me kicking. As I looked back at Birdy, I saw another guard cuffing him, and then my hood was lowered. I saw no more.

Good heavens! I had been too careless in my need. My boot heels kept catching on uneven cobblestones, and I careened from side to side like a spooked carriage horse, off to an unruly gallop with no heed to the traffic. "Stop! You're hurting my wrists! My ankles will snap!" I yelled.

"You should have thought of that before you broke the rules. No cavorting 'round with other prisoners. We guards are not fools!"

Fast Step dragged me inside, along one hallway and down a flight of stairs to a lower floor stinking of mildew and sewage. This alone would have been bad enough, but he pulled me down a second flight. Panic overcame me because when I reached out to touch the walls, my hands came away cold, slimy and dripping. This lower cellar leaked. "Where are you taking me?" I yelled desperately "Please, return me to my own cell. I'll stop causing any trouble at all!"

Fast Step launched into donkey brays. "Much too late for that, Witch. He took out a clanking set of keys, unlocked a latch, swung open a rusty door that squealed and hauled me into what I feared was the *hole* that prisoners spoke of in quivering whispers. Even through my hood I breathed in dank, stale vapors of the kind that could render even a healthy man ill. With sharp, brutal movements Fast Step chained me to a chair and fastened my feet in leg irons.

"Stay put," he ordered.

"Where are you going? Please sir, please let me out. I will not survive this."

It might have been better if he'd just stayed away. For when he returned minutes later, he unleashed bucket after bucket of freezing water upon my head.

I shrieked. I choked and struggled to breathe for the water kept coming and coming relentlessly. It gushed past my throat into my windpipe, which made me gag and cough. He was merciless. At least eight more buckets came. I strained to hold my breath, but after a time I had to let in air. The water rushed down into my beleaguered lungs. I would have wept from the cold but did not have the breath. After that, I lost count of how many more buckets of icy water he threw.

By the end, I struggled to remain conscious. My head was as heavy as a cannonball on my neck. My limbs were limp. My lungs were burning and freezing all at once. My clothes were sopping. I shivered violently.

I sensed the beasts in the dungeon advance—hungrier, coarser rats than at Dowdrick's with slavering snouts, snakes that itched to inject their venom in frail flesh, carrion beetles that skittered forth to feed upon the promise of death. They smelled my fear—like spoilt milk.

Do not harm me. I am an ally and will not kill you. Let me stay in this place for some days. I thank you, for it is your home not mine. It was not my choice, but I need to stay alive. If you come close can it please be to warm me? I beg of you, wild beasts, I am not your foe...

Fast Step had hurried out and secured the door before the beasts could swarm him.

I sensed the creatures pause and then advance, only to pause again—sniffing, scratching, slithering and running forked tongues over the wet rocks.

In and out of lucidity, I had visions of my mother talking softly to me at the small kitchen table. This was followed by an unhappy image of her grayed, thinning face, and her coughing and hacking out phlegm. The visions switched to my brother Todd and me laughing as we skipped down Sansom Street in the summer under the gently arching trees, rich with green. Todd and me cuddled in bed as Mama read to us. Then, my chest pinched as I saw my mother again, fading from cholera on her deathbed, the room reeking of camphor and sweat.

Another vision took over, of Dr. Dowdrick strutting into Conklin's Tailor, his pink melon face pinched in a tight frown. "Where are my pressed vests?" I heard him shout. "You forgot to include them in my bundled order. Is that your brother in the storeroom? If so, he should be let go. He is very disorderly. This is not the first time he bungled my orders!"

Teeth chattering, I startled into awareness. "The practice!" I gasped. "It is tonight. I cannot miss it!"

I shook my wrists to free them from their iron cuffs. Useless. Every move made me tremble for it pressed my cold, sopping prison dress against my already chilled skin. One more time I rattled my leg chains to determine any point of weakness. None.

My prayer! I had to imagine the stars above as I recited it

for it was pitch black in this dungeon. I could not see my arms or even the ball of my nose jutting from my face.

The sojourner gazes upward through the Eye of God to a place beyond words.

The stars tell tales of soaring, skipping light.

The birds create poetry in their circular flight.

Even here, in this bleak prison, the night is illuminated.

Its last line I murmured again and again until I faded.

18

My eyes blinked open but saw nothing. Enveloped in such tarry blackness, my breath came in short, terrified stabs. I was all but frozen. I tried to wrap my arms together to warm myself but was stopped by heavy irons. The full horror rushed in. I was in the dungeon, the hole, the place most feared even by the hardened convicts.

I forced myself to calm down because panic would do me no good. *In, out, in, out, take slow breaths.* As I breathed, I became aware I was not alone. I sensed tiny crouching beasts, sniffing me out, waiting. And I recalled the ones from before—snakes, carrion beetles, feral rats.

I saw pinpoints of greenish light—eyes peering at me. Again, I forced myself to slow my breathing. For these were new beasts to me, and being unfamiliar, they raised my fears. As a mage with a growing awareness of the peculiar balance between humans and other beings, I knew fear was a killer. Fear and panic would upset the delicate balance I needed to *talk* to the beasts. I sensed they were hungry, starved in fact. Food was not as plentiful in the penitentiary as at Dowdrick's, for man or beast. *You need to eat. I know.*

What else do you need? I asked them. Listening with no expectation was another key to their respect, if one could call it that.

Food was all they replied. *Food.*

I pushed away my desperation for this was something I could not provide.

They crept closer.

Wait. I will not harm you. Wait. I can provide better things than my flesh. Wait.

I startled at the grating sound of the door opening. It let in a tiny sliver of light at which I spied Fast Step carrying a saucer of bread and glass of water. The critters scurried back under the cover of darkness.

"Eat," he ordered. His lantern lit up his red-lidded eyes as he glared at me. Waiting, as the beasts waited. More vicious than the beasts that so far had left me unharmed.

"I will. Please put it by my hand."

He did. Then he went out, leaving the door ajar. As best I could, I drank the water then broke the bread into crumbs and tossed them here and there. The rats and beetles and snakes skittered out and gobbled the treats.

Just before he returned, while I still had light, another tiny beast scurried forth and leapt up by my hand. One of my own mice! He nudged forth a folded paper. I was more famished for this than any heel of bread. Birdy had scratched a note in his own blood.

E, sorry I pressed us to break rules. I was in the pit, too. A kiss. B

So, they had also punished Birdy! He must've gotten out sooner than I in order to find a shred of paper to write upon. His sending me a kiss healed the worst of my despair. Smiling, I stroked my mouse's head and sent him a silent command:

Dear messenger, run upstairs, for I cannot guarantee your safety here.

My mouse lifted his snout and rippled his whiskers. Perhaps he sensed the furtive beasts in the corners, for he skittered out the door just as Fast Step entered.

Fast Step charged over and dumped another icy bucketful on my head. "That'll teach you to carry on like a wench in a bawdy house." He had more lined up and after ten I lost count, for I was again sputtering and gasping for air.

I recall nothing more save for the grinding of the door shutting and clasp being locked.

The next time I awoke I had pissed myself and my entire body was shaking. I discovered that Fast Step had removed my leg irons so I was free to move about. In the dark, I felt my way over to a chamber pot and did the rest of my business. Chattering and shaking, I crawled over to the opposite corner and curled into a ball.

The carrion beetles had begun to scuttle over me. Their greenish eyes staring.

Beasts, take a care. I have fed you all, as I was able. All I ask is that you not devour me or inject me with venom. I beg you; I need warmth.

My lids lowered and I fell into a fevered lethargy.

Again, I dreamt of my mother. Already skeletal, she pleaded for me not to die. "Dear God, keep the last of my children alive. Hold Evalina in your hands and heal her, for my heart cannot take more deaths." The voice shifted to Birdy's as his face floated in view. "Fair Eva, I send you kisses, kisses, kisses. We shall meet again soon. Do not give up. My love will be a vessel that keeps you afloat." But then

Dowdrick's impatient whine and puffy face accosted my mind: "Where is the obstinate wench? She has not kept her part of our bargain. If she intends to make a laughingstock of me by being a no show, I will see to it she never sees the light of day."

I launched into a rattling laugh that became a rattling cough. "How droll, for already I see no light of day," I muttered and went into a fit of wheezing and choking until I recalled no more.

Startling out of a black void, I wondered how many days had passed? My belly had gone beyond hunger into a dull shrivel like the drying of a mushroom. The green pinhole eyes had moved much closer. I forced down a shudder of pure terror, for something had shifted. The beetles no longer tickled my neck and shoulders.

No harm had come to me—yet.

I was warm! Reaching out, my hand touched a luxuriously smooth, yet scaled being. It was coiled round my hips and sides. My fingers counted one snake, two. Finally, I determined that four distinct snakes embraced my body. Somehow, in their nearness they were able to pull from me what remained of my own body heat and give it back. They had slithered down to the chilly depths, unusual for such cold-blooded beasts that required outer warmth, and had granted my desperate wish!

Thank you, beings! If I get more food, you shall be the first to taste it.

I gingerly stroked their backs. Surprising how firmly built they were. They responded by curling ever more snugly. My lungs itched to expel phlegm. I felt a deep, worrying rumble at every breath but I did not want to disturb the snakes. The dank chamber and icy water had done their damage. I faded again, cradled in serpents.

The next time I awoke I was out of darkness! Light shone down on me through the Eye of God. Oh, Blessed Life, I was back in my own cell. I tried to rise but fell back. It wasn't that I was cuffed but I lacked the strength. A brown skirt whisked past and then settled by me. Amity was studying me. Her hazel eyes lit up when she realized I was awake.

"Stay still, Evalina. Thou has had some difficult days. Thy fever is high."

In my headstrong way I again tried to rise, to no avail. I launched into a coughing fit, which required Amity to come running with a bucket. Choking on phlegm, I spit up and then coughed some more.

She tossed it down the flush toilet, came back over and sat. She began to softly stroke my head with a blessedly warm cloth, smelling of eucalyptus. I knew this herb from Sumac.

Sumac! Dowdrick! I struggled to sit, but only plunked back down unceremoniously.

"I must ... I must, needs—" I began.

"Shh, stay calm. Thee need not speak." Once again, Amity stroked my head with the fragrant cloth. My lids lowered of their own accord and I fell into a stupor ripe with visions.

In it, my mother was stroking my forehead. We were in my childhood home. I was in bed and she was by me. "Evalina," she explained, "You have a touch of croup. Don't fret.

Hot tea and a mum's touch will have it gone in the blink of an eye."

The images switched to Sumac and Dowdrick arguing about snakes. "I refuse to indulge your passion for poisonous serpents," Dowdrick shouted with rising hysteria. "You are ignorant," Sumac retorted, "The venom is useful. I have a nice green viper snake here, would you like to see?" "No!" Dowdrick yelled, recoiling. "Take that hideous thing away from me!"

The image of Sumac waving the snake in Dowdrick's face was satisfying. Dowdrick deserved it. And after my ordeal in the hole, I needed a chuckle. Amusement quickly soured though as memory boiled up about my missed practice. Lord! Dowdrick must have sent at least a couple of notes that went unanswered. Had he come to the prison to inquire about my welfare? Had Blackbeard steamed the letters open? My gut twisted at the thought.

When I opened my eyes, Amity was leaning over me with a bowl of fragrant beef broth in one hand, a tablespoon in the other.

"Can thee sit?" She set the broth aside and returned to help hoist me, which made me cough, though with less rasping.

It took all of my strength, but I wriggled up until I could sit, propped with a pillow. When one was sick, nothing could be taken for granted. Not even the ability to sit, talk and stand. She spooned the broth in me as if I was a baby. It brought tears to my eyes.

"Shh, dear Evalina, thee needs thy strength. Pay mind to the broth. I brought it to thee special." Amity sounded so much like my own mama that I sniffed back more tears, though a couple did spill into the soup.

When I was done, a rush of wellbeing rippled through me. I gave Amity a smile. "You are so kind. Thank you."

"I was terribly worried," she admitted. "I visited twice to an empty cell before the bearded guard told me where thee was. They would not allow me to down there. I asked and begged them—"

"Oh, Amity, I'm glad you didn't. It was pitch black, cold and treacherous! You would have been horribly scared."

She let out a delicate laugh. "Thee might be surprised to know how daring I can be."

"Really? For example?"

She tipped her head and grinned with a mischief in her eyes. "I ran down the lane after a thief who stole a chair from my husband."

"You could have been badly hurt. Even stabbed!"

"That is what my dear husband told me." She tipped her head the other way. "I have also reported unscrupulous vendors on Market Street, and given this penitentiary director a stern talking to about the unfair incarceration rate and treatment of Negro inmates. By the by, in working on Samuel Barton's case, I found a weakening in the Fugitive Slave Act. In a case called Prigg versus Pennsylvania, states that could formerly protect runaway slaves, now must return them." A defiant fire appeared once again in her eyes. "This means that Quakers must break laws in the service of a higher morality. In Samuel's case, for instance, I may have to ferry him away in the cover of night," she whispered.

"Oh, you are bolder than I."

She shook her head. "Undertaking humane acts is simply part of the Friends' practice."

"There is nothing simple about it though. It takes brass resolve."

She nodded. "I heard thee slept with snakes in the pit.

Rats too! I heard not a one took a bite out of thee. That is quite bold if true."

"Tis true. Every word."

We sat there, admiring each other for a few triumphant moments.

"I heard thee endured the water punishment," Amity ventured. "It was quite injurious to have given thee such a cough and fever."

"It was like choking to death. It was cruel."

"I am not in favor of this." She looked down at her hands. "Yet thee must be careful to follow the rules. No speaking to fellow inmates in the yard. I would not like to see thee endure any more severe punishments."

I wasn't sure I could go without speaking, though no more kissing Birdy here. Humans were not meant to be in solitude for years, or even months. I sighed. Amity and I had already struggled through this topic. I forged ahead with a different one. "For how many days was I down in the hole? How long have I been sleeping?"

"Thee was in the pit for three long days. They saw from the crumbs that thee had spread the bread to the animals instead of eating it. They saw as well thee grew terribly sick so they brought thee back up here." She placed the empty bowl back on my table and returned with the warm cloth. "After the pit, thee was in and out of a fevered sleep for the better part of a week."

"Oh, no! What is today's calendar date?"

She looked up at the skylight as she thought. "Why, it is March 11th."

"Only four more days until the Ides! Good Lord!" I must send out a message..." I tried to throw off the covers and shuffle over until my feet were off the bed, but I was terribly weak.

"Thee must sleep, dear Evalina. Thee must conquer the fever before thee rises from the sickbed. I insist."

Again, she reminded me of Mama, who had also made me stay tucked firmly in bed while ill when all I wanted was to play. Or of the sister I longed for but never had. Or, perhaps a devoted new friend, if that was not too much to ask.

I blinked away my ache, for I needed to think up a solution to the problem of communication with Dowdrick. I could not reveal my plans to Amity. Not yet.

Amity rose. "On the topic of messages, thee received letters last week."

I tensed. "Do you have them?"

She walked toward the cell door and pulled two folded envelopes from a chink in the ledge. "I tucked them here. Would thee like me to read them?"

"No! No thank you," I exclaimed. "If you would be so kind as to bring them to me, I shall read them after a restorative nap."

She frowned, but said, "Very well. A nap is wise."

I tucked them under me and yawned, feigning exhaustion.

"I will visit again tomorrow. Rest, dear Evalina."

"I'll try." My feigned sleep was soon real. For my body was fighting hard to push the croup from my lungs. The letters would have to wait.

I slept around the clock to the next morning. When I awoke I was covered in sweat. The fever had broken! I still had a cough, but even that had improved. Next, I tried my legs, swinging them carefully over the edge of the bed. I held onto the bedpost as I rose to a wobbling stand. I took an experimental walk back and forth a few times to build my strength. And then, I remembered the letters I had slept on. I nearly fell in my haste to read them.

Witch, where were you the other night? The moody guard was no help. He refused to say. If you do not hold up your end of the bargain you will experience dire consequences. H.D.

And the next:

The bearded guard finally broke his silence and confessed you were down in the pit. How stupid of you to get in trouble so close to our performance! You have caused me a world of worry. This is bad for my health. I will send only one more note before I am forced to figure out my own presentation. In anger, D

This was terrible! I had to figure out an immediate solution. After a time of clutching my head and rocking, I came up with an idea. I cocked an ear to the hall. No footsteps, even padded ones. The only noise I heard was Dolly Rouge, dragging a chair.

"Dolly! Can I speak with you?" The dragging ceased.

"You are back! I saw the short, cruel guard seize you. You've been as quiet as one of your mice. The date grows close. Are we still on for the plan?"

"I hope so." I pressed my face close to the largest chink in the wall to ensure she heard every word. "Dolly, I need your help. Please do not say no before you hear the entirety of my reasoning."

"Belt it out, Eva!"

"I must get a note to Dowdrick. The only way is to send Blackbeard. And the only way he will do it is if we pay him. Dolly, I know he's given you coinage. I promise to reimburse—"

"No!"

"I told you to keep an open mind," I said sternly. "Do you want to send Dowdrick off to prison or not?"

"Yes," she said grudgingly.

"This is the only way. Dowdrick is furious I missed two practices. He is worried I will be a no-show. I must reassure him and convey details … such as your *outfit*." I let this float in the air, hoping she would snatch the bait.

"My outfit? Will he buy me a gown?" Her tone took on a remarkably renewed enthusiasm.

"Why of course, Dolly! Do you think we could blend in with a genteel crowd of physicians otherwise?"

"You have a point. Ooh, your mind is such a crafty steel trap! Hold on …" I heard her scraping a piece of furniture along the floor and then the loud clinking of coins being dumped on a hard surface. "How much might you need?"

"You know Blackbeard better than I. You also have a sharp, wily mind, as well as a charm about you."

"Why, yes, don't mind if I say so," she clucked.

"So, I will compose a note and my mouse will carry it to you. Call out for the guard as soon as you receive it for there is no time to waste! And what color gown do you fancy?" I added to strengthen her mettle.

"Crimson," she said with no pause. "It complements what's left of my pretty red hair."

"Say no more. You shall have it."

I sent the note and called for my mouse. The largest one came forthwith. His whiskers twitched as I directed him to the chink in the wall and sent a mental picture of the red-haired madam. I also thought of her sounds. For Dolly was a concerto of thuds and clangs and scrapes.

After this, I composed a note to Samuel Barton to stay put and not perform at Dowdrick's. I said the same to Dowdrick. For what Amity had said about the laws, and her probable need to break them, weighed heavily on my mind. I did not want to harm Sammy's chance of freedom by prodding him into a perilous limelight.

This task exhausted me, and I fell right back to sleep, dreaming of little Lewin, waiting for his knock on the underside of the carriage that never came. "Where are you?" I asked as I dreamt. He did not answer.

I awoke hours later, wondering how he was and where he was sleeping, and praying his silence in my dream did not foretell tragedy. As I dressed, I heard the hum of two people talking. Straining to listen I picked out Blackbeard's bass and Dolly's higher, yet brassy tone.

"Why should I?" Blackbeard was asking.

"Because it is *I* who asked. Because I trust only *you* to do it well. Because you know you likes your Dolly and your Dolly likes you!"

To this, I heard his gruff laughter and then the smooching sounds of a kiss. I sighed with relief for when Dolly was convinced of a plan's worth, she delivered the goods. I closed my eyes, waiting for sleep. This would be the performance of my life. If I was not recovered it could well kill me.

19

The big day came. At dawn, I wrote Amity a long note, sealed it and pictured it surrounded by protective light so it might reach her and no other. In it, I told her I'd seen Lewin outside the prison and I confessed my plan for the symposium. It fortified me that she had admitted breaking rules; that civil folk could do this in dire times in service of a greater good.

When I heard the clink of my door lock and Blackbeard's bellowing for me to stand against the wall, I knew that my note had reached Dowdrick. With the help of my mouse, Dolly had squired a few precious coins over to me through the chink in the wall. I held those coins in my trembling hand. "Please sir, I ask only one favor. That you give the sealed note on my table to the Quaker matron, Miss Amity."

"Why would I do that?" he scoffed.

I reached out my hand and showed him the coins. "It's not much but it's all I have."

He grunted as he took them. "I'll see what I can do," was all he said before he cuffed and hooded me. "A mystery client sent for you and two others. Must be something of note! Make haste."

In the carriage I dared not speak to Birdy, though we boldly touched boots from across the seats. Dolly came in after. My chest buzzed as if a thousand bees were trapped inside, and my lungs, only halfway healed, rasped like a broken bagpipe. I prayed my nerves would not consume me.

Inside, Dr. Sumac whisked the others to a separate room, while telling me to wait in the foyer. A red-faced Dowdrick awaited me, gussied up in a silk pinstriped suit with a double-breasted vest set with gold buttons. It unsettled me that I still knew his suits. "So, the careless inmate has been unearthed from the murky pit! About time! Do you remember all of your lines? Every move? Have you instructed your players precisely?"

"Yes. For realism, I shall have one doubting Thomas who, after sampling the tonic shall be transformed into an astonished convert. This, as you say, will top any drama at the Walnut Street Theater."

I was awarded a peevish smile. "Very well. Manage your players during the morning events. They should have aliases. They will mingle but watch them closely for it is up to you to insure they make no faux pas."

I nodded blankly, unsure of what *foe paw* meant.

Dowdrick continued. "There will be an opening lecture and morning presentations. After a luncheon, the afternoon presentations will proceed. We shall have tea breaks—very British of me," he concluded with a self-satisfied chuckle. "Our big moment is the grand finale. We shall send them off with a bang."

Like the slamming of the prison door on you!

"Now, run along, and get dressed. Make sure your nightmare of tangles get thoroughly combed out. The others are already getting fitted in the anteroom off the parlor. It's a small room off to the left, and halfway down. You'll hear the clamor. Condor has been shopping for ladies' fashions," Dowdrick chirped, a malicious gleam in his eyes.

Stepping into the enormous parlor, I gasped to see it converted into an elegant ballroom, festooned with bouquets billowing from exotic Asian pots, round dining tables set with white linen tablecloths, porcelain china and silverware of the likes I'd only seen in the best shop windows.

It saddened me to see Sumac in a cook's apron, fretting over a large tray of morning crumpets. I tapped his shoulder. "Dr. Sumac, good morning."

He swung around. Under his apron he had on a pressed black suit that complimented his swarthy complexion and ebony hair. "Ah, buenos dias, Evalina. I am happy to see you better from the croup. I heard about your … difficult time. What a shame the wardens did not give you a cup of my healing botanical tea."

I shuddered, recalling the stupor I fell into with the first drink he gave me. "Can I help?"

"Gracias, mi amiga. But you are needed in the anteroom. You must get dressed. Dr. Dowdrick hired two maids at my insistence, but not until yesterday." He made a pained face. "Neither is trained for this work and so I end up doing it."

After our private conversation, we had formed a sort of mutual complaint society, which gave me as much comfort as it seemed to give him. "Best of luck. Don't let Dowdrick steal your thunder," I said. His brooding look softened.

The maid walked in, a thin, frowning girl that I recognized as the daughter of a Market Street vendor. She glanced at me nervously before scurrying around to adjust the already set cutlery. Dr. Sumac and I exchanged exasperated looks.

The anteroom was abuzz with activity. Another maid, the girl's stout sister, was struggling to button up the back of Dolly's crimson gown.

"Don't fasten my skin in the dratted closures!" Dolly wailed. "You're pinching me!"

"Dolly! You're a beauty," I said to distract her. "Your hair looks lovely as well." It was true. The maid had managed to tame her flyaway mop, pile and pin it up so the gray roots were hidden. She topped it off with a stylish red hat adorned with purple feathers and grapes. Coquettish netting floated over Dolly's heavily painted eyes. I could see what a stunner Dolly Rouge must have been in her prime, for this remake had trimmed fifteen years from her.

Birdy stepped out from a changing room curtain. My heart galloped at his long-limbed male beauty. The maid had shopped well. His waistcoat and pants were of dark gray wool, and his vest a rich navy. Under this, was a crisp, white shirt, and around his neck a plaid navy ascot set off his dark eyes. "Do I look the part?" he teased.

"Every inch the genteel doctor!" I longed to hug him, but business was pressing.

After I dressed it was his turn to gape. The maid had outdone herself, choosing for me a pale blue gown with a modest white collar trimmed with pearl buttons. Down the bodice and the along the sleeve borders were appliques of navy blossoms, and the dress was cinched with a tight belt. She brushed my hair as best she could, pinned it up in a twirl and topped it with a fashionable sea green hat trimmed with silk daisies. I wished we had the luxury of getting our photograph taken for I wanted to preserve this rare moment.

Before they hustled us out I went over our aliases once more. Birdy was Dr. Bertram Davies, a country doctor from Humphreysville in the Welsh Tract. Dolly Rouge was Mrs. Susan Rogers, an assistant to a nurse caring for homebound Mennonite patients in the Germantown area. She had a special interest in botanical remedies. And I was Miss Eve Fallon, a nurse-in-training, from the heart of the city, Elfreth's Alley.

By the time we were led into the Discovery Symposium, a trek to the end of the vast parlor and through sliding pocket doors into Dowdrick's laboratory hall, the room was packed with doctors. They were in their best suits, chatting and sipping tea. Another one of Dowdrick's hired help, this time a burly man, ushered us to our seats. Birdy and I were separated but at least I could see him from across the row. Dolly sat two seats from me.

The room grew quiet as Dowdrick walked to a podium to the left of his long table. He cleared his throat, straightened his ascot and began. "Morning salutations to the esteemed doctors and practitioners of medicine in this great city of Philadelphia. I am Dr. Horace Dowdrick. As the director of the Eclectic Medical College I welcome you to the first, of hopefully many, Discovery Symposiums. Our college focuses on botanical remedies. Though today we are thrilled to welcome luminaries such as Gunter Hohlstein, master of Pennsylvania Dutch Pow Wow treatments, Charles D. Meigs, professor of obstetrics at Jefferson Medical School and Dr. Thomas M—" Dowdrick appeared to choke on the name but recovered. "—Dr. Thomas Mutter, professor of surgery also at Jefferson Medical College. Dr. Hunt will explain Homeopathic Medical College's Hahnemann System of Therapeutics. Also, today will be a lecture by Dr. Farmington from The Pennsylvania Hospital for the

Insane, on "Biological psychiatry" cures for terrors of the battlefield and other strong anxieties. Rounding out the afternoon program will be a demonstration of *my* newest revolutionary elixir, debuted here!"

I gritted my teeth as he glanced my way. So much depended on my upcoming performance. Tension was already cramping my every muscle. It would be torture to wait until the afternoon—for my beasts, too. For my turmoil would run through them.

Looking out at the sea of doctors, he went on. "My formula has almost magical properties to eliminate house-hold pests, with *you* as the Pied Piper!" He chuckled. "You will not want to miss this presentation so make sure to stay for the entire symposium!"

The room broke out in surprised chatter, and Dowdrick waited gleefully for the clamor to settle before introducing Dr. George McClellan, director of the medical department of Pennsylvania College, who spoke of worldwide news.

I caught most of it, though my mind was fretting over our upcoming show.

"Some of the exciting developments are by our northern neighbors in New York City," McClellan was saying. "Bellevue physicians are promoting their "bone bill", which legalizes the dissection of cadavers for anatomical studies in medical schools." This was followed by enthusiastic claps.

"Also, up in Manhattan is the Nursery for Poor Children, the first of its kind has recently opened on Saint Marks Place ... While across the Atlantic in England, Alexander Wood has developed a hollow needle, and is now using what he calls, the hypodermic syringe for subcutaneous injections. Such an exciting time!" More approving clamor arose.

"In our own city of Brotherly Love, Dr. Samuel Hahnemann's system of therapeutics, or the wisdom of "like treats like" lives on with the recently opened Homeopathic Medical College of Pennsylvania." Loud cheers went up for this. "Female Medical College on Arch Street is another recent opening. It will provide talented women their first medical degrees."

Dolly and I exchanged open-mouthed gapes, though this news was met with tamer claps, for the room was almost exclusively filled with men.

When the keynotes were done, my attention was lured back by the first presenter to take the podium. He was a wiry man in elegant but colorful clothing—a pink cravat, a salmon-hued vest, and an impeccably tailored beige waistcoat festooned with a showy pocket watch on a golden chain. In contrast to Dowdrick's gaudy attire, Mutter looked stylish and modern. The audience went wild in their applause before he even began his lecture. So, this was Dowdrick's most threatening competitor. Clearly this doctor was well loved. I glanced over at Dowdrick, who sat in a chair near the podium. He was scowling.

"Greetings, esteemed doctors and interested parties, I am Thomas Dent Mutter, third chair of surgery at the Jefferson Medical College," the doctor began, his movements reminding me of a squirrel's—quick, eager, sharp. "Today, I will discuss my novel method for restoring the normalcy of the face, which for too many women cooking over open stoves, has been utterly destroyed by fire. Forgive me in advance, for I affectionately term this as *fixing my monsters*." A stunned murmur welled up.

Mutter continued. "It is not *I* who see these wonderful patients as such. Rather society, who fears a deformed face. At any rate, I have developed the art of "plastic operations". I must find healthy skin to patch into the disfigured area. Yet surgeons well know that if one cuts a piece of skin completely off to use as a patch, there is necrosis—the tissue usually dies. It must be connected to a source of blood flow in order to live until the skin can adhere and form new vessels. In this, I have developed the Mutter Flap.

He mounted a diagram on an easel and pointed to the illustration of the deformed face, where the chin had melted into the neck from burns. He explained the process in detail, after which he said, "Mrs. Davidson, please join me at the podium." Mutter held out his hand to welcome her.

I gasped as she strode out from a side door to thunderous applause. Her face was flawless—a strong jawline, and a gentle sloping neck. No frightening wrenching down of the skin under her eyes and cheeks as before.

To some it might be gruesome. To me, it was astounding. I was grateful to my mother for reading to me, for always teaching me things. I was never "too little" for a full explanation of terms, of dense novels such as Hawthorne's *The House of Seven Gables.* Its wrongful hanging of a witch scared me, yes. Yet it taught the consequences of greed, and that wrong could be made right, no matter that it might take generations. Because of my mother's persistence, my mind was open, and complex ideas could take root, as Mutter's Flap did.

Despite the nefarious reasons for my being here, I was thrilled, for my mind was hungry. I thought of Birdy, and looked over at him. He gazed back at me with gleaming eyes. Excitement was catching. I had a sudden determination. I would talk to Mutter during a tea break.

After this, Charles D. Meigs took the podium and spoke of difficult infant deliveries. In the question and answer period, Mutter spoke sternly to him.

"Many patients under your watch have died due to unsanitary conditions."

"Malarky!" Meigs shot back, "Wearing street clothes and washing my hands or not has nothing to do with the success of a surgery."

"To the contrary, it has everything to do with it," Mutter insisted. "The midwives who practice using sanitary hand-washing have a much reduced record of maternal deaths from chilblain and other mortal infections."

They continued to argue as a loud ruckus went up in the audience, and it shocked me, especially since they were professors at the same medical college.

I was no doctor, but I knew, even from cooking in a kitchen, that if one did not scour dishware and if one ate off of a soiled plate one was at greater risk of falling ill.

When the recess was called I rushed over to Dr. Mutter and waited in line as other admirers crowded around him. Finally, it was my turn. "I am Eva Fallon, a nurse-in-training, and I am quite interested in your plastic operations."

"Why thank you, Miss Fallon, it is an obsession of mine." Mutter grinned, revealing an impish set of dimples. He then cracked his neck to one side as if relieving it of stress. Up close, every hair was in place, every hint of whisker shaved flat. He smelled of clean laundry.

I screwed up the courage to continue. "Um, I have a friend who was injured in a terrible explosion while working on the railways."

"My sympathies."

"Yes, and well, the charge damaged his feet. It turned one of them inward, so he walks with a lopsided gait. The other foot, also damaged has to take on most of the work. Can injuries like this be fixed with your plastic operation?"

"Quite possibly," Mutter replied. "I'd have to examine the foot."

"How much might it cost? My friend is of very modest means."

"I'd have to have to converse with your friend. There is a cost. Yet nothing is set in stone," he added when he saw my downtrodden look.

"Do you have an address for your office?" I said brazenly.

I was stunned when he handed me his calling card. I had no pockets on my gown so I stuck it under my hat and hoped for the best.

Glancing around, I was horrified to see Dowdrick glaring at us as he walked toward the adjoining den set up for tea service. He stopped in his tracks, and cornered me as soon as I wove through the room to find Birdy.

"What do you think you were doing?" he growled.

"Pardon me?"

"You know what I am referring to." When I continued to stare blankly at him, he said, "Your little session with Dr. Mutter."

"What, pray tell, is the problem with conversation? You told us to play the social butterfly and blend in." I glared at him.

"True, but not to corner the doctors who are presenting."

"Why ever not?"

"Because ... because they are busy! They don't need some girly buzzing in their ear, and distracting them."

I was ready to slap his priggish face to kingdom come, but I held in my rage. The beasts though, came alive just under the surfaces, rumbling, scratching, ever my protectors and sensitive to my reeling emotions. I pushed out a breath filled with hatred, and only said, "Keep a mind to who your performers are."

Then I stomped away.

In the adjoining room, groups of doctors were engaged in lively dialogue as they sipped Sumac's tea and nibbled on fruit and biscuits. I snaked here and there until I found Birdy. He gave me a wink. "Ah! Here comes Miss Fallon," he explained to a rotund doctor with an impressive white moustache. "She interns in the nursing trade, did I recall that correctly?"

"You did." I said to Birdy. Turning to the man I asked, "What is your interest in the Discovery Symposium?"

"Why, I came to see the Amish doctor. Scuttlebutt says he can cure warts, get rid of snakebite venom and fever with his folk chants. He's on after the break."

I had my doubts but nodded, anxious for time to speed up.

"Are you a practitioner of Pow Wow yourself?" asked Birdy. "Some of the Welsh Quakers out my way are inclined toward it."

"No, I am a homeopathic doctor following the path of Hahnemann," the doctor explained. "He taught that a substance which causes symptoms of disease in healthy folk cures similar symptoms in the ill."

"Which substances?" I asked.

"I use tiny doses of what some deem as poison, but to cure. So a small peck of diluted arsenicum album, commonly known as arsenic can actually cure arsenic poisoning! It also helps those with stomach upset."

"Well, shucks, I'm astounded!" Birdy crowed. "I shall try arsenicum on my patients."

Inwardly I cringed, for Birdy was hamming up his performance to the point of parody. Luck was with us, for the call rang out to reconvene. As we took our seats I glanced over at Dolly Rouge, down the row from me. I would have to check on her next. This was part of my task. If Birdy was wavering on his performance, God only knew what hijinks Dolly was up to. I also wondered where Dr. Sumac was, for I hadn't seen him since we arrived.

The Pow Wow doctor took the podium. A gigantic man with the bushy beard of an Amish, he was stuffed into an ill-fitting suit where the sleeves came up halfway to his elbows.

"Greetings fellow doctors of Penn's great experiment," he said, as he fumbled through his papers. "I am Gunter Hohlstein, a practitioner of the Braucherei. We know each disease has a recognizable pattern, with its own form of treatment, and yet, as modern people we often underestimate the power of prayer, plant remedy and the impact of charms. We let others take control of our healing. Let us reclaim the responsibility of getting healthy and staying healthy. As in Samuel Thompson's Vermont botanical method, we may well have best results with a combination of herbal, spiritual and water and heat based therapies than simply undergoing surgery, where we depend on the knife to cure all. One might argue that our method smacks of quackery."

At this, I glanced at Dowdrick, wringing his hands. I was nervous, too. Because this very afternoon we would attempt a momentous act of quackery! I had to focus on the goal: justice. If it didn't work… well, it had to.

Holstein continued. "Yet can any doctor claim to cure all ailments? Take for instance, the esteemed Benjamin Rush and his theory of the "Unity of Fevers". His claim that the simple "letting of blood" can cure any illness could also be deemed quackery. As many now suspect, the draining of blood causes weakness not strength! No one doctor has a claim to perfect practice. Therefore, why not utilize a mix of tools proven effective over time?"

I peeked at Dr. Mutter, who was nodding. Some folk remedies made sense to me as well.

"Hear, hear!" someone shouted.

"Quiet down," someone else scolded.

Hohlstein's assistant wheeled out a gurney with a groaning child of about five on it.

"This poor boy suffers from intestinal bloating," Hohlstein explained. "We powwowers call this condition hidebound, or to use our own language, of being *Aagewaxe*. For we believe this problem often occurs from the liver attaching itself to the body cavity."

A disbelieving hubbub arose, but a few doctors shushed the dissenters. Hohlstein produced a large bottle of oil and rubbed some on his hands. Then he lowered the sheet, placed his hands on either side of the crying child and pressed firmly, chanting in German. After firm kneading and chanting of prayer, the boy became peaceful, and said he felt much improved.

It was similar to how I coaxed animals—a communing of energies. I thought of the beasts under the floorboards, how loyal and patient they were. And I sent them my unspoken thanks. Waves of warmth enveloped me as they returned the emotion.

As Hohlstein finished his lecture to a smattering of applause, Dowdrick rose briskly from his chair by the podium and rushed toward the parlor, clutching his belly. Was he suffering from indigestion? I wondered if this powwow treatment would help him. Eating fewer cookies would work even better. I glanced at Dr. Sumac, now sitting by Dowdrick's empty chair. Sumac craned his neck to see where Dowdrick had gone. Suddenly, he leapt up and took the podium—a curious move because he wasn't one of the scheduled presenters. Doctors in the audience glanced at each other with confusion.

"Buenas dias, estimados doctors, I am Dr. Condor Sumac, a professor at the Eclectic Medical College and colleague of Dr. Horace Dowdrick's. I am not listed on this morning's programming. However, there is an unexpected opening, so I will show you a revolutionary way of putting a surgical patient into a painless twilight state, in part awake." He pulled a bottle from his waistcoat and held it up. "This is a rare mix of herbs and flowers from my country, Peru. A groundbreaking powder that will replace ether, from which one can easily die, and nitrous oxide, which renders a patient dizzy, nauseated, even in a dangerous hallucinatory trance."

Confusion turned quickly to excitement. The crowd bellowed, "Show us!" and "Incredible!"

"There is no time for an unscheduled display before the luncheon," complained the elderly man Birdy had spoken to.

"Ignore him!" someone else shouted.

"Let us see it!" called a doctor near the podium.

Surprising how rowdy the medical establishment is.

What was Sumac doing? If Dowdrick came back and saw this, Sumac would be ridden out on a rail. Surveying the doors to make sure Dowdrick had not yet returned I recalled telling Sumac to seize his moment in the limelight. Was he following my advice? All at once I was jittery with nerves for the bold Peruvian doctor.

The stout maid who had dressed us pushed a patient in a wheelchair to the podium. Dr. Sumac took one of his hands and raised it. He pointed to a concerning apple-sized growth on his forearm. "This will be gone in moments," claimed Sumac.

"When I administer my Peruvian powder this patient will be awake and yet fully tolerate the surgery." Sumac gently tipped the man's face upward and then blew powder he had tapped onto the bottle cap into the man's nostrils. Within moments, the man's eyes rolled up beyond his lids and his head lolled sideways. Dr. Sumac wiped the area around the engorged cyst with a cloth smelling of herbs and alcohol. Then, he carved a deep, unwavering incision around the growth. Blood spurted forth but the patient did not make a peep. Dr. Sumac removed the cyst, staunched the bleeding and quickly stitched up the gash. During the whole ordeal, the man hadn't moved a muscle in his reclining wheelchair.

"Now, watch and listen," said Sumac. He turned to the patient, still seemingly dead to the world, and asked, "Are you in pain?"

"No," the man drawled.

"Do you know what happened?"

"No," said the man slowly yet clearly.

Sumac studied the stunned crowd. "Despite his twilight state, the patient can converse. He is pain-free yet I did not have to administer so much that he fell unconscious or ill. Afterward, he will have no memory of our talk. No memory of pain. No lingering side-effects."

Sharp gasps erupted around the room.

"What the devil is this?" an all-too familiar voice exclaimed.

I spun around. Dowdrick had finally returned from the powder room after what must've been a good half an hour. His scalding glare could have started a barrel fire. His face had gone from baby's rump pink to furious red. I began to tremble, remembering that crazed look from when Dowdrick choked Todd. My beasts rumbled and chittered under the floor.

It's not time, not yet. I strained to settle my own boiling emotions.

Leaning forward like an enraged bull Dowdrick charged Sumac. Though as heads turned his way, he seemed to realize he would be the target of shameful gossip. Abruptly, he slowed his gait, yet marched on until he had retaken the podium. "That will be all, Dr. Sumac, thank you." His sharp order sounded like he was chewing on broken glass.

Sumac wheeled his patient halfway to the side door, when a bunch of doctors shouted, "Dr. Sumac, wait! Tell us more about this Peruvian flower."

"Is your powder available at the druggists?"

"How soon do you expect this twilight medicine in surgical wards?"

"Come back!"

Dowdrick thumped his brass walking stick on the podium. "Order! Order, good people. You will have ample time *after* the symposium to speak to the doctor. For now, luncheon is served in the ballroom. Make haste!" He banged the stick harder.

I had no idea where Sumac had gone, but I was already fretting over his fate. Then I remembered, Sumac had willingly drugged me. He was not my friend, simply because he had shown me a few thoughtful moments, or shared vengeful chuckles. I hurried to the ballroom to grab a seat and calm my nerves in preparation for the performance that would govern my fate.

20

Dolly Rouge was chatting up a storm when I took the chair next to her that Birdy had saved for me at the large round table. "May I get you a drink, Miss Fallon?" he asked as if we were strangers.

"Why yes, thank you..."

"—Dr. Bertram Davies," he replied, with a lopsided smile that coaxed out his dimples. "They have cider, coffee, tea, hot chocolate or bourbon."

"Cider would be divine, thanks." As tense as I was, the prospect of food and drink that wasn't cooked in a prison had my mouth watering.

Birdy went off, and I veered around to hear Dolly. "Why, I'd love to attend the new female medical school," she was saying to a gentleman with wavy red hair that matched Dolly's bright ends. He had a pleasingly round face, which no doubt made him look younger than his age. "I have a great sympathy for what a poor, single mother heavy with child suffers if she has illness during pregnancy," Dolly said. "Why, it could drive her to the poorhouse! For that matter, I have nursed many an older, bedridden women back to health." I detected, from her bourbon-laced breath, that Dolly was in her cups. Glancing at me, she remembered her manners. "Dr. Fussell, this is …" she circled her arm at me in a gesture of forgetful confusion.

"—Miss Fallon," I finished, and smiled at the doctor.

"I am Dr. Edwin Fussell. Pleased to meet you. I was telling your friend, Miss Rogers that I am a founding member of the Female Medical College for Women near Seventh and Arch. Miss Rogers is impeccably suited to enter as a first year student. She tells me she is a quick study and has learned all that she can up in Germantown."

"Yes, from what she has told me, she is a talented nurse-in-training. Your college sounds grand. Yet, I lack the means," I said frankly.

"Ah." He nodded sympathetically. "Well, then."

Birdy returned with the cider. I took a sip and brazenly licked my lips.

We were served a lavish lunch of pheasant with gravy, green beans and yams. On the side were buttery rolls. I could barely touch my dessert of chocolate cake, for not only was I as stuffed as a Thanksgiving turkey, I was again worried about the upcoming performance. My cough had returned, and with it, an early exhaustion. Birdy must've noticed it, for he kept his warm gray eyes on me even when he was putting on a show of talking to yet another doctor.

The skittering of mice also disturbed me. During the first course, one came along the floorboards as fast as a shooting star. I glanced around the crowd but everyone was engaged in lively conversation. Then, came a second mouse, dashing boldly right under our table.

Dolly saw it and yelped. "Foo! Get gone!" She batted it away with her linen napkin.

Another person at the table, a Dr. Toby quipped, "Looks

as if we need Dr. Dowdrick's Mesmer tonic immediately if not sooner!"

"Yes," I said, "the doctor has an infestation." I attempted a lighthearted smile, but inside, I was in turmoil. While others were busily engaged, I pretended to search for a napkin I'd dropped. I lifted the hem of the tablecloth for a peek. The mouse was on its hind legs, staring right at me, a bit of something drab green in its maw. He placed it on the floor and dashed off.

My stomach dropped when I realized what it was: rotting herbs from one of the bags in the cellar. My beasts did not drop random tidbits by my feet. This meant something.

I must figure out what's amiss. Time is draining away!

Send me another clue, I pleaded to the mouse and the other creatures, listening.

The carriage horses neighed loudly outside the window. A rumble began under the floor—an echo from the wild beasts. The mystery unnerved me terribly.

Birdy leaned in while making a ruse of wiping chocolate icing from his mouth. "Miss Fallon, whatever's the matter?"

"The beasts are trying to tell me something," I whispered back. "I have not figured it out. But we must be ready for our act, for we may need to perform early. Are you prepared?" He gave me a solemn nod, and seamlessly returned to conversing with Dr. Toby.

"Yes, along the lines of ancient remedies, Dr. Davies, I'd love to talk with Dr. Sumac regarding his incredible Peruvian powder," Dr. Toby replied. "Where is the good doctor?" he asked as he surveyed the room.

"I've no idea." Birdy shrugged.

The doctor next to Dr. Toby with the white moustache who couldn't be bothered earlier to take the time to see

Sumac's demonstration chimed in. "This Peruvian doctor will be a wealthy man from his powder. In fact, I'd buy some right now! Where is he? He has not eaten his lunch. Quite odd, wouldn't you agree? All of the other physicians are present."

Where was Dr. Sumac? For that matter where was Dr. Dowdrick? I turned to Dolly who had stopped chatting with Dr. Fussell and was now polishing off her cake with the smacking of her lips. "Dolly, are you ready to perform?"

"Is a cat ready to pounce on a mouse?" she joked. Then she prodded my arm with a finger and whispered, "Lookie here! This old Madame has won the jackpot." She reached down her dress in between her voluminous bosom and pulled out a half dozen calling cards.

Despite my worries I chuckled. "Dolly, you are a talented social directress."

"Why thank you, Miss Eva ... I mean Nurse Fallon."

Just then, Dr. Dowdrick entered the room and announced that the afternoon lectures would begin, and for everyone to retake their seats.

His eye caught mine in a questioning way, to assess my readiness. I gave him a faint nod. He looked unusually frumpy. His collar was half turned up, and his white hair, always impeccably groomed with the nauseating oil looked if he'd just hiked in an October gust. I shivered with an ominous dread. My energy ebbed, and I began to cough.

Our wordless exchange was over when a group of doctors approached Dowdrick to ask where Dr. Sumac was.

"He did not appear at the luncheon," said one.

"Is his twilight powder available for purchase at the Eclectic Medical School store?"

"We've been waiting an hour to speak to him about his miracle powder," said another impatiently.

"You will have to wait weeks, even months," Dowdrick snapped. "Dr. Sumac was called away abruptly for a family matter of extreme urgency."

What? When pigs fly!

"So sorry to hear of it," the first doctor said. "Do you know his return date?

"Or his address down in Peru?" another boldly asked.

"We do not release private addresses," Dowdrick replied, a dangerous edge to his tone I knew all too well. He frowned, while giving me another directive nod. "It is past time for the afternoon program. Gentlemen, ladies, get seated forthwith." He marched into the lecture hall with a group of doctors following like ducklings to their mama.

When I sat, the wild beasts resumed their own secret march. Ants began to zigzag around my chair, bringing with them more clots of the wilted herbs. I cringed when a few people crushed the insects under their heels.

The basement. I smelled these mildewed plants when he locked me down there. *Something is in the basement.*

The next to present was Dr. Farmington from The Pennsylvania Hospital for the Insane, on "Biological Psychiatry cures for terrors of the battlefield and other strong anxieties". I was far too distracted to listen, even when his patient described recurring nightmares of "dead soldiers who still moaned."

For there were more mice underfoot, and they carried new things in their snouts. Two of them congregated under my chair. I reached down as if to stretch my legs. One had a gnawed-on bit of fabric with a faint odor of citrus. I took it and reached for the next mystery item in the other mouse's snout. Blond hairs.

Lewin.

Sitting back up, I launched into another coughing fit.

Birdy looked over from the next row. The horses neighed like banshees outside, and somehow a bird got in a window. A starling it was, and it swooped down toward me, and then over to Dowdrick as if it longed to peck his eyes out.

Not yet, I warned, not yet!

The stout maid was trying to sweep the bird out of an opened window with swipes of her broom as another one flew in. Her wiry sister called, "Shoo! Away!" while rustling her apron at them. The starling took refuge on a ceiling beam. The other bird stole a cookie and careened about with the confection in its beak. This prompted some in the audience to stand and crane their necks at the sources of the disturbance.

Amidst the hubbub of the birds, Birdy darted over. "What is it, Eva?"

"I am sure Lewin is in the basement. Dowdrick must've captured him!"

"Good lord! How did you find out?"

"Mice came to me with a lock of Lewin's hair."

For a second, Birdy wore his skeptical look. But then, he shook it off. "What can I do, Eva? Am I still to be doubting Thomas or has my act changed? Just say the word and I'll—"

"The cellar entrance is guarded by a padlock. Dowdrick has chemicals in his lab. I know nothing of them but—"

"Chemicals, eh? I shall see if any are useful."

"Audience. Be seated!" Dowdrick roared. "The birds are being removed by staff."

As people returned to their seats, I whispered one more thing before Birdy left. "Hurry! I'm about to do my act and you'll be needed as part of it. The cellar door is off the ante-room where we dressed." He slinked off.

From the corner of my eye I saw Dowdrick, already

piling his lab table with Monster Mesmer bottles in their colored categories. The display looked like a carnival table advertising sugary drinks. Far from it, the bottles were fakes with nothing more than fizzed water and diluted off-brand whiskey one could buy at any flophouse bar.

I gave Dolly a sign.

Dowdrick had collected himself enough to straighten his collar, but I sensed his vitality and balance were off. Looking around I saw the crowd had filled out quite a bit. This included what looked to be students of Mutter, McClellan and other doctors.

As Dr. Dowdrick began his lecture, the mice had already resumed their activity, causing uproar when one dashed along the front row toward the side door. My throat clenched. If the beasts rampaged too soon... if I could not control them...

Take a care, little creatures, save your strength for the final act. Soon, but not yet!

"You see that even our esteemed Eclectic Medical School could use a pest extermination. We all could," Dowdrick was saying. "How many times have mice fallen in your stews, gnawed on your precious stores of bread and grains? Even the best of us are plagued. That's why my Monster Mesmer product is so essential, so revolutionary." He held up a bottle. "No need to lure the vermin to the poison. We all know that city rats have grown too canny to be trapped in this way." This earned Dowdrick many "Hear, hears!"

He lapped up the attention and continued. "Monster Mesmer is especially good in the surgical ward, for it keeps it free from vermin who spread the worst filth. Consider the Black Plague." Horrified murmurs rose up. "As I explained in my opening speech, with Monster Mesmer *you* are the Pied Piper. You lure the pests to cages and slam the door on them." He pointed to the two large wire cages he had set up by the wall, doors opened and waiting. "It's up to you whether to throw the cages in the Delaware and drown them, or simply release them along the riverbank." He paused again to soak up the appreciative laughter.

My anger spiked and I sensed the beasts slavering. No one should show this degenerate one sliver of attention or respect. *He* was the Monster in Monster Mesmer. *He* was the vermin!

I snapped to particular attention when Dowdrick said, "Don't take my word for it. Let's get a couple of audience members to try it!"

An enthusiastic clamor arose. "Don't cheer loudly," warned the doctor, "or you'll scare the rats back to their hidey-holes." With that, the audience became subdued, expectant.

I raised my hand along with a few other volunteers. Dowdrick pretended to survey the crowd and pick me at random. I marched to the podium and Dowdrick asked for my name.

"Miss Fallon," I replied, my heart drumming.

He made a great show of popping open a newly sealed bottle. "Orange tonic is for extremely wily critters like rats. I admit; I have seen a rat upon occasion in my cellar." Uneasy mutters rumbled through the hall. He shushed them by holding a finger to his liverish lips. "Miss Fallon, open wide." He wore a puckish grin as he poured a brimming tablespoonful down my throat.

The cheap whiskey and carbonation burned. I swallowed hard. Extending and shaking my arms, rolling my eyes and breathing hard, I dramatized the look of the mesmerizing. This made me cough, and it was hard to stop, for I was already tired. But I needed to conjure the beasts before I let all hell break loose.

The mice retreated as the rats scurried forth. Big, scruffy rats with bug eyes and jerking tails. The crowd cried out in horrified fascination. A few people screamed and ran through the pocket doors to the safety of the parlor. The energy was chaotic, yet I managed to silently guide the rats to rise onto their hind legs and sniff at the air. I had conjured a good twenty. Some were as big as raccoons from grazing on the herbs downstairs. Folks gasped and stepped back, many on the toes of the people behind them, which produced more yelps.

Go into the cages, dear beasts. Let's give them a show of obedience before the mutiny.

I uttered fake chants such as, "Stream forth! Congregate in the cage. Obey!"

The rats came down on all four legs and skittered inside. The audience went wild as soon as I closed the door.

"You see how powerful my tonic is!" said Dowdrick triumphantly. "Even a young lady with no expertise can control the vermin with her commands."

"But how does the elixir work?" called a man with spectacles I recognized as Dr. Toby.

"What are the active ingredients?" asked a medical student.

"No secrets exposed here. Not yet," Dowdrick said.

Secrets, bah! I am the secret!

"Can she kill them, too?" asked another doctor a touch too gleefully.

"I shall not kill them," I announced firmly. "I am squeamish." I opened the door to screams and people jumping in panic as the rats fled every which way to their dens.

"Such control she has with the tonic!" exclaimed a woman I recognized as Dolly Rouge.

"Impossible!" yelled none other than Birdy, who had worked his way to the front. "I don't believe it. What is her treachery?"

"No, treachery!" claimed Dowdrick, a dark grin spreading on his face. "No tricks at all. In fact, since you are such a doubting Thomas, why not step up and have a go at it? Come, join me at the podium." Dowdrick waved Birdy to the front.

With the two men side by side, there was a clear contrast between Birdy's assured manner and Dowdrick's deceitful, darting ways. But this was no time for leisurely thought, for I was sure Lewin was trapped downstairs, and who knew how dire his condition was. I gathered my flagging energy and focused it to help Birdy's performance. This would be the end of all fakery if I could help it.

Dowdrick had Birdy swallow a large dose. Birdy did a star actor's work of raising his arms and shaking them, rolling his eyes back and chanting, "Come forth, vermin! Enter the cages. They are so very enticing!"

It took mammoth strength for me to coax the beasts out, for they had already performed once. Their reluctance was clear in weary tremors that traveled from my feet to my spine.

We're tired, they said, *we're hungry.*

Dearest beasts, I know your pain. This cause is worthy. I will feed you soon!

As I strained to convince them, one by one, they ventured out. Whiskers quivering, they glanced my way. They seemed to be wondering what in the world I wanted with them a second time that I hadn't gotten the first time. Yet more crept from the corners, the chinks, the open knots in the floorboards until there were almost forty strong. Gruff creatures with sharp, crooked teeth. I lured them toward the cages.

This time the crowd was spellbound. Not a sound was heard but the scrabbling.

Dowdrick stood by the podium, self-satisfied, leaning on his walking stick.

Birdy's jaw was slack from shock. He must have been harboring one last drop of doubt in my ability until this moment. We exchanged a look of solidarity.

Dowdrick broke the silence. "So, you see, even the Doubting Thomas can be a conduit for the Monster Mesmer elixir and send the pests to their death."

Birdy glanced at me to determine my mind. I narrowed my eyes, which were glazing over, and drew my last strength.

Circle the man who smells of rancid oil. Run around him as if you are a living rope. Run fast, my wild beasts, so fast he cannot catch you or beat you with his metal stick. Keep on running. We must trap the bad man, but do not bite.

The furry horde changed direction so rapidly their pink tails switched in unison. They circled Dr. Dowdrick, who made desperate attempts shoo them away from his leather shoes. The rats were far too fast. A whirring gray carousel! The audience erupted in cries of astonishment as the doctor yelled, "Go! Leave me be!"

"Look, they're so fast they're only a blur!" someone exclaimed.

Other creatures emerged in droves: ants so thick the floor looked black, buzzing flies and even a grasshopper that came hopping from heaven knew where. Outside, the neighs of the carriage horses sounded like a chorus of dying cows.

"Off! Away!" Dowdrick screeched, holding his arms high so they wouldn't bite them.

I took this moment to mount the podium. Doctors turned toward me. Who was this girl? A mere volunteer who was now daring to speak! "I must make an important announcement," I called. "Quiet, please!" Now all eyes were on me. "This doctor is a fraud!" I yelled and pointed to Dowdrick, still fending off rats that now tugged at his boots.

"What are you saying?" asked one of the doctors.

"Don't listen to her. She's lying!" Dowdrick exclaimed. "Help me!"

"Drink your own snake oil, you sham!" I screamed. "See how far it gets you."

"Dowdrick," shouted Dr. Toby, "you said this tonic provided control over the vermin yet they are in utter chaos."

Someone else yelled, "Even the horses outside are rampaging!" The audience rumbled in agreement.

Birdy joined me at the podium. "This crook Dowdrick knows nothing about pest control," he insisted loudly.

"He only knows he wants your money," I added to the growing uproar of the shocked audience. Then I cocked my head in the direction of the cellar to hint that Birdy needed to try and crack the padlock. He ran off straightaway. I stared at the doctors, their students, at Dolly too. "You see, the power to lure the beasts is all in me. *I* am the one sending them."

"Impossible!" and "You're joking," and "I knew this was fishy," the crowd exclaimed all at once.

"It is all in *you*, but how? What exactly are you saying, Miss Fallon?" Dr. Mutter had stepped to the front and was staring intently at me, the rats, at Dowdrick, and back at me.

"I'm saying that *I* am the medium! I am the person who

reads the minds and hearts of these wild beasts. Meanwhile, this tonic?" I held up the opened bottle. "It's cheap whiskey and carbonated water. It will never make you a Pied Piper, though it might make you a drunkard. Try some for yourselves!"

"Poppycock!" yelled a doctor from the back of the crowded room. "You are no animal mesmerizer! That is the stuff of fantasy books."

"Is this not proof enough?" I pointed to the cycling rats, the haze of zigzagging ants. "*I* did this. And if you're not careful I will send them your way!"

"I believe in animal mesmerism," said Gunter Hohlstein, the Powwow doctor, glaring at the naysayer in back.

By this point, a few daring souls had stepped up to seize Dowdrick's Monster Mesmer and try it for themselves. "Rotgut whiskey," one determined. Another man was trying to lure one of the rats to another location with a cookie. Of course, the rats kept running around Dowdrick's ankles.

Dowdrick roared, "Miss Stowe, if you hold the power then stop this nonsense! Tell these vermin to cease their running and return to their dens."

"For you?" I shook my head. "Not a chance!" I addressed the audience. "Fakery is not the only thing this man is guilty of."

"What else has he done?" asked a medical student, plainly enjoying the drama.

"Yeah, what?" The audience crowed.

"This man is guilty of abducting prisoners from Eastern State," I said. "He hauls them to his lab to endure dangerous medical experimentation."

The audience went wild. "What?" "Live prisoners?" "That's against the law!" ""Why, it's inhumane! Even criminals deserve a modicum of decency."

"Lies!" screeched Dowdrick over the clamor, his face blood red. "She's an absolute lunatic!" He clamped his feet together so the rodents wouldn't totally destroy his good boots in their frantic running. "Seize her!" he yelled to no one in particular. His unwilling servant, Dr. Sumac was nowhere to be seen. And there were no police, nor night watchmen keeping order.

I needed to prove my point. Finish this off. My life force was fading. If I expired my beasts would rebel, rampage. Lewin was trapped downstairs. "Dolly... I mean Nurse Rogers, please step to the podium," I yelled.

"Gladly." She trounced proudly to the front, her fancy red skirt swinging.

Dowdrick howled. "Someone stop these hussies!"

"This crook performed risky surgery on us without our permission. Show them, Dolly."

"Dolly?" exclaimed the ginger-haired Dr. Edwin Fussell. "She said her name was Susan Rogers."

Dolly gave Dr. Fussell a coy grin. "I made up the name. Who knew what type of forward man I would meet at this symposium? A girl's got to protect herself, don't she?" Shamelessly, she pulled her sleeves to her armpits to show the ragged scars. The crowd gasped.

"That's what this vile man did to me." She pointed accusingly to Dowdrick. "What's more, he gave me a barrelful of that Peruvian powder. I lost my memory for over a week!" She gave Dowdrick a glare that could peel paint off a wall.

"He did that?" Dr. Fussell gasped. "What a demented monster!"

"I was also operated on against my will by this rapscallion." I turned my back to the audience and lifted my skirt to just above my knees. The sight of my exposed skin along with the knotty scars down my calves made the audience roar in shock. "Dowdrick dosed me with the same poison powder. I woke up, shackled in one of his holding cells. The same padlocked chambers he holds another victim in right now!" Gasps turned to shouts of outrage.

"Who? Are you certain?" yelled a student.

"Where are they?" boomed another.

I sensed the rats reaching the end of their tether. I was also beyond weary with a dizzying return of my sickness. My knees wobbled, my eyes blurred and my lungs burned. This dark pageantry must soon end, or I would faint dead away.

Just then, there was a riotous flurry of activity in the other room—a slamming of doors, hammering footsteps, shouts and frenzied objections.

"Where is Miss Stowe?" asked a woman whose voice sounded quite familiar.

"In there," one of the maids said in a quivery voice.

"She and her army of Quakers made me drive her here," a gravelled voice complained.

Blackbeard and Amity. By God, Amity has come!

"Amity, I'm in here!" I called.

"Madness!" Dowdrick was saying. "Evalina Stowe is a hardened criminal from the Eastern State Penitentiary. She was in on the whole con. She was accused of witchcraft. You can plainly see she's put a hex on these vermin that plague me. Someone with a firearm please shoot these devil's familiars!"

"Hear, hear!" yelled the stout man with the white moustache, reaching for something in his waistcoat.

"Don't you dare, you French-poxed whapper!" shouted Dolly as she batted down his arm.

Blackbeard, who had sidled up to Dolly, erupted in raucous laughter. "You tell him, wench!" he crowed.

Dr. Mutter stepped forward. He raised his arms wide. "No guns will go off in this crowd," he ordered as he formed a human blockade between Dowdrick and the audience. "No one will take any frightful actions until this is sorted out! Doctor's orders!"

"I second that." Dr. Toby stepped up to join Dr. Mutter.

Waves of terrified laughter burst from the crowd, who had probably not seen such life and death theater, even in the surgical wards.

By this time, Amity had found me and rushed over. It was huge relief. "No harm shall come to this woman," she insisted, seeing White Moustache again aim his pistol at the swirl of rats, and who knew what would be next in his crosshairs. "I said no harm!" she yelled so fiercely I was stunned. Cowed, White Moustache lowered his firearm.

Two men had run over and were flanking her. Both wore the wide brimmed black hats, the suspendered black trousers and beards of the Plain people. "Stay put. No violence. The police have been summoned and are at the door," warned one.

Birdy tore in. The police as well, looking bewildered and a bit frightened when they saw the circling rodents, the mad skitter of insects.

"Cuff that man!" Thomas Mutter said, pointing to Dr. Dowdrick.

Wild beasts scatter! Thanks for your help. Now you shall rest. Treats soon!

This was the last message I sent, for my legs buckled and I began to sink down. My Birdy noticed, and grabbed my arm. He held me by his side as we watched the rats and insects swarm away. The policeman cuffed Dowdrick despite his angry protests and orders to seize 'the two vile women convicts'.

Abruptly, a deafening explosion rocked the building. Bottles of Monster Mesmer toppled to the floor and smashed.

"What the devil?" Dr. McClellan exclaimed. He and others rushed to the parlor.

"A boy is in the cellar," I rasped. "He's being held prisoner."

"Over here! This door! I blew the lock off sir," Birdy explained as the policeman chained Dowdrick to a table and dashed toward the parlor, followed by dozens of doctors and spectators.

As we trundled down the narrow basement stairs the anguished cries of little Lewin rang out. "Help! Someone!"

His voice snapped me back to life. "We're coming to let you out!" I cried.

"Hang on!" Birdy called.

The basement reeked of mold, fetid water and swamp weeds. As I walked, I dropped crumbs for the beasts from the rolls I'd slipped in my pocket during the luncheon.

At the sight of Lewin slouched over tears sprang to my eyes. For as Lightning, he was ever the defiant rebel. He had given me strength when I was living on the streets. Now it was my turn to give it back. When the policeman turned the lock with a skeleton key Lewin limped out and clung to me for dear life.

"I tried to help you, Eva," he cried. "I tried but the sawbones catched me one night by the stable. He beat me bloody."

"Shh, it's all right now." I stroked Lewin's matted hair, which had turned from blond to brown it was so soiled.

"My Lord! Over here!" someone was yelling. I looked up

to see none other than Dr. Sumac in a barred chamber ten paces from the first, slumped over as if dead with froth bubbling from his mouth.

"Oh, no!" I exclaimed. It dawned on me: the citrus scented fabric the mouse had dropped earlier was from Sumac's waistcoat.

"It's the Peruvian doctor with the wondrous powder!" someone shouted.

"The poor man. Is he still alive?" asked Dr. Toby.

"His product made Dowdrick mad with jealousy," Dolly chided.

"Good Heavens!" Mutter exclaimed. "So that's where Dr. Sumac disappeared to. Not exactly a family emergency. Is there a pulse?"

"Stand back," the policeman warned the horrified crowd.

Sumac had dark red handprints around his neck. It brought me back to the ghastly day that my brother lost his life at Dowdrick's hands. "He strangled him!" I screeched. "Just like he strangled my brother Todd to death! Dr. Dowdrick is a murderer! A murderer, I tell you!"

After this, I cannot recall every moment, for I was in a fog, passing in and out of clarity. I remember Birdy taking charge and holding me up so I would not fall. I remember the doctors crowding into the cell, taking out their stethoscopes and listening intently to Sumac's heart. I recall them nodding, and I thanked our lucky stars they did not have to cover his face with a sheet. For Sumac might be a villain, but he was a warmhearted one.

I recall Amity's sweet voice saying, "Thee will be healed soon. Do not despair, brave Evalina. Thee does not deserve punishment for being led to do noble work. My husband,

John has found thee and thy friends a public defender. A date will be set. Thee needs only rest now."

The last thing I remember of the night is Blackbeard loading me in the carriage with Birdy, Dolly, Amity, her husband, the other Quaker man and little Lewin. Lewin sat on one side of me, clinging to my hand. Birdy sat on the other, pressed up close and comforting.

With these good folk—my tribe—I had renewed hope I would survive any difficult days ahead.

21

Like other early spring mornings, I woke to the peach-pink sun streaming in the skylight. Yet this day was as different as night to day from the ones that passed before.

For everything *had* shifted on its axis.

Dowdrick was in prison awaiting trial. I had done that with the help of my friends and my beasts. For this I would ever be grateful, no matter if I spent the rest of my days in Cherry Hill.

Fast Step slid my breakfast in through the mailbox-sized opening in the door and the mice that slept by my side scattered. The trencher contained porridge, a mealy apple and lukewarm tea. It tasted like manna. I was still chewing the last bite of apple when slower footsteps approached.

Blackbeard rapped on my door, yelling, "The famous witch has a visitor! Make haste. Back against the wall."

"Why don't *I* have a visitor?" Dolly thundered from her cell.

"Hold your darn horses, wench. You'll have old Whiskers a visiting you in a bit."

"Huh!" she huffed, but calmed down.

I hurried to the back wall and plastered myself against it as the door opened. I nearly fainted when I saw who it was.

"Dr. Thomas Mutter," the man said as he adjusted his perfectly folded pink cravat. "Do you remember me, Miss Stowe?"

"Why of course! I could never forget you!" I studied his impeccable ocean blue suit that fit like a second skin over his wiry frame, his pocket square that matched his cravat and his gold pocket-watch that sat gleaming on a chain atop his vest with feather patterns. Mutter, like Dowdrick was a complete dandy. Yet, he was day to Dowdrick's night. "I am honored you thought to pay me a visit," I said when I remembered my words.

Mutter gestured to the chair. "Come. Sit, Miss Stowe. No skulking against the wall. I have a business proposition for you."

My heart began a fierce and relentless hammering. "Whatever do you mean?"

"The Quaker matron, Amity Wistar filled me in on your true story. I know you are not Nurse Fallon. You are prisoner number 113." Mirthful twinkles played in his blue eyes.

Wistar. Amity's surname! "I'm so sorry I pretended to be a nurse. I've embarrassed myself."

"I told you, Eva. Never say sorry!" Dolly bellowed from her cell.

"This lady is right." Mutter chuckled. "Yours was an ingenious plan! How else with your confinement were you to defeat a dangerous villain?"

"Well... yes. It was the only way I could think of."

"Dowdrick is in prison, as is Dr. Sumac, though the doctor from Peru is not in for murder. They are questioning him, as a corroborating witness to Dowdrick's crimes. After that, they will send the man back to his home country."

"So the police believed me when I said Dowdrick murdered my brother, Todd? But why?"

"Lewin Derr. The boy claims he saw it through the tailor's window. He also relayed instances where the doctor beat innocent children. And kicked his own mother."

"Oh, my God!" My hands shot up to my mouth, and tears slid down my cheeks. "No child should have had to witness all of that. Is Lewin all right?"

"Yes. He has rested and eaten. He asked about you." Mutter cracked his neck and readjusted his cravat with the artful fingers of a surgeon who sewed up tiny veins, rearranged faces. "At any rate, you described a man with deformed feet. I would happily perform surgery on your friend in one of my plastic operations, if you might consider working for me to pay it off. I am rather fascinated by your assertion of being an animal sensitive. I relish the study of medical anomalies."

I gasped. "I am in prison behind bars. I cannot. Your offer is too—"

"Take the blasted offer!" Dolly called through the wall. "No questions asked!"

Mutter laughed. His laughter was refreshing, like the burbling Wissahickon creek. "We will work on getting you out of here. I believe Mrs. Wistar has already started the process."

"But how?" I gaped at him forgoing my manners entirely.

"I will leave that to Mrs. Wistar. She should be here presently." He stood and straightened his waistcoat. "What is the man's name who requires foot surgery and where might I find him?"

"He is prisoner number 407." Mutter did not even flinch that it was another convict so I went on. "He was at the

Discovery Symposium posing as Dr. Bertram Davies. His real name is Bertram Castell, or Birdy for short. His feet were terribly injured while setting off a charge to blast rocks for the Reading Railroad."

"Ah, carving out the Philadelphia granite to build the railway, quite a worthy cause. What a boon it will be to travel out to the country and all along the coast."

"True. I'm afraid though, that the explosion killed a fellow worker. Birdy was horrified by it."

Mutter shook his head. "Calamities befall men at random. Life must go on."

Mutter was so humane that his warmth radiated out to the whole chamber. "Birdy is a fortunate man," I remarked. "And of course, I would be incredibly honored to work with you if I ever get out of here."

"Wonderful. I trust you will. Mrs. Wistar's determination impressed me greatly when we spoke." He leapt up, reminding me again of a nimble rabbit or squirrel. "I must go speak with your Birdy." He shook my hand. After a rapping on the door to indicate he was ready, the guard showed him out. I was left sitting at the table, stunned by the turn of events.

"Eva, oh, Eva!" Dolly trilled.

"Yes, Dolly?"

"Seems we are both graced by Lady Luck today."

"How's that?"

"Do you recall Dr. Edwin Fussell?"

"The one with the red hair at the Discovery Symposium."

"Precisely. Well, I just got a special piece of mail from him. Dr. Fussell offered me a scholarship to his new female medical school. I'm pushing forty but it's never too late to reinvent yourself, is it!"

"Of course not! Oh, Dolly, that's wonderful!"

She chuckled. "As you may recall from my colorful deck of calling cards, I had other offers but his was the best. No more Madam Rouge, bawdyhouse proprietor. Now it will be Nurse Rouge!"

"Congratulations, Dolly! I guess our playacting got us both new roles."

"We are formidable, Eva! Now Dolly just needs to be freed from this hellhole."

"You will, Dolly, you will." It wasn't exactly fact. But today it seemed anything was possible.

Only a short while later, Amity came calling. I jumped to the back wall and pressed tightly to it. For once, Blackbeard did not announce her arrival with a sarcastic joke. She looked prettier than usual as she wore a bonnet adorned with gray ruffles. She wasn't alone.

"Thee might recall my husband, John Wistar from the other day at the symposium," said Amity. "And here is Mr. Nat Emlen, one of Philadelphia's few and best Quaker attorneys." I shook their hands. Amity's husband, John was a handsome man with auburn beard and curls. The portly lawyer, Emlen had jowls like a Bassett Hound and wore wire spectacles. Under them sat an impressive set of crow's feet, which crinkled when he smiled.

The men perched like great birds on the table edge. They discussed my case, and a little about the ones for Birdy, Dolly and Samuel Barton. We would all appear in civil court in three week's time and Mr. Emlen would labor to get our sentences commuted. This way, we could avoid a brutal trial. He said we had a good chance, seeing as we helped catch a swindler who preyed on vulnerable patients. Moreover because the doctor had murdered my brother and Lewin had witnessed it, even if the boy was a petty thief, with his word slightly sullied. Dowdrick had tried to murder Condor Sumac as well, thus attempted murder was added to the line of argument. Mr. Emlen asked if I had any character witnesses besides Amity. I thought long and hard.

"Sir, my parents have departed this earthly plane and my brother as well. But I did have one friend at Somerset Farm who may vouch for my innocence. Her name is Betsy Ainsley. She is a Scottish girl who worked flushing out birds as I did."

"Good, good." Mr. Emlen jotted this in his leather journal.

When we had reached the end of our legal planning, the two Quaker men left so Amity and I could have a moment together. I was so grateful for what she was doing for me I did not know what to say. At first, we stared at each other from across the table. Then, my words came pouring out.

"How can I ever thank you? I never thought anyone could care the way you have for me."

She smiled and looked down, ever modest. "I could not do anything else, for I was led to it, dearest Evalina. When I read thy note, it broke my heart to know what thee was led to do, the perilous path thee would take for justice. Thou are so courageous, Evalina. I'm sorry I doubted thee."

"Doubted me?"

"I worried thee were a witch. When I first began visiting thy cell. I was filled with fear. I worried thee would put a hex on me."

"Why did you keep on visiting me then?"

She shook her head and as she did two tears fell on the

table. "I wanted to fight my own darkness, I suppose. My own dread of evil."

"I don't know exactly what a witch is," I admitted. "Yet I know that whatever they—we—are, they are not all bad. Like poor Maule, accused and hung in the *House of the Seven Gables* so a greedy old man could seize land that wasn't his."

Amity brushed away more tears. "Perhaps the Salem witches were no more than wise women wrongly accused. The early women healers who cured using plants, the midwives who in delivering babies, came across one or two that the lord would have carried up to his heavenly kingdom anyway. But the parents, in their grief, wanted to blame someone for the infant's death. So the woman—the witch was accused of murder."

"I misjudged you too, Amity."

"How so?" She looked up.

"When you first came to visit I thought…" I was trembling. I wrung my hands.

"Go on," she said softly. "I will not judge."

"Well, I suspected you were eager to scold and condemn me; force me to memorize bible verses for no more reason than to punish."

Amity lowered her head again. "Does thee still see me this way?"

"No. I started to see things differently when you taught me the mustard seed prayer. It hit me like dynamite."

She laughed and looked up. "Hopefully, not as punishing as dynamite."

I closed my eyes as I recited the parable. "Again he said, 'What shall we say the kingdom of God is like, or what parable shall we use to describe it? It is like a mustard seed, which is the smallest of all seeds on earth. Yet when planted, it grows and becomes the largest of all garden plants, with such big branches that the birds can perch in its shade.'

It's beautiful," I said, opening my eyes, "but more than beautiful, it is *true*. 'Therefore, Bring forth fruit worthy of penance,'" I finished. "It is my greatest hope, aside from gathering a family and keeping them close. You helped me see this. Thank you, Amity." I was quiet for a moment, mustering courage. "I longed to be friends with you, but we came from such different worlds... yet now? I feel we could be."

"We are, dear friend, we *are*." She rose and we hugged. It was sweeter than the time she stroked my fevered head, for I believed that if and when I got out of prison, we truly could be equals. Our friendship was hard-won but genuine. I felt it as fervently as the beating hearts of beasts.

"Soon," she whispered. "Soon thee shall be freed." Then she called for the guard and left.

We went to the yard once more before our court date. It was a splendid April morn with a breeze that carried the tang of unfurling leaf buds from the lanes outside the prison. We got to plant seedlings, which brought me back to when Birdy and I first met. My heart pattered with excitement, for I had not seen him since the symposium, though Amity and I had discussed his case.

They lined us up along the planters as before, and told us we could remove our hoods. I suppose Mr. Dicken's treatise on the dangers of solitary confinement had made a big impact. Or perhaps they knew we all needed sun to brown our ashen winter faces. Whatever the reason, it was lovely to look down the row and see my fellow prisoners. Dolly's hair had grown grayer but the ends still shone red and her eyes shone most of all. She was looking over at Blackbeard, who was winking at her. Lewin looked ever the spunky boy he had before his time in Dowdrick's jail for even though he had washed his hair and scrubbed his face, he still wore his rebellious grin. I gave him a sneaky wave back. Sammy, bless his heart, held himself tall and distinguished. I worried that the prejudice against Negroes would keep Sammy here in jail, but I had to keep holding him in the light, as Amity had taught me.

The best I saved for last: gazing across the planter into Birdy's handsome face. To see him looking back at me with adoration sped up my breath.

Birdy mouthed the words *Fair Eva.*

I mouthed the words *My Birdy.*

And then we set to planting. This time taking a blunt trowel and chopping up the hardened peat, making it supple to welcome and nourish new roots as if tucking a small child into bed. The crescents of my fingernails darkened, and my limbs lost their kinks in the effort of honest labor. It was bliss to see Birdy's long fingers work the soil across from me. I imagined those fingers entwined in mine, us walking out in freedom, together. Imagining it was almost as good as the real thing.

Almost.

"Soon, Eva," Birdy whispered as he leaned in to straighten a plant. "When we get out, will you be my bride? I love you. Marry me, fair Eva."

Had I heard him right? I stared into his caring gray eyes and knew I had. My heart swelled with such sweet happiness.

"Yes. A hundred times yes."

22

The morning I got out of Cherry Hill to attend court Amity brought me a clean black dress with gleaming black buttons down the front. I had washed my long hair and plaited it, so as to look properly serious. She brought me nice leather boots as well. I owed her and now the debt was raised. The only thing marring my appearance were the handcuffs, which I 'd grown accustomed to. Yet out on the public streets where shopkeepers and professional people walked, the cuffs felt shameful.

Happening on my reflection in a shop window as we walked down Chestnut Street toward Courthouse Square I gasped. I was older and thinner with a haunted look as if I'd lived with ghosts. Amity waited while I paused to stare. Upon closer reflection, I decided I looked wiser, with a new patience and calm in my eyes.

Birdy, Dolly, Lewin and Sammy met us with their own guards in tow. I suppose we could not be trusted to travel to the hearings together. Birdy wore the same suit as when he pretended to be Dr. Bertram Davies. Lewin looked very grownup in a tan suit and his blond hair combed neatly back. Dolly had piled her hair again in a tasteful bun, and this time she wore a respectable navy dress, which hid her ample bosom. Sammy seemed distant, pensive. Perhaps because he knew that the scales of justice were not tipped as favorably toward Negroes, even in this city of Brotherly Love.

I gathered my nerve to say, "Best of luck, Samuel. If anyone can help, Amity and her Quaker lawyer can." He nodded, but stayed silent, out of public propriety.

I longed to speak more with my friends but we were here for vital reasons. Our guardians led us inside.

The building had elegant marble staircases, carved balustrades and ceilings soaring skyward with domed windows, streaming in light. When we reached the second floor, we were ushered into a room filled with wooden benches and men in black waistcoats milling about. Amity's lawyer, Mr. Emlen began to whisper to another gentleman. One by one, Mr. Emlen brought us up in front where an imposing man with a snowy white beard and flowing black gown sat behind a raised desk.

When it was my turn, I tried to be brave but with so much at stake I was petrified. From the corner of my eye I saw Betsy Ainsley approach the bench. I was shocked that Mr. Emlen had found her, and she was willing to be here. She held herself stiffly and her eyes were wide. I felt badly for her.

The judge asked for my name and if I knew what I was in prison for. I told him I knew it was for witchcraft.

"Did you kill a Mr. Gaul, who owned Somerset Farms in Kensington?"

"No, I did not, your honor."

"How did he die?"

"A bird flew down his throat."

"A bird you owned?"

"No one owns the wild beasts of the field, your honor."

At this, he hiked up his wire spectacles and jotted something down. Had I said the wrong thing? I had uttered the truth, as Amity had told me to do.

The judge then addressed my old friend. "Your name and profession?"

"Betsy Ainsley, your honor," she said in a pinched voice. "I work as a Bird Girl at Somerset."

"Ah, who runs the farm now that Mr. Gaul has passed on?"

"His son, Galen, your honor."

The judge wrote down something else. "What can you tell the court about Miss Evalina Stowe during the time she worked at Somerset Farms?"

"She was a nice girl. She loved the animals and did not like to harm them. She never hit the cornstalks hard for fear she would kill a bird."

"Wasn't that her job?" he asked. "Wasn't it expected that birds would be hit?"

"I suppose sir. But Evalina could not harm a flea."

"What about a man? A man she did not like?" The judge studied Betsy intently through his thick glasses.

"No sir. She would not raise a hand to a person either. Evalina had a heart warm as pie. She cared for everyone and never said a nasty word. Even when Mr. Gaul beat her."

"Beat her?"

"Yes, your honor. Beat her merciless with his metal stick."

The judge wrote more notes. As he did, Betsy snuck a peek at me, and gave me a smile. I smiled back, grateful for her testimony.

Amity was called next as a character witness. She

explained how she taught me bible verse and parables, and that I was always willing to learn. She said I was a devoted gardener, worked hard in the yard and that I had never broken the rules other than to expose the extreme villainy of the doctor. "This doctor not only swindled many but he murdered Evalina's brother."

The judge nodded without expression. He jotted down more in his book. I thought of the note I had saved from Dowdrick and wished I hadn't forgotten it. At least this wasn't a trial with opposing arguments. In this, we were lucky.

The judge then called up Lewin, who vouched for Todd's murder, in fact seemed to relish explaining. "Through the window, I saw the no-good lay his hands around my friend, Todd Stowe. The nasty sawbones squeezed and squeezed until the life left Todd. Sorry, Miss Eva," Lewin added at seeing my tears.

"That will be all. Take your seats," the judge said, still pokerfaced.

I watched Birdy and Sammy and Dolly all take the bench, accompanied by the tireless Mr. Emlen. We watched as the lawyers conferred with the black-robed judge. A few arguments broke out but the men quieted down too quickly to eavesdrop.

It took four hours and by the end of it I had bitten all ten fingernails to the quick, twisted each side of my hair from their plaits and gnawed my bottom lip bloody.

One by one, the judge called us back to the bench. Dolly was free in two week's time with the understanding that she would never again slip into to her bawdyhouse ways, and would immediately enroll in Dr. Edwin Fussell's new Female Medical College. She released a triumphant holler, which the judge scolded her for. But I secretly think she charmed him, for that was her way.

Birdy's sentence was commuted as of two week's time, as was Lewin's with the understanding that Amity and her Quakers would find them temporary homes.

Sammy was not as lucky. He was serving his time for murder, and though there was no direct evidence the judge did not set him free. "Your sentence will be reduced to serve one more year, Mr. Burton," he announced. At least he lopped off two years.

"Thank you, your honor," Sammy said with a nod. My heart sank for this polite, brave soul, and I wondered how much harder my life would have been if I were simply guilty of being born with brown skin?

I was called up last. The judge regarded me through his spectacles. "Mr. Emlen tells me that you have been hired as a personal assistant to Dr. Thomas Mutter over the Jefferson Medical School. Is this true?"

"Yes, your honor." My heart beat so forcefully that blood pounded hither and thither between my ears.

"Well then, your sentence is commuted as of two week's from now if you agree to let Mrs. Wistar find you temporary lodging."

"Yes! Thank you, your honor."

The judge did not smile. He only nodded, closed his journal and readjusted his glasses. I felt sorry for him. Clearly, it was forbidden for judges to show human emotion. Luckily I did not have that constraint, for I burst into tears of pure joy.

23

Two Years Later

Five months after our freedom was granted, Birdy and I were married in a Quaker ceremony at the Arch Street Meetinghouse. To prepare, Amity and I gathered daisies and lilac sprigs to decorate the normally plain, but sun-filled chamber. I wore a beige gown trimmed with lace that a lovely friend of Amity's had sewn. Birdy walked evenly and proudly down the aisle, for my employer, Dr. Mutter had performed his plastic operation on Birdy's damaged feet, and restored them so well there was only the mere trace of a limp.

Dolly Rouge enrolled in medical school and married the old prison guard, Blackbeard. They came to the wedding and at first I didn't recognize him. He had trimmed a good thirty pounds off his belly, and his beard was neatly shaved to a gentleman's goatee and sideburns. I knew that Blackbeard had a wry sense of humor, but finally, I could see what Dolly was so enamored of on the outside as well. Dolly sparkled, too. Her hair was hennaed red, with nary a gray root showing. She wore it pinned up, as she had at the symposium, and her dress was a forest green that set off her flaming hair. We hugged and hugged, and she relayed barrelsful of naughty gossip about the professors and women at the school.

I promised her my lips were sealed.

Sammy Barton could not make the wedding but for good reason. He was released from Cherry Hill a year prior and Amity's network of Friends had ferried him up Boston way. Word was, he opened up a barbershop and married a women he met while strolling in Boston Commons. Birdy and I were over the moon for him.

And little Lewin, yes, he was there. But for Lewin, I shall skip to the end.

Late on Friday afternoon was a favorite time because Birdy and I got off work early, and it was our way to stroll together through the labyrinth of cobblestoned streets, watching and listening to the lively chatter of people, large and small, young and old. I never tired of it, especially after my extreme prison confinement.

Birdy and I collected Lewin from his new employ, Independence Stables on North Third Street, a hop, skip and a jump from the Friends Meetinghouse. John Wistar housed his horses here, as did many of the prominent local politicians.

Lewin was proud he had started at the bottom, shoveling pile after pile of manure, and working his way up to stable boy and then finally to shoeing and handling the saddles.

He ran out to greet us, blond hair flying. "I got me a fat

raise!" he exclaimed, digging in his pockets and hauling out fistfuls of coins.

"Very nice, young man," Birdy said and clapped him on the back.

"Are we going to Market Street?" asked Lewin.

"Yes," I said, mussing his hair. "I am proud of you too!"

"Thank you," he said, and dashed off ahead of us.

Birdy and I held hands. I never tired of that either. We turned up Market Street, where the circuslike profusion of awnings dazzled. The stout girl and her stick thin sister who Dr. Sumac had hired as maids on that fateful day now owned the vegetable stall their mother had run.

Lewin rejoined us. We picked out four potatoes, a handful of carrots, and a pretty red onion. Next, we stopped at the fruit-seller. Birdy loved apples, I loved grapes and Lewin liked peaches. We added those to our bag. After that Lewin ran ahead again.

We strode by a vendor of fish, and a vendor calling out "fresh chocolates by the dozen!" There was a woman selling men's bowler hats and scarves, and one selling leather belts.

"Where is our little lightening bolt?" Birdy joked. At seeing a streak of his flaxen hair through the crowd, we hastened our pace.

Lewin was at the flower stall, where we seldom went for we considered it a luxury. He was counting out his coins very intently and placing them in the flower girl's opened palm.

"Lewin, whatever are you up to?" I asked.

He grinned from ear to ear and held out the bouquet of phlox that the flower girl had just wrapped in wax paper. "For you, Mama and Papa! On account of I got me a pay raise. I'll never have to swipe food from the vendors again. Never!"

He thrust them in my hands. I leaned over and hugged him. Birdy took Lewin on his shoulders and pretended to gallop. Lewin might be almost nine, but he was still a boy and loved horse rides from his father.

I have gathered my family.

Singing songs like 'Row, Row, Row Your Boat' and 'Jeannie with the Light Brown Hair' we walked up Market, turned right at North Fourth and finally took a last right turn onto Cherry Street, all the way to our narrow house with red shutters. How fateful it was that I had been locked in a cell at the Cherry Hill prison, and now I was free on little Cherry Street. Our humble house had two doors: one on the right for Birdy's blacksmith shop, and one on the left for my business. We lived above.

My work with the eccentric Dr. Mutter had been inspiring. I got to examine and label many oddities for his growing menagerie: bone malformations, brains of every stripe in jars of alcohol, wax molds of eye diseases, two-headed piglet embryos and the like. He got to examine me and how I was able to speak without words to the creatures in his lab: his cats, his ornery Boxer, and a horde of mice he wasn't even aware he had.

Thomas Mutter and I formed a great friendship. After a year, he recognized my need to strike out on my own and offered to set me up in a business. Of course, I gratefully accepted the offer. Thus, *Evalina's Pet Parlor* was borne. I sold kittens, puppies and parrots but I also helped to figure out why someone's dog could not sleep or eat, or locate a lost pet. To help people see beasts as companions of the earth rather than enemies, this was the unique fruit I brought forth from that single mustard seed.

As Birdy turned the lock, I said, "There is one more surprise for us today."

"What is it? What is it?" Lewin asked, leaping up and down.

Birdy gave me a quizzical look.

"I have made enough money from my store to get a puppy for us! I have a mind to name him Charles Dickens, for it was because of his treatise against solitary confinement that we were able to spend time together at all. What do you think?"

"Charles Dickens." Birdy laughed. "Yes! Sir Charlie."

"A puppy, for us? Where is Sir Charlie?" Lewin screeched.

I ducked into my shop and came out with a wriggling, jiggling beagle that leapt upon Lewin and licked him all over.

While Lewin knelt down to hug the pup, Birdy swept me up in a kiss.

So warm and sweet; like light beaming down through the old skylight.

I remembered lines from my last poem in Cherry Hill.

Winter shall pass into spring.

With it, the blossoms shall open to the sun.

***

If you enjoyed this novel, try Catherine's historical fantasy, Witch of the Cards, set in 1932. An excerpt follows:

Witch of the Cards
Fiera ✪ 1

This was my first time walking the beachfront strip at nightfall. Before this, I'd stuck to the wicker rockers on the porch of the Asbury Park Hotel, where rich, respectable ladies and their paramours lounged. I had neither—the respectability of a large purse or a paramour. At least I'd made a new friend. Dulcie and

I had chatted the first two mornings on the porch as we sipped sweet tea and ate blessedly free hotel crumpets. That was when I found out she was rooming across the hall from me.

Now, strolling on the boardwalk past a line of bright stores with twinkling lights, we paused in front of Peter Dune's Tarot and Séance. A sign in the window with showy, curlicue headlines gleamed golden in the moonlight.

"Look, Dulcie!" I pointed to it. "Fortuitous timing. This shop owner's celebrating his first month in business by conducting a table reading. Let's go in."

She screwed up her heart-shaped face. "You sure, Ivy? Don't card readings scare you?"

I linked my arm in hers and gamely tugged on it. "They might. But it's vacation time. Let's have an adventure."

"I suppose." She gave an uncertain nod.

"We'll have so much fun!" I exclaimed, my heart pumping faster. I adjusted my little summer hat with its leaves brushing over my right cheekbone. I'd made it out of felt and feathers from a penny sales bin on the Lower East Side, but no one needed to know.

The summer of 1932 was a frightening time. Bread lines in Manhattan snaked around for blocks, and some folks even camped out right in the parks. I was lucky. I had a job as a nanny, but I kept a strict watch on my purse. These days, one never knew how long her job would last. "Do I look all right?"

"More than all right," Dulcie said. "Your bob is glamorous, especially with the hat." She sighed and checked her own image in the plate glass. "How about me?"

"You look pretty, like the bee's knees," I reassured her as she smoothed her white-blonde hair over her expensive pink dress with its sailor's collar.

I adjusted my sparkly earrings—cast-offs from my employer. Who knew if I was truly pleasing to the eye? All I knew was that in addition to the rich, these beachfronts attracted the riff-raff who craved the unusual.

That would be me.

I wanted tales of sprites and magicians, along with odd food like escargots with coiled March ferns, weather thick with damp mists, and thrillers featuring unhinged killers.

My daily drudge was minding Mrs. Cuthbert's small son, Terrence, on Manhattan's Upper East Side, but my spectral curiosity had led me here. That, and Mrs. Cuthbert's generous offer of a week's lodging; I could never have afforded this Jersey shore vacation on my wages—not even with the decent ones she paid.

In truth, she was a difficult boss. Her rules and persnickety customs were exhausting to remember—crusts cut off all the bread, shoes shined only from tip to heel, furniture polished twice a week at ten am sharp and only with her castoff stockings so the mahogany wouldn't scratch. Those were a few in her long litany.

So, if I only had a week in this glorious place, I wanted to catch up with sleep and plunge into as many escapades as possible—even bewildering, outlandish ones.

We walked in to the jangle of Mr. Dune's door chimes. I skated around, ogling the floor-to-ceiling shelves brimming with leather-bound books on cosmic mysteries, spiritualism, and witchcraft. Two immediate standouts were *Ten Ways to Practice Mentalism* and *Dona Bella, Memoirs of a Southern Witch*. These were my fare, similar to a favorite book at the public library—a tome on dark magic. The most stirring part was about each witch dynasty having its own grimoire, a sort of magical recipe book. I had no clue as to why dark tales tickled me so, and often wondered about my taste.

Still, I read everything I could get my hands on, even boring books that drifted me right off to the Land of Nod. At my nanny job, I was so desperate for stories I even read the tedious articles about cooking and how to throw a proper cocktail party in Mrs. Cuthbert's *Reader's Digest* and *Home Arts* magazines.

Mr. Dune strode toward us. His handsome aura and towering presence intimidated yet thrilled me. He was dressed in crisp, charcoal gray pants and a vest with a double-breasted pinstriped jacket. "Are you lovely ladies here for the séance?" He held out a long, elegant hand, studded with a silver ring. I barely collected my wits enough to shake it and nod. Dulcie's hand whooshed out and hardly touched his before she clamped it protectively back to her side.

No doubt about it, he was the most striking man I'd ever seen. His thick mop of dark hair tapered into long side-burns, rendering his jawline a tad dangerous. I guessed he was in his mid-twenties. When his coffee-brown eyes gleamed at me, my breath caught, and a heat greater than any moonshine fired through me.

We paid the dime admission. He escorted us to a round, wooden table with lion-footed legs where we joined a heavyset older couple and a reedy gentleman with thin, blond hair. His lime-fizz eyes darted over to Dulcie, and then away. Two empty chairs still beckoned.

Dulcie looked terrified, so I smiled at her. She calmed enough to take a seat.

Mr. Dune strode to the window, loosened the crimson curtains, and lowered their heavy velvet over the windows, lending the already-pensive storefront a mystical aura.

His assistant, who he introduced as Opal, was a waifish ragamuffin of about seventeen with mussed hair and freckles the color of nutmeg over drawn-in cheeks. Her wise but sad eyes seemed to track our movements. I felt sorry at seeing two rips in her lace bodice, and I wondered how long it had been since she'd gotten a new dress.

She placed a candelabrum on the table. Its reddish glow flickered up the edges of the audience's chins and cheekbones, settling ghoulishly on the sockets of their eyes. Dulcie glanced over at me with a worried frown. She was from a well-to-do family who'd surely never seen a bohemian card reader. I'd never seen one either, but I was uncannily calm. I shouldn't have pushed her into this. Though when I gave her hand a squeeze, she eased back in her chair.

Opal poured a round of grape juice from a cut-glass pitcher. Its spicy, pungent aroma wafted up and stung my nostrils. Good heavens, was it real bootlegged sherry? We exchanged shocked glances that glided into sneaky grins, but no one said a word. Its liquid fire burned inside my chest with my first sip, amplifying the heady warmth that the strange proprietor had already started in me.

The chimes jangled again, and a tall woman in strappy heels strutted in. She had an unearthly beauty, as though she was composed of violets, wishes and sultry clouds. Her hair, the color of midnight, was swept up in a twist and cinched with a purple, grosgrain ribbon, save for her long bangs. Gleaming, black garnets dangled from her ears. She was even fancier than the rich ladies at my hotel, who fanned themselves as they rocked in their best summer lace.

As though she'd done this many times, she took a seat without addressing Mr. Dune. But wasn't this his first month in business? The woman's gray eyes with golden slivers stared shamelessly at me. Did I know her? How could I? It was only my second night here in Asbury Park. Yet her gaze was so keen I had to avert my face.

"Let us begin then." Mr. Dune settled into the last empty chair, straightened his jacket tails, and scraped closer to the table. His presence gave a sense of gravitas and calmed me from the unsettling flurry our new arrival had caused. "Introductions first," he said. "Tell us your names and where you're from. Whom you're hoping to hear from, if you like. But no more," he cautioned. "I'll divine the rest."

Out of a pensive silence, the older man spoke for both his wife and himself. "We are Mr. and Mrs. Parson, from Short Hills, New Jersey."

"I'm Tim Stevens, from Sandy Hook," the reedy guy exclaimed. His gaze slunk over to Dulcie again. She didn't seem to notice.

I said I was Ivy Lorena from New York, and Dulcie said she was from Madison, New Jersey.

The beautiful latecomer said only, "Alyse Bone," as if she were so important, everyone should know where she was from without her telling us.

Introductions over, Mr. Dune extracted a Tarot deck from a leather briefcase and shuffled it with an expert hand. I studied his ring in more depth—a raised wolf's head. A ripple of fear mixed with longing passed through me at the odd contrast between Mr. Dune's civility and the snarl on the wolf's muzzle. "Which brave soul will be first?" he asked.

Mr. Parson spoke up as his wife twisted a rumpled hand-kerchief. "If you please, we hope to hear from our son, Harry, who passed last year."

Mr. Dune nodded. "Ma'am, we don't always hear from whom we're expecting, but we shall see."

Mr. Parson chose each card from the ones Peter Dune

spread in front of him, and then Peter placed them, one by one, in a cross pattern. They were large cards with brilliantly hued illustrations. Most were royal figures swathed in robes, some holding staffs, others clutching cups. I'd seen pictures of the arcana in books but never in person. They were spectacular, and some deep urge in me longed to touch them. Of course, I held back.

While Mr. Dune perused the cards, I felt a gust of ill-disposed air aimed my way. Looking up, I saw Alyse Bone peering at me through her long bangs. She quickly adjusted her expression into a regal smile, yet I could sense her unseen emotions—moody, frosty and guarded.

Far more than I liked or understood, these powerful intuitions often came to me unbidden—a sense that a certain lady would twist her ankle on a loose plank on the way out of the neighborhood bakery, or a ripple of worry that the gentleman reading his newspaper on the subway would get fired that day. What was it about Miss Bone that stirred a sudden draft up my sinuses? I pressed my palm against my chilled nose to warm it. Maybe this card reading would give me a clue into my unknown origin and strange hunches. I wanted to either understand them or banish them from my life because they made me feel downright loony at times.

I refocused my attention on Mr. Dune as he pointed to the first card—a young man wearing a mask and holding a staff. "I'm seeing a figure," he explained, tapping the next card, a skeleton with alabaster eyes. "It's a small boy. He's crying . . ."

"Our son!" wailed Mr. Parson. "What's he saying?"

Dulcie gasped and clutched my hand.

"He's saying he didn't mean to run out into traffic. It was—"

"That's not what happened to him," Mrs. Parson snapped in a tight voice. "He expired from diphtheria."

Dulcie's hand flew up to cover her gaping mouth.

"I told you we shouldn't have come here." Mrs. Parson rose and grabbed her scarf. She glared at Mr. Dune. "Tell it to Sweeney, you con."

The very air in the room was stammering. I wriggled my right leg to get rid of the strange force also jittering through me, and I looked over at Mr. Dune to see how on earth he was going to weasel out of this mess.

"True, that wasn't what did him in," Mr. Dune insisted in a defensive tone. "Nevertheless, he *did* run out into traffic one day."

"Do you think we're saps?" Mrs. Parsons' face had grown red with sadness and fury, and she shook a fist at Mr. Dune. She was sitting right next to him, and I feared she would grab for his neck and strangle him even though he was stronger. "We've gone to other mediums. We can tell a charlatan from an honest one. We want our money back," she hissed.

Mr. Dune moved his chair away from her and made another big show of trembling. Just as I was convinced he was a shoddy, grade-B actor, conning us out of dimes like we were Dumb Doras, he began to shudder with such force that he knocked over his sherry. The thick drink rushed onto the table, pooled around the cards, and then the goblet rolled and crashed to the floor. Opal ran over with a broom and a dirty rag to sweep up the sticky shards.

Suddenly, Mr. Dune stood up as if an invisible being had grabbed him by the back of the collar and shoved him right over the table. His shocks of dark hair flopped into the spilled sherry. Mrs. Parson let out a high-pitched squeal, and her husband's jaw wagged at the sight.

"What's happening to me?" Peter Dune mumbled as his handsome face contorted into a pained grimace. "Be careful," he slurred. Then, jerking upright, he reached across the table for me, as his dark eyes glimmered with fear. "Be careful, Fiera," he warned, louder this time.

"Did you say Fiera?" Alyse Bone asked in a tone as if everything was as routine and normal as tapioca pudding with whipped cream, but somehow, the cream had toppled sideways. Her catlike gray eyes narrowed at him as she dug her long fingernails into the rim of the table.

I was just as shocked. The sound of the name set my whole being on fire. *Fiera? Really?* For me, this name was anything but routine. Had I heard him correctly? "Be careful of what, Mr. Dune?" I managed to utter. People gaped at him as his eyes rolled up in his head. "Mr. Dune? Are you all right?"

Opal wavered in the shadows, one hand holding the broom, the other pressed to her skimpy chest. Clearly, she couldn't fathom how to help. Which meant that this was no regular occurrence at Peter Dune's Tarot and Séance.

Tim was the first to leap up, his eyes full of worry. "Peter, old boy," he called as he waved his hands in front of Mr. Dune's face. "Don't you see me? Over here!"

"Are you friends with this man?" I asked Tim. "Can you run out and get him a doctor? He's shaking like an epileptic."

Before Tim could take any decisive action, Mr. Dune stumbled toward me, the heels of his polished wingtips nicking against the floorboards. "Fiera," he wailed again, low in his throat.

Dulcie whispered something too, but it didn't register over the roiling in my brain. So, I *had* heard him right the first time. How could he know Fiera was my private name? No one was ever called Fiera. Except me. My baby name was the only thing the orphanage had ever revealed to me. They said my real mother had nicknamed me that. Due to the unfortunate circumstances of my infancy, they'd renamed me at once. I'd begged them to tell me what circumstances they were referring to, but they'd only smiled sadly at me and shaken their heads.

So, all of my life, I was simply called Ivy Lorena. How could this shuddering man know more? My heart rang like a gong against my ribs.

Was this a con game? Had Mr. Dune done research on me, and if so, why? How had he pulled off this caper? My senses told me otherwise.

In the few moments I'd been lost in thought, he'd moved so close his hot breath now heated my cheeks. He was staring at me, yet through me, and his eyes scorched me with their raw beauty, their unhinged emotion. I grabbed him by the shoulders and gently shook him, desperate to startle him from his stupor. "Why do you call me that? What do you want from me?" I murmured.

He didn't answer, but started to groan as his face contorted in a horrified grimace. "Fiera, Fiera, I'm choking, Fiera!" Reaching out for me, he wrapped his substantial arms around my shoulders. As he clung on, I must say it inspired a wave of heat and excitement in me, highly inappropriate for the moment.

Inside my uncanny vision, a monstrous, frothy wave rolled up. It was so real that its marine scent stung my nostrils. As it continued to barrel forward, the invisible wave seemed to overtake him. He pitched forward and crumpled onto the Oriental rug, where his shaking disappeared as swiftly as it had come.

Everyone stood stock-still, breathing hard, with glazed

expressions. Only Tim took a slug of his sherry before plunking it back on the table.

I knelt down and wriggled Mr. Dune's shoulders. "Mr. Dune? Can you hear me? What happened to you? Do you need an ambulance?" He rubbed at his eyes. They looked amazingly clear as they stared up at me. But they also looked blank, emotionless. As if he had no memory of what had just happened.

Picking himself off the floor, he straightened his suit. "What was—?" He never finished his sentence because Opal scurried over to brush the dust from his back.

"Well, I never!" Mrs. Parson stood up and wobbled to the front door. She turned to her husband. "Are you coming?" Mr. Parson followed his wife, regret splashed across his porcine features as if he preferred to stick around for the next circus act.

"What *was* all that?" Dulcie asked me, the blood so drained from her face that her pastel pink dress was now rosier than her cheeks.

"I'm not exactly sure."

Opal brought Mr. Dune a goblet of water. He sat down, drank a few sips, and slowly shook his head from side to side as if he wasn't sure it was attached to his head. "I've never drifted off like that. I'm so embarrassed."

"Don't worry. We're glad you're back with the living," I answered with a shudder. It felt odd being the one to comfort him. I was longing to ask where he'd conjured up my private nickname, but with Miss Bone standing inches away with her sharp curiosity, something told me to save my queries.

"Shall we head on back to the hotel?" Dulcie implored.

"Let's do." I gave Mr. Dune a motherly pat on the shoulder. "Feel better, sir. Get a bit of sun tomorrow. This place is awfully dark. Sunshine will do you justice."

He nodded thoughtfully, attempted a grin, and took another sip of water.

Miss Bone beat us to the door. As she did, she performed a theatrical turn, which sent her dark skirt rustling. "Lovely to meet you, Fiera," she said, exaggerating my secret name. And then she clicked out on her heels, the chimes loudly jingling.

"It's rude to stare," I blurted before I could stop myself.

If she heard me, she didn't show it, for she kept on walking.

"Oh, Ivy?" Mr. Dune implored from behind me.

"Yes?"

He grabbed a card deck from a wicker basket on a side shelf. In three long strides, he was in front of me, looking as imposing and dashing as he had when we'd entered his establishment. "I want you to have this." He held the deck out.

One of his illustrated Tarot decks wrapped in cellophane! A hot flush of pleasure and embarrassment shivered up my neck. "Oh, I couldn't, really." I didn't even know him, and why would he do this? "It doesn't seem right. I can't pay you."

"I insist." He held it out further, the light glinting off his silver fox head ring.

Dulcie was looking faint, and I needed fresh ocean air too, so I put the deck in my purse and thanked him. With one last peek into his smoldering eyes, we fluttered off like quivering moths in the night.

Get Witch of the Cards, and find more book information on Catherine's website. Join her mailing list at catherinestine.com for news of sales, launches and events.

ACKNOWLEDGMENTS

This novel is my love letter to Philadelphia, where I grew up. It also satisfies my longstanding fascination with the Eastern State Penitentiary, a revolutionary prison at the time, built in the shape of a panopticon, where all cell halls run out from a central core like the petals of a flower. It was built in 1821 on the hill of a former cherry orchard (which is why my characters call the prison Cherry Hill). Opened in 1829, it was equipped with skylights, central heating and some of the very first flush toilets, and inspired by the Quakers' belief that solitary penitence could quell an inmate's urge to commit crimes.

Eventually, this theory was proven false, as people grew to understand that solitary confinement was brutal to a person's body and mind. Nevertheless, it was an improvement in incarceration of that time. Eastern State's predecessor, the Walnut Street jail, threw everyone, including children, into one giant holding pen.

I'm thrilled that an earlier draft of *Witch of the Wild Beasts* won second place in The 2019 Valley Forge RWA Sheila contest for YA. Thank you, Valley Forge judges, all. Ironically, I've since determined that this novel is adult rather than YA. In fact, the novel now fits squarely in the historical romance/fantasy category, alongside my other book, *Witch of the Cards*. I reached this decision in part with the help of my talented editors, Amy Tipton of Feral Girl Books and Meredith Rich, to whom I owe serious gratitude. I'm also grateful for insightful input from writing group members Maggie Powers, Holly Kowitt, Shawne Steiger, Emily Damron-Cox and Mary Kate Pagano. And nobody whips up a witch book cover like the enormously talented Regina Wamba. I can't wait to see what visual magic she'll conjure up for the next cover.

Witches were some of the original wise women, who could cure with their herbal salves, intuit the causes of sickness in body or spirit, and communicate with the beasts of the field as my Evalina Stowe did.

Catherine Stine
    Catskills, Jan 2020

ABOUT THE AUTHOR

Catherine Stine is a *USA Today* bestselling author of historical fantasy, paranormal romance, sci-fi thrillers and young adult fiction. Witch of the Wild Beasts won a second prize spot in the 2019 Valley Forge RWA Sheila Contest. Other novels have earned Indie Notable awards and New York Public Library Best Books for Teens. She lives in Manhattan, grew up in Philadelphia and is known to roam the Catskills. Before writing novels, she was a painter and children's fabric designer. She's a visual author when it comes to scenes, and she sees writing as painting with words. She loves edgy thrills, perhaps because her dad read Edgar Allen Poe tales to her as a child. Catherine loves spending time with her beagle Benny, writing about supernatural creatures, gardening on her deck, traveling and meeting readers at book fests.

To get book and event news, join her mailing list, and visit her website:

www.catherinestine.com

facebook.com/authorcatherinestine

instagram.com/kitsy84557

bookbub.com/profile/catherine-stine

pinterest.com/kitsy84557